D1575882

PERISH

A Novel

LaToya Watkins

THORNDIKE PRESS
A part of Gale, a Cengage Company

East Moline Public Library
745 16th Avenue
East Moline IL 61244

Copyright © 2022 by LaToya Watkins.
Thorndike Press, a part of Gale, a Cengage Company.

ALL RIGHTS RESERVED
This is a work of fiction. Names, characters, places, and incidents either are the product of the author's imagination or are used fictitiously, and any resemblance to actual persons, living or dead, businesses, companies, events, or locales is entirely coincidental.
Thorndike Press® Large Print Black Voices.
The text of this Large Print edition is unabridged.
Other aspects of the book may vary from the original edition.
Set in 16 pt. Plantin.

LIBRARY OF CONGRESS CIP DATA ON FILE.
CATALOGUING IN PUBLICATION FOR THIS BOOK
IS AVAILABLE FROM THE LIBRARY OF CONGRESS.

ISBN-13: 979-8-8857-8384-2 (hardcover alk. paper)

Published in 2022 by arrangement with Penguin Books, an imprint of Penguin Publishing Group, a division of Penguin Random House, LLC.

Printed in Mexico
Print Number : 1   Print Year : 2023

For Cameron and Colby.
And all of those who saved me.

I
SEED

I

SEED

HELEN JEAN

THE FLATS

1955

Helen Jean sat on the hole inside the musky outhouse and pushed her palms flat against the bench, willing her body to do the work she needed it to. She waited for the heavy knot to begin to throb and her bowels to break. For the familiar pain to erupt from the core of her stomach. She had followed all of Ernestine's orders, just like the first time. Nothing to eat all day but toast. Nothing to drink. Not even water. But all she felt was nervous.

She tried to remember exactly how it had happened before. Last time, she had been early on when she went to her cousin for assistance. This time, a tight knot had already formed on the inside of her belly, a knot that she was beginning to notice on the outside. A knot her father and three brothers had likely noticed, too. The one they all chose to ignore because it told each of them too much about who they were.

Ernestine had warned her, *It might be too late, Helen Jean. Can't give you too much cause you be dead, too. Got to be just enough to ruin the seed but not you.*

Helen Jean had prayed to the God of Moses that it would work. She reminded him that she had never gone to the Mr. Fairs Pleasure Gardens with the other girls and boys her age. She reminded him that she'd never sat on any of those benches, letting boys wrap their thick lips around her neck or touch her in the places that were meant to be secret. That she had been a good girl. Obedient to her parents, her father after her mother was dead. She promised God that if he spared her the hell of carrying the thing growing inside her, she would leave Jerusalem, Texas, and find a place where she could fully serve him. A place where no one knew her.

She inhaled and clenched her teeth and then let all the air out of her body in one powerful push. She couldn't hold the grunt, almost a scream, that came out with the push.

The last time she'd taken Ernestine's turpentine, her stomach had cramped up while she was serving her father and brothers turkey necks and beans. It happened just after she popped open her father's can of

12

Hamm's beer. It was unlike the cramps from her monthly and felt more like the time she had drank too much castor oil to relieve herself of a bad case of constipation. She'd wrapped both arms around her stomach and almost toppled over right there. Without moving his head, her father allowed his eyes to shift to her from peering down at the spoon of beans hovering in front of his mouth.

She'd excused herself to the outhouse, which, unlike the one in her current situation, was a two-holer that her father had wired for electricity. The outhouse was the thing her father hated most about their shotgun house. He always complained about indoor plumbing and how it would never reach the blacks in the Flats because nothing was expanding for them, being built for them.

On that night, the last time it happened, Helen Jean sat down on the hole just when she thought her bowels would explode, and, to her surprise, she felt a slimy mass pass through her womanhood instead.

This time, however, nothing was happening. No horrible stomachache. No slimy mass. Just dry pushing, gas, and grunts.

"Did it come out?" she heard Ernestine's squeaky voice ask from outside the door.

She didn't answer. She turned her mind to Jessie B. It was setting in that she'd have to accept his marriage proposal. That she'd have to say yes to the nowhere man. She wanted to cry, but she just sat there breathing hard and staring in the direction of her feet. It didn't matter that she couldn't see them through the darkness. Just like the seed growing inside her, she knew her feet were there. If she had been her usual self, she would have been concerned about snakes being curled up in the corner of her aunt's outdated outhouse. But she wasn't her usual self tonight.

She exhaled again and reached down to pull up her panties. Her chest began to tighten and her breathing became rapid. For a moment, she sat there with one hand down at her ankles, gently tugging at her panties, and the other over her heart, as if she would say the Pledge of Allegiance. And then the breathing turned to panting and then loud gasping for air.

There was light knocking on the door, and she could hear Ernestine calling out to her, almost crying but still whispering, begging for a response. But Helen Jean couldn't speak. She was struggling to catch her breath, to breathe, a thing that had always been easy. *Dear God of Moses,* she thought.

What I done now? You gone kill me for trying to right this wrong? She asked him to take the monster growing inside her. The abomination it would be.

And suddenly, her ears felt stuffed, blocked, except for the sounds inside her. She opened her mouth wide and tried to force out a yawn. Everything outside of her felt distant, quiet, and she heard a faint whisper growing from inside her ear, like a mouth inside her head trying to crawl its way out. *A life to repay the last one,* it said. *You can't keep killing them. Bear it or perish yourself.*

Her eyes widened and she knew. She knew that God was not with her this time. The sounds around her returned. She could hear herself gasping for air and she could hear her cousin calling her name from outside of the outhouse. She fell to the floor of the outhouse and rolled to her back, raising her knees into a pyramid. The moon slithered in through the splintered wooden slats that were the roof of her aunt's outhouse. The tin had blown away years before, during a tornado, and the poor family had simply replaced it with wood from around their land. She hadn't noticed the glow when her eyes had been on the darkness around her feet.

15

It had been still all night, but as she lay on the floor, a strong, long wind seemed to come through and rattle every plank that was holding the outhouse together. The wind coupled with Ernestine's shaking the outhouse door made it feel like the end of days was happening outside.

Helen Jean kept her eyes on the moon's glow. It was beautiful. Like what she imagined the God of Moses looked like. And then, she made out a face through the glow. It was a narrow heart centered by a long, slender nose that was slightly humped in the center, like her own. For a moment, she thought she was seeing her own haint. She'd heard the old folks say you see yourself most clearly right before death. But the softness around the eyes allowed her to recognize her mother's face, and Helen Jean's breaths began to come so quickly she thought her heart would explode. This was it. She wouldn't be allowed to see herself clearly in this life. Not even in her own haint. The God of Moses had sent her mother to carry her to the Promised Land.

She wanted to tell her mother something first. She wanted to tell her that things had been hard. She wanted to ask her why she didn't fight for her mind. To stay herself. To stay with her children. She wanted to ask her what possessed her to leave them on that cold night. Why she had been so close to the lake when she couldn't swim. If she had meant to drown. To be found days later with her lungs filled with water, with her eyes wide open and void of life and her lips curled into a smile. If she had meant for them to suffer as they had. Helen Jean wanted to tell her mother about the thing inside her and how much she hated that it was there. She wanted to tell her that she wouldn't allow it to break her. She was stronger than that. That she was stronger than *her*.

On the floor of that nasty outhouse, with the scent of feces and urine closer to her nostrils than she wanted them to be, unable to catch her breath, she thought she would die, but she turned her head from the moon's glow, from her dead mother's face, and she made promises to God anyway. She wouldn't kill the monster inside her. She promised to never try it again. She'd give birth to any seed to ever grow inside her womb. She would stay with the things that passed through her. She would protect them. All she asked for was life. She promised she'd give it if hers was spared.

And just as quickly as the attack had come upon her, it ceased. She stayed on her back

17

EAST MOLINE PUBLIC LIBRARY

until her breathing leveled and then she responded to Ernestine's voice. "I'm all right, Stine. I'm all right."

After a few minutes, she rose up from the floor of the outhouse, pulled up her panties, and opened the door. Ernestine's wide, stout body blocked the exit. One of her hips sat higher than the other, so despite her wide girth, she appeared fragile, leaning against the wooden stick she used for a cane. She was only twenty-six, ten years Helen Jean's senior, but due to the slight handicap, she carried herself like she was older than that. Her tight eyes became two straight lines on her face as she attempted to take all of Helen Jean in before she finally asked, "What happened in there? It come out?"

Helen Jean shook her head and stepped down from the outhouse. "Nawh, still there," she said, and she could hear a low grittiness in her own voice.

"Well," Ernestine began. "Maybe you was too far gone for turpentine. Momma in the house. Can't do it now, but if you come back tomorrow when she go to Ms. Dorothy Ann's, I can get it out with a wrench for you. Got Reesa's out like that last week."

Helen shook her head again and walked past her cousin. "Nawh. That's all right. I'm

18

EAST MOLINE PUBLIC LIBRARY

gone go see Jessie B. in the morning."

Ernestine grabbed her arm, and Helen Jean stopped walking. The moonlight was shining bright enough for her to see her cousin's toffee skin perfectly. Her hair was rolled into pin curls and Helen Jean knew bobby pins were holding the perfect circles in place.

"You sure, Helen Jean? I mean, I think Jessie B. a catch. Shoot, wish I could go find him and tell him yes for myself, but you . . ."

Helen's lips began to quiver and she felt her knees going weak, so she stomped her foot and said the first thing that came to her mind. "Shit," she said. "I'm sure. This what I got to do. This how it got to be."

And she told herself that this *was* how it had to be. Jessie B. was a silent man with no family and he just seemed to appear from nowhere two years before. His face was hard-set and mean like he didn't want to be bothered, so no one dared ask him where he was from or about his family. There were all types of stories about him. Most of them centered on some type of rage or murder, but Helen Jean simply thought the way he carried himself garnered respect. He was always dressed nicely and had a quiet, stoic quality about himself. She had seen with her own eyes how white and black men tipped their hats at him in public. They respected him. Feared him, even. As far as they were concerned, he came from nowhere in the world.

The people of Jerusalem didn't understand that. Most of them had come from families that trickled in from the smaller surrounding towns at the turn of the century. Family histories were shared things. Known things. Even those silent shames.

Jessie B. was mysterious in a place where most folks didn't have a clue about how to keep themselves to themselves. So that mysteriousness was something the people envied more than feared, but most folks didn't know the difference.

Helen Jean found that he was easy enough to talk to, but he had taken the few words she'd ever spoken to him and turned them into a marriage proposal. A month before the night at the outhouse, when she first discovered she was with child, she sat in a booth at the Hut Café on 33rd, nursing a Coca-Cola and shuffling the Hut's famous fries around her plate. She didn't even see Jessie B. approach, but when her puffy eyes looked up to find him standing over her, it seemed that he'd been standing there holding his hat to his chest for a while.

"Evening," he said, nodding toward the

seat across from her.

She replied, "Hello," and turned her face back to her fries without responding to his request to take a seat.

"Little gal," he said, sliding into the seat anyway. "I was over yonder having a bite and looked over here and saw the saddest thing in the world. Beautiful young lady, having dinner on her own. Face looking like she done lost her very best friend."

She looked at him and took in his dark skin and beady eyes. His hair was cut low, but she could still see that he was balding at the top by the way his cowlicks reached toward the back of his head. She had seen him from a distance many times, and pegged him for someone close to her father's age. She'd never seen him this close up, so she hadn't noticed that he was missing her father's frown lines, crow's feet, and other hard marks and lines that time and real evil create on faces. No. He wasn't that old. Close up, he was in his late twenties, maybe even his early thirties, but he wasn't her father's age. He wasn't in his fifties. He was younger than that. He wasn't her father.

"I don't have no friends, sir. All I got is me," she said, before dropping her eyes to her lap. And she wasn't sure why she even said that much to him, but she felt like she could've gone on if it hadn't been for the knot forming in her throat. The knot threatening to make her cry.

He didn't offer comfort. He didn't reach across the table and pat the backs of her hands. In fact, his silence was so thick that she looked back up at him to make sure he was still there. The hardness that folks were afraid of, that she hadn't noticed earlier, was in his jawline, in which she saw a slight twitch. She thought of her father. Of his twitching jawline, and pulled her hands from the table into her lap.

As if it suddenly reoccurred to her that Jessie B. was there before her, she tilted her head and asked, "What you want with me, sir?"

He placed his hat on the table, and, leaning in closer, circled his arms around it.

"I know you, Miss Helen Jean," he said. And her eyes widened because before now they had never spoken. Sure, he'd nodded in her direction at the Piggly Wiggly a few times, but they had never verbally exchanged so much as a hello.

"I know you enough to know somebody or something hurting you. That you need some protecting. So I figure, me and you got something in common. I'm a man that can only be defined — only live his life — if

22

I'm responsible for another, and you a woman that need somebody to be responsible for you. To take care of you. You be my wife, give me purpose, I'll do that. I'll protect you." And as if he expected her to decline or protest, he took her moment of shocked silence to ease out of the seat, stand, and place his hat upon his head.

He adjusted his jacket and looked down at her. "Take your time, Miss Helen Jean. Take your time. I'll wait. I rent a room from Ms. Gerty in Hyde Park. Come see me when you ready." And then he was gone.

Ernestine turned her head and her face became thoughtful underneath the moonlight. "Who this baby for, Helen Jean? Surely not Jessie B. Who you pregnant for?"

Helen Jean snatched her arm away from her cousin. "Anybody ever ask you who father all them you keep getting big with and giving over to that hole?" she said through gritted teeth. And she immediately felt bad. Ernestine and her family had accepted Helen Jean as an honorary member as much as they could, considering their limited resources. Helen Jean knew that her aunt, her mother's sister and Ernestine's mother, felt bad because they couldn't do more for her and her brothers after their mother's death. The family of ten rented a small three-room house on a couple of acres of land, and they didn't have things like running water or electricity. But whatever they had and whenever they could, they tried to welcome Helen Jean to it. It was through their family that Helen Jean came to know the God of Moses, as her father had never been a religious man. Had never allowed her mother to be the religious woman her family had meant for her to be.

Ernestine gasped and put her hand on her chest. "Helen Jean," she said in a whiny voice. "That ain't called for. All that ain't called for. I'm just trying to help. Trying to —"

"I'm sorry, Ernestine. I'm sorry. I just ain't gone talk about this no more," Helen Jean said, raising her hands in surrender. And she meant it. She meant to stop talking about all of it forever. She meant to move forward, because looking back changed nothing and hurt more than she could stand.

Embittered by the failure of the turpentine procedure and her new covenant with the God she had no intention of continuing to pray to, Helen Jean turned away from her cousin and walked into the darkness, determined to at least keep her promise. To be a woman of her word. To live and give life.

When she snuck out of her father's house later that night, when she made the short trek over to the pen that housed his hogs, when she shoved her narrow feet into his feeding boots and sloshed through the pen in search of the deformed piglet that the old sow would not nurse, when she took the tiny piglet into her hands and sliced through its soft flesh and let the blood warm her, when she stuffed it into the potato sack and doused it with kerosene, when she set the match to the dead thing and watched it burn against the night, she thought of the thing inside her and all of the dead things it meant.

■ ■ ■ ■

II

HARVEST
2018

■ ■ ■ ■

EAST MOLINE PUBLIC LIBRARY

1
LYDIA

I feel my phone vibrate from the pocket of my robe when I enter the room that was supposed to hold our children. My husband, Walter, calls this room the "mothering den." It's really just a nursery, but I understand why it looks like a den to him. The warm colors, the comfortable couch in the corner, and the panoramic window give off that vibe. I wanted the room to be a place of comfort. A place of peace. So I get it. I get what he sees. But all I see anymore is the picture we hung on the wall. In it, I'm six months pregnant and cradling my oversized stomach, looking happy and so in love with what's growing inside me. I'd adored that photo when we first got it taken. I was the one who had it framed and insisted Walter hang it on that exact spot on the wall so it would be the first thing I'd see every time I walked in the room.

Now, I can hardly bear to look at it. So I

walk over to the window before I pull out my phone. I see the 806 area code in front of the number. Jerusalem. For a moment, I consider ignoring the call. Instead, I sigh and tap the green icon on the screen and before I can get the phone all the way to my ear to say hello, words are spilling out, like water.

"It's bad. It's real bad, Lydia. I had to call you —"

"Hello, Auntie," I say. Even though it's been years since I've heard her voice, I know it anywhere. It's grating and nervous and always in a hurry.

"Shit," she says. "I'm all she really got left. I mean, your momma. But you know I can't count on her."

"What's going on?"

"It's Momma. She in the hospital dying, and I just —"

"Grandmoan? Grandmoan's dying?" I wonder why she's calling me with it.

"Hmm-hmmm." I hear Aunt Julie B. exhale deeply. "I need you to get here. Need you to be here."

"In Jerusalem?" I ask.

"Of course in Jerusalem. This family, girl. Don't never forget where you come from," she says, as if that's something that I could ever actually do.

30

She sounds authoritative in a way I don't remember her being. I feel like I should tell her that now is not a good time for me, but I doubt it will mean anything to her.

Instead I ask, "What happened?"

She sighs and clucks her tongue against the roof of her mouth. "That artery finally gave out. Been living on just that one for longer than she should've been able to. She waiting to hear from you, Lydia. I know she is." She lowers her voice to almost a whisper. "This be good for you and Jan. Y'all can be here for each other, like when y'all was kids, like — like sisters, you know? Y'all can be there for each other, like sisters."

I close my eyes. I haven't spoken to my cousin in close to a decade.

"I don't know, Auntie," I say.

She is silent. I pull the phone away from my ear to see if the call has dropped or ended, but her number is still on the display so I put the phone back to my ear. "Hello?" I say.

"Yeah. Yeah. I'm here," Julie B. says, and sighs. "She somebody momma, Lydia. You hear me? That woman is somebody momma, and right now, she need all her children."

Her words are unemotional and empty, and I don't expect them to touch me in the way that they do. I don't know if it's a good touch, but it's been so long since anyone has wanted me, I mean really wanted me. Just to be there. Just to sit beside them in a room. So I nod and say, "I'll see what I can do, okay?"

She exhales. "I know you gone come. I know you will. And we gone gather around her and show her some love. Burn a hog for her when it's time. Send her out the right way — her right way."

I jump a bit when she says that. The ghost smell of burnt meat is in my nose.

"We gone treat her like what she is. Somebody momma," she says.

I don't have the heart to tell her that I don't know what that means. It's been a long time since I've seen what that is. From what Mother says, from what I know and can only imagine, Grandmoan wasn't really the mothering kind. I guess because of that, Mother was never one either. And me . . .

I'm nobody's mother.

After my aunt's call, the first person I think of is my husband. I wish he were here being what he'd been before things became what they are for us. Before we lost so many things, before he let go of me. I almost dial his number and tell him to come home. Tell him I need him. But I don't. Instead, I call Quail Oaks and tell them that I need to see Mother. They extend an emergency after-hours visit to me, and I get dressed, get in my car, and make my way there.

I put Mother in Quail Oaks the week after Walter asked me to marry him. The drive to see her is less than an hour, but I only make it twice a year. During the holiday season and on her birthday. I drive from my place in Dallas to Fort Worth and spend the day with her at an upscale mansion-sized home for people diagnosed with chronic mental health disorders. There are fifteen other residents here, and though most of them come from wealthy families and are used to lives vastly different from what Mother has lived, she is around others with similar needs. Others like her. This facility, which sits on about seven acres of lush green land, is a beautiful place that helps me forget that I haven't had a mother in a very long time.

"I was surprised when you called," Tashé, the only black tech, the only black anything on staff at Quail Oaks, says to me while holding the door open to let me in. "I hope what you got to say ain't bad news. Momma can't handle no bad," she says, and just like that I'm reminded that Tashé isn't from this place. Her words and usage always take me to her island. She pronounces things differently. Her *th*s are *d*s and I often find myself trying to sound like her after my visits. She looks around to make sure we are still alone in the oversized foyer, which doubles as a reception or welcome area.

Everything about the place is warm and elegant. The butterscotch marble flooring and the deep brown couches draped with throws and huge pillows. It's different from the sterility of Chapel Hill State Hospital, where Mother lived off and on before Walter and his money. At Chapel Hill, there were no caring Caribbean women like Tashé. Women with full lives behind them who had worked hard to get to where they were. Women with children my age. Women with a clear understanding of what it means to be there for a woman like Mother.

The girls at Chapel Hill were young and rude to me and, I'm sure, Mother. When she was there, the situation necessitated three to four visits per week, which was difficult when I was in college and later working. I am grateful for Tashé and this place.

Tashé's tired eyes change to something a bit more pleading, which makes her gray Afro look ancient. "Come see your momma more," she says. "I won't be here always. You a good daughter. Come check on her more," she adds, opening her hands to the room. I look down at my shoes because I don't want to make a promise I know I won't keep.

She leads me to the visiting room, which is set up nicely, like an elegant living room. There is a television and couches and even a small refrigerator filled with snacks and soft drinks. "Have a seat. I'll get Momma," she says before leaving.

The last time I came here, Walter wanted to come along. I told him that I was making a day of it, taking Mother shopping for her birthday. I knew he wouldn't come if I said that. We've been married for almost a decade, but he's only been around Mother a handful of times.

Family is big to my husband. I met Walter at his law firm. I was a paralegal and he was up for partner. When he made partner, his family came to Texas and celebrated with him for a week. After we started dating, when he asked about my parents, I told him my father had died when I was just a girl and that my mother was ill. Still, he wanted to meet her. When he finally persuaded me to let him, I cooked dinner at the apartment I shared with Mother when she wasn't at Chapel Hill and invited him to join us. And I warned him that she'd just returned home from a weeklong stay at Chapel Hill. That she was ill — would always be ill — and begged him to forgive us in advance. He was gentlemanly in a way that was funny, considering who Mother had become. I apologized a lot that night, and I cried some too. Most especially, when he kneeled down in front of my mother and asked her permission to propose to me.

I'll never forget how handsome he was, so distinguished kneeling there with his perfectly trimmed salt-and-pepper goatee against his dark skin. I can see why Mother confused him for my father, why she tilted her head to the side and placed her hand on her heart, why she blushed and said, *Awh, Soweo.*

If I hadn't been so caught up in the "my moment" part of it, I'd have known to jump up and save him. But before I could even think to pull him up from that kneel, to explain her confusion, she had placed her hand on his cheek and was going in to kiss him.

Since then, I've monitored how much time she spends with us and we spend with her. He saw her at our wedding and I brought her home for a few visits. That first Christmas we spent together in our new home and after the first baby died. I was always right there, guiding her actions and words because I understood how uncomfortable she can make others. We lost our whole family because she couldn't be whole. I didn't want to lose Walter because of that too.

I can hear Tashé's voice in the hallway before they enter. *Got a big prize for you, Ms. Ruby. Real big one tonight.* Eventually, she guides my mother into the room where I am waiting.

When Mother walks into the room, it's as if she hasn't seen me in years. She puts her hands together, like a prayer, and presses them against her lips and stands there with her eyes watering up like it's been forever.

When she approaches, I wrap my arms around her tiny frame. She hasn't always been so tiny, so frail, but the days of her thickness are far behind us, among the things she lost with my father. She holds on to me and breathes into my neck, as if holding me is a normal thing — something she's always done.

I finally manage to pry her body away from mine, and she sits down on the couch, but she doesn't allow her back to rest into it. She sits up and rocks her body forward like she has to go to the bathroom.

Tashé tells me to call her if I need her and

points to the phone on an end table in the corner. She turns to walk out the door and calls back over her shoulder, *Enjoy your daughter, Ms. Ruby. Enjoy her well well.*

I make small talk with Mother. Ask if she's all right.

She nods and I sit down next to her.

"I have something to tell you, Mother," I say. "Aunt Julie B. called and —"

"My dear sister," she says, and smiles at me. "She all right? She ask about me?"

I shake my head and watch her smile slide away.

"I mean, yes. Yes. Aunt Julie B. is fine. It's your mother. It's Grandmoan," I say, softly.

Her face is blank for a moment, and then a shy smile breaks through her quivering lips. "My momma killed my man, but I ain't gone never let him go." She pats the back of my hand and sighs. "We all got to go that way, child. We all gone die, but Soweo gone always have my heart. Every bit of it beat for him."

"Mother, I need you to listen to me," I say, locking eyes with her to make sure she's focused. "Your mother is dying. She's close to the end," I say, but she's smiling at me as if I've not said anything. I shake my head and sigh.

I don't know what I was expecting, coming here tonight. Don't know what I thought telling her would do. What it would mean to me. She won't hear me. She never really has, so I just sit here, allowing the silence to be soaked up by the both of us. And then she leans over and puts her lips so close to my ear that, at first, I'm afraid she might bite me. She's done it before. When I was young. Before Quail Oaks, before Chapel Hill, even. She thought I was someone else, she said. Leaned over me while I was sleeping and almost took my ear off.

Now I can feel her hot breath on my face and when she whispers, her voice is so low I have to strain to make out her words. "Some people can't have children for a reason. Lord know my momma didn't need a one, but he allowed her to lay down and push them out just the same," she says. "Seem like we ought to be able to listen to God. What we got and ain't got in us ought to be enough for us to hear him talking." She places her hand on my cheek and, tilting her head, looks at me for the first time in a long time. When she speaks again, her voice is wet with tears. "Like you . . ." she says, letting her words fall away.

And I can't hide the horror on my face. "What?" I say. "How do you —" I stop my own words and clasp my hand over my mouth. I feel tears forming inside me, like some type of violent storm. I want to ask her how she knows about my pregnancies. My losses. But then I see that there are tears in her eyes too, and her face looks so very old.

"And your momma," she says. "Bless your heart, child. She ain't never want to have nothing to do with you. You shouldn't have never been born," she says this so matter-of-factly that I can only agree with her. "None of us should've."

I exhale. She doesn't know what I thought she knew. She isn't talking about my babies. She's talking about me. She's sitting here wishing I didn't exist because of who she is, and, as much as I want to understand that, it pisses me off.

I smack my lips. "But I've always been good to you, Mother. Haven't I always been good to you? Even when you couldn't be good for me, I was a good daughter. I kept us out there free in the world." I pinch my lips and grit my teeth. "Not him. Me," I say patting my chest. "Why can't I be enough for you?" I take a deep breath and clear my throat. "Why did you keep me, Mother? Why didn't you just abort me if you didn't want me?"

She tilts her head to the side and shakes

it. "Cause my sister had the most beautiful things and cause I thought me and Soweo deserved beautiful things too. You was supposed to be the light of our world." She sighs, shrugs, and peers at me. "We all deserve beautiful things," she says. "Soweo deserved you, even if you wasn't really his."

I run her words back in my head. Try to understand what she's saying. And when I understand them, I peer at her, as if I'm searching for something that can be found on the surface of her face, and I place my hand on her thigh. I can feel tears on my face as I search her with my eyes. "What, Mother? My father? Mother, are you saying my father isn't my father?" I ask.

I can't say that Mother's words ever leave me unaffected. Even with my knowing who she is and how she is, she still has the power to break me with words. Like the time she told me she wished she could love me the way she was supposed to or the time she told me that she'd always felt more responsible for the fates of her brother and my father than she did for me.

But this. This is different. This isn't some hurtful thing that comes from her hurtful things. From her hurting heart. This is something that comes from her mind. It's a knowledge, and it's not often that she dishes

41

that out. Her words most often come from the heart and never the head, so I am curious enough to be disturbed by them. To believe them.

She smiles without spreading her lips. "Member how much you loved *The Cosby Show*? You thought you was gone marry Theo Huxtable," she says, laughing. She places her hand on top of mine again. "I thought you deserved him cause you deserve good things too, Lydia. You deserve all the good things too."

I pull my hand back from her thigh. She's still smiling, but I'm sure she sees the confusion my face. I place the palms of my hands flat against the seat and push myself up.

"She gone be dead, but he ain't gone never die," Mother says, as I collect my handbag from the seat. "You hear me, child?" she says, putting her hand on her chest. "Soweo gone live forever in me. Always and forever in me."

I tune out her voice as I stand there, digging through my handbag, until I feel the zipper on my wallet. My hands shake as I open it and flip to the bill slot. I pull at the small photo, but it's tightly tucked away. I pull harder and it gives. The edges of the photo curl and peel just a bit, and it looks much older than it did the last time I pulled it out.

It's the only thing I have to remember my life before it fell apart. I keep it tucked away in my wallet. I hardly ever pull it out to look at it. I just like to know it's there. In the photo, my mother is holding me in her arms, tight, like she doesn't want to lose me, like I'm something important. I look less than a year old. I'm chubby with no hair. Mother looks young and healthy. She's smiling up at my father, and he is beautiful. His skin is smooth and creamy. His teeth are perfect and I've always felt that, in the photo, he's looking down at me as if I am the only person in the world.

When I was in the third grade, Laverne, the girl who lived across the street from my grandmother, went missing. She returned home a few days later, but she had been tampered with and defiled in ways that could not be reversed. My father was accused of the crime. He was arrested and never returned to Mother and me.

We had a good life before that — before my father was sent away. We lived in Jerusalem, where he had a good job as a cook in a hotel kitchen and Mother worked as a packer for the bread company. Grandmoan and the rest of our family lived on the east

43

side of Jerusalem, while we lived on the west. We were considered well-off because of that. Though we were separated by four or five miles, we lived close enough to see our family every day. But that all changed after my father was gone. We moved away to Dallas and started living in a low-income apartment, far away from the only family I'd ever known. So in the end, I pretty much raised myself. My father died in prison just a few months into his sentence, and Mother was never Mother after that.

Though she proclaimed his innocence — still proclaims his innocence — after he was gone, she never really looked at me again. Even now, after all this time, he's still the only thing that matters to her.

Sometimes, I get that. He's the only father I've ever known. The only parent really. And I know what they said he did. I know it was wrong, but my father was always right to me. Always everything I needed. I don't doubt my mother missed him, but nobody missed him more than me. I've tried hard to protect the memory I have of him. And I get that Mother missed him, but I don't get why or how she stopped looking at me. How she forgot about me.

A tear drops on the photo and it covers my entire little face. I wipe it away with my thumb and gaze at the three faces before me. My father is still beautiful in the photo and my mother is still gazing at him. I bring the photo closer to my face. It no longer looks like he's looking at me like I'm the only person in the world. His eyes seem to be asking a question. I seem to be a wonder.

I nod at the photo. "Yeah, me too," I say. "I want answers too."

When I stuff the photo back in my wallet, Mother is still talking about him living forever. I let her speak those words to my back as I leave the room. When I'm outside of the door, I lean against the wall and let my body slide down into a squat. I cup my face in my hands and I weep.

2

JAN

I want to holler in there and tell her to quit splashing like that — to quit wetting my floor like I know she doing, but I ain't got enough energy left in me to say nothing. I been going all day. On top of all that, my car giving me trouble but I ain't even got time to worry about it. Had to meet Tonya at the housing authority, and after that I had to go to the library and get help writing the notice out to my leasing office. Tonya say I been a good tenant this far; ain't no point in ruining that now. Me and her done become something like friends. I went from calling her Ms. Gipson to Tonya. She the first one I told about getting out of Jerusalem. She the one who told me how to do it. Told me I could take my benefits until I don't need them no more. Told me the real stunt is that's what they supposed to be used for: to help people what's down get on they feet.

Writing a thirty-day notice, letting them know I'm leaving, gone keep me in good standing with the tenant-tracking folks. Finished that and Javon had a appointment at the doctor and Jazera needed to be picked up right after that. Then I had to go to the store to get the nacho stuff for dinner. Ain't had time to sit down and process nothing. Don't even know about turning this letter in to the leasing office. That'll make it for real. Make it final. I don't know about taking a step like that.

This move, I want to make it happen more than I want to breathe my next breath, but I'm scared everything gone fall apart the minute I do it. I been looking at Grandmoan a year, trying to figure out how to make this work. Trying to figure out how to make her being wise with money — a super saver of sorts — work for me. Figure out how to get some of that money from her and leave this place for good.

Jazera in there making all that noise in the tub, and I'm at the kitchen sink scrubbing dishes like I can't hear her, like I ain't even in the apartment with her. I can't bring my mind down from thinking about Dallas. From thinking about picking up and just leaving. My hands feel warm swimming around in the sink water, seeking knives and forks that I ain't had a chance to scrub clean. But I ain't looking down. Don't need to. If I can't do nothing else, I can clean my kitchen. Clean up after me and mine.

My momma called and said it's the end. Said Grandmoan gone die. I was cubing up the cheese for the nachos when my phone rung. I saw her number in the ID and almost just ignored it. Don't know why I went on and picked it up. Maybe I wanted to hear her voice. Wanted to maybe say some things. But she just blurted it out before I could even say hello. Before I could greet her like both of us humans. *Momma dying on us, girl. She about to get on up out of here.*

And it knocked the wind out me. Not cause me and Grandmoan close but cause her dying right now don't work for me. I didn't say nothing at first. I always want my actions to be Christ-like. All my actions should be for the perfecting of saints, the work of the ministry, and for the edifying of the body of Christ. I didn't want to be thinking all selfish like I was. I wanted to find a way to make my feelings fit the right way, so I just didn't open my mouth. And I didn't really want to ask her about the money. My momma ain't never had nothing outside of what Grandmoan and welfare give her. If she knew about some money, maybe she'd think she was owed something, too.

I don't want nobody to think I'm begging for nothing. I ain't never been like that. I done always did things on my own. God say be the lender, not the borrower.

She cleared her throat on the other end of the line and said, "You all right? If you need me to be there, I can be on my way. I know y'all had got close. I can come sit for a little while."

My eyes darted to the digital clock on the wall. I didn't want her coming by, so I said, "Nawh. Don't come over. I'm all right. We all right."

"You sure, Punkin?" she asked, and that made me kind of jump a little. She ain't called me that since I was a little girl. Since I really felt like I was somebody Punkin. "If you need me to be there, I'll be there for you," she said. I shook my head, like she could see me, and tears welled up in my eyes.

She said she could be there again and I couldn't say nothing back to her. I couldn't talk or everything inside me was gone come out.

I put the phone on speaker and laid it down on the counter beside the cutting

49

board. I went back to cubing the thick, smooth processed cheese. And I listened to her voice call me over and over again. *Punkin. Punkin. Punkin. Punkin . . .*

Grandmoan die, I won't never find out where she keep that money. If she live, I probably won't find out either. She ain't been herself in a long time and I'm coming to realize she might not never get back to being herself. I wonder what that mean to me and my kids. To my momma, who I got a mind to take to Dallas with me. My momma ain't never been the kind of momma I am to my kids, but that don't make her any less than what God done made her to me.

"Momma." My son call me from his bedroom, and it make me pause with my scrubbing and let out a weak "Huh?"

"Is Jazera done yet?" he ask, and it get on my nerve that he rushing cause I know he just want to play that video game. When we pulled up after I got my groceries from the store, I told him: "Don't ask me to play no game till you done your homework, ate, and got your bath." Now he rushing and I want to go in there and get on him, but I'm gone ignore him cause he done rushed through everything to get to that game. Rushed through his homework; rushed through his chores; rushed through dinner. Everything.

Everything ain't about having fun. I want him to know you can't run all over others, rushing to where you want to be. He gone consider others.

Me and my friend Keesha walk Canyon Creek Park once a week. Neither of us can afford a gym membership. I have problems keeping my weight up, but Keesha need any kind of membership she can get. After five babies, her body done had it. She ain't lost the fat from the last one, and he almost five.

Me and Keesha walk that park cause it got steep rolling hills, and she figure that's good for her burning fat and I figure it's good for my muscle building. Ain't nothing scenic about Canyon Creek Park, though. More dirt than grass and trash all over the place, but it's the only park on this side of town that the white folks ain't come and took from us. They set they eyes on something, decide they want it, they do everything in they power to keep us out. Whole east side used to go out to Buffalo Lake on Juneteenth. I mean, it was huge. Parades, music, and community barbecues, and it was always a weekend-long ordeal. It was like manna from heaven, too. Nothing never ran out cause the whole east side be done collected money and raised funds for it all year long. It was good to see everybody come together like that. They kept it up without the city help for a long time too. Folks went to drugging and thugging and it seem like the city just watched the whole park go to waste. Like they was waiting for it cause they knew how much value was in that place. White folks decided they want Buffalo Lake and they let it start looking bad enough to take it on the count of us not wanting it. Now, the police won't even let us get on the grass at that park without taking somebody to jail. The whole east side done abandoned our big Juneteenth celebrations. Most of our kids don't even know what Juneteenth is.

Anyway, me and Keesha walk and talk and catch up and encourage each other about being struggling mothers. Keesha husband is best friends with my kids' daddy, Omar. Me and Omar ain't lived together — ain't tried nothing like that in a long while — since I been saved, probably. So when she got to telling me about the new girl he messing with last week, I acted like I ain't care. But that's on my mind, too. I done put it with my move stuff. Something else to get away from.

"Momma," Jazera call. "Momma, tell Javon to leave me alone."

And it don't sink in with me at first. I keep scrubbing the cup I'm working on. Start to open my mouth and tell Javon I'm gone beat his butt, and then I remember she in the tub. He ain't posed to be nowhere near there. Everything go quiet for me. Like my ears closed up and I done gone deaf.

I drop the cup in the sink and water splash on me and on the floor, but I don't care. I want my heart to be still cause not in my house. Not never in my house. I almost slip on the spilled water trying to make my way to the bathroom, where I can see the back of Javon head and his orange T-shirt moving like he doing a dance. When I come closer, sound come back to me and I can hear him. He saying, singing, "Ah ha, ah ha. She ain't coming. Crybaby, crybaby."

When I get close enough, I slap his back with my open palm so hard he fly forward and trip on the rug. His head barely miss the side of the tub, but I ain't worried about that. His scared eyes don't move me or make me softer. I bend over him and pull him up by his shirt.

"What you doing in here?" I scream in his face. "What you do to her?" I ask. I can feel his body trembling under the weight of my grasp. I can feel my own body trembling.

I don't know what's going on. Javon and

Jazera both know the rules. I ain't never put them in the tub together. I don't care that it's just a few years between them. They ain't never allowed in the bathroom when the other there. They ain't never allowed to see each other nakedness.

"I — I," he stutter, but don't say nothing else, so I look over at my daughter, who sitting in the tub with her black Barbie doll suspended in midair. Her eyes wide with fear and it make me want to hurt the child under my hand.

"What did you do?" I say, grabbing both his shoulders between my hands and trying to shake the truth out of him.

"He was throwing toys in here, Momma!" Jazera say so loud she shouting at me and about to cry at the same time. "Momma, don't kill Javon! He was just playing! Don't kill my brother!"

And I look at her and how scared she is and I look at my boy and how scared he is and it make me sick to my stomach.

"Oh," I say, releasing my grip on his shirt. "Oh. I thought . . ." And I can't say it.

I straighten up his shirt, which done got wet from the floor, and I want to bend down and wrap my arms around him, but I'm too shame. I turn my head and see my own face in the mirror. It's flushed red and my nose snotting, like I done ate something spicy.

I take a deep breath and look at my babies. "Javon, get your tail in there and get ready to bathe. Quit aggravating your sister and stay out of here till she done."

He still look a little scared, but he squeeze past me and my heart almost break at how he trying not to touch me.

"Jazera," I say. "Get out of here. Now. And scare me like that again for nothing. Watch what happen."

I walk out the bathroom and go straight to my room, close the door, and start throwing the pillows off my bed. I make my bed every morning soon as I get up. Soon as I climb out, I turn around and fix my mess. And I make it perfect, too, like something in a department store that ain't never posed to be slept in. But right now ain't for beauty. Right now is for something else.

My mouth is open and I'm screaming with no sound. I pull the comforter off the bed, swirl it into a ball with my arms, and throw it toward the dresser. I peel the sheets off and drop them at my feet.

I think about the acceptance letter I got from that college in Dallas. I think about my dream — my nightmares — and start stomping on the sheets. I keep stomping on them, like somebody marching off to something, until I get tired of how they just there.

I crawl up into the center of my bed and I ball my fists up and pound the bare mattress, like a child throwing a tantrum. And then I just stop and lay there, scratching my nails against the clean floral print under me.

The kids was in bed by nine. They was quiet after the bathtub thing. I was too. We moved around the apartment like we was trying to keep out of each other's way, like we was invisible to one another. They didn't even really want to ask me to sign they agenda books for school tomorrow. I don't know why Jazera was scared. She got a sunshine sticker and was named Queen of Goodness today. Maybe it's just that she ain't used to me snapping like that. I don't usually holler or put my hands on them. I whoop them, but only with a belt or a switch. I don't never touch them with my hands. That's anger. Or fear. And you can't go around putting your hands on nobody with one of them spirits on you. Bible say be slow to anger and fear nothing and nobody but God. I want to raise them like the Bible say. I want to be like the Bible say.

I want to be a elephant momma to them too. What God put in them is a wonder to me. Human kids don't know they born blind like little elephant calves. They think they can see cause they got eyes, cause they can look in your face, cause they can reach out and touch your lips when you blow kisses at them. They don't know my eyes and everything I see and done seen is my trunk. That I'm leading them with all that. They don't know that I'm there to grow them safe. And I know it ain't God-like to want this, but I think everything the elephants have — all that peace — would be possible for us if we could live like elephants. Without the influence of men.

Javon was scared to show me his agenda cause he got a negative comment. He usually hide the agenda until right before he crawl into bed. Tonight he brought it out, like he always humble and agreeable. He thought he was gone get a whooping. I ain't even say nothing to correct him on the negative comment, though. Instead, I thought about the book of Matthew where it talk about being sorry and saying it and then giving a gift to mean it.

After I signed my name in the little signature box under the date, I extended my hand to give Javon the agenda and when he extended his to reach out for it, I pulled him into me. I know he was scared. I could feel his heart pounding up against my chest.

I could feel Jazera holding her breath on the other side of the den. I wrapped my arms around him tight, so tight I could feel his breath against my neck. I nuzzled my face into his neck and smelled his clean body. I kissed him loud and then blew a raspberry into his flesh and he laughed. Just like that, he laughed.

"Momma sorry," I told him when I tucked him in his bed a few minutes after that. "Just follow Momma rules, okay, baby?" I said.

He nodded, and when I went to his sister's bedroom, she opened herself up and let me kiss her, too.

Now, I'm in my bedroom cleaning up my mess.

When I told Keesha about the college in Dallas, she asked me why I want to go away to go to college when we live in a college town.

I wanted to tell her it's too close to Grand-moan house to seem like another world. I wanted to tell her it would be too hard on me to leave hell every day only to come back to it after my classes. I wanted to tell her that it's a whole lot of stuff she don't know about me, but I ain't say nothing. I just shrugged and said, "I need a change — a whole change, girl."

She didn't think I was serious. Shoot, I still don't know if I'm serious. I been trying to find the words to talk to my grandmother for a while now, and she done gone and collapsed on me.

Saying my words to her, telling her what I want, sometimes, one time, it meant something good to me. Before Lydia — before Lil and them left. Before Alex and Marie was gone, me and Lil used to love the idea of going to the hog pen. On the count of Grandmoan having way more nos than yeses in her vocabulary, we was always scared to ask her.

One day, me and Lil stood under that carport all day, trying to practice getting the question out in unison. And when we finally did, when her and Granddaddy finally come through that door and head to the truck, we just blurted it out. "Can we help y'all at the hog pen?" Granddaddy started laughing so hard that I think it caught in Grandmoan throat cause she started laughing too.

When she said, "Come on, gals," and waved her hand for us to come, you could've bought us for a penny. From the moment we squeezed in that truck between her and Granddaddy, Grandmoan was so nice that later that night we hoped she wasn't dying. Lil said her daddy said folks always come nicer right fore they die. She let us feed the chickens, showed us how to milk the cow, and let us call Sooiee as loud as we wanted.

When we pulled back up to the house that night, she thanked us. Actually said, "You little old gals sure did help Grandmoan and Granddaddy tonight. We sure appreciate it. Y'all some hard little workers."

I don't know why she said yes that day. Sometimes, I guess like anybody else, she felt good about something. Maybe Victor and Nikki got back together on *The Young and the Restless.* Maybe she got some money she'd been waiting for. Or maybe she just remembered something beautiful and wanted to be like that for the rest of the day. But all it took was that one yes to set Lil and my smiles for days after that.

And it ain't sitting well with me that my time done run out. That I can't never ask her nothing again.

After I clean up my messes, the one with the kids, the kitchen, and my room, I climb in bed and think about Dallas. About how I can't afford that university *and* living with two kids. Not even with housing assistance and food stamps, I can't afford it. I'll need a little job and all the financial aid they'll give me to help me out, and even with all that, I still don't know. I think about how bad I need that money Grandmoan put away, and I try to figure out ways in my head to make it work, but I know it's pointless.

So many things swirling around in me. "Lord," I say out loud. And I don't mean to do nothing but call out to him at first. But the more my insides swirl, the more I feel I need. "My Lord, my father, who art in heaven," I say. I think about not being able to sleep in the dark; about the bathroom light shining for me, a grown woman, now. I feel my lips beginning to quiver. "Hallowed is your wonderful name," I manage to say. And before any more words come out my mouth, I shut it. I feel tears gathering, like rain clouds inside me, but I refuse to cry.

3
JULIE B.

I sit up on the edge of the bed and listen to how empty the house sound without the humming from Momma oxygen tank. I want to lay down and go to sleep, but I ain't had no good night sleep since Punkin left home. That girl don't know how far I done carried this love for her. Ever since the doctor first placed her little pumpkin head in my arms. She was posed to reset something in me. In all us. She was posed to make the crooked paths straight, like some sort of promise that wasn't never given, like something ain't none of us deserve. She don't know how much hope I drove into her. She don't know nothing about why and I ain't never tried to tell her.

I only call her Punkin in my head these days, since that day she told me what her real name was, like I wasn't the one to give it to her. She'd just turned ten and I wanted to do something nice for her. It ain't never been like me to keep no steady job. I ain't lazy; I just ain't cooking, cleaning, or nothing else for nobody that ain't mine. But for Punkin, I got a job at the chicken shack on the east side and held it down for a whole month before walking off it. During that month, I saved until I was able to get her this custom-made T-shirt and baseball hat that had *Punkin* airbrushed on it in fancy cursive.

When I gave it to her, she didn't look like she hated it or nothing like that. She just sat it on the bed and said thank you. A few months later, I asked her if she was gone ever wear it and she said she wanted to go by her real name. She wanted to be called Jan or January. Reminded me that Punkin wasn't her name. I ain't tell her that's all I done ever called her. That I wanted her to stay my little Punkin. I just nodded and told her I'd call her whatever she wanted to be called.

Since then, since Punkin turned herself January and eventually left home, I just struggle to sleep good. I specially can't sleep tonight. Not since I was told what I was told today. Not since I had to call Lydia and Punkin. I thought about calling my son, too. About telling him that everything gone end real soon, but then I remembered he

63

was working. Remembered I was gone have to wait. Now I'm up with that.

All this got me thinking about my sisters and my brother. About how we could've been so much more if we knew anything about being more. Ruby Nell was so smart — so bright in school. She loved science. Could've been some sort of doctor or scientist. And the baby of us all, Marie, even being born the way she was, she could've known she was loved and cared for and beautiful. And Wayne. My brother, Wayne, was such a sweet thing, but he wasn't allowed to be nothing beautiful. Nothing like what he probably could've been. Nothing like them pretty pictures he used to draw. He was my favorite when we was little. Before Momma wouldn't let him be nobody favorite. That boy would smile so wide when we played in the yard that you could count every one of his teeth. Sitting under the gaze of our father, Jessie B., made us feel safe. Made us feel saved.

I remember falling down on the paved part of the driveway one time. I must've been about seven or eight, which mean Wayne was about nine or ten. My knee scraped real good when I fell. So good, you could see the white meat of it. It was Ruby Nell what was chasing me. I fell running from her. But Wayne made it to me before our father or Ruby Nell could. In my mind, I remember him being there before I could even really hit the ground. And when he looked down and saw all that white and then all that blood, he looked at my face. He put his hand on my cheek and offered a weak smile, and I could see his eyes getting all wet with tears. When he opened his mouth, it sounded like he was gone break, like the very thing holding all the wet inside of him was about to spill out between the both of us.

It's okay, Sister B, he said, calling me by the name only he called me. *Daddy gone fix it. He fix everything.*

And he was right. After our father talked Momma out of whooping Wayne, after he convinced her that Wayne hadn't pushed me down, he bandaged me up and I ran with my brother and sister all day. And sometimes I miss them days. I miss them to myself, though. Can't rightly miss Wayne or love him out loud. That ain't never been no said thing, but it's a known thing.

I'll be sixty-two this year and feel like I'm just now figuring myself out. I heard Momma say things usually click for women right at thirty. Then she said it don't never click for some. I didn't never look up to see if she was looking at me when she said it, but I reckon she was. I think lying to yourself is what slow the clicking down. At the end of my sixtieth year, I just didn't see no point in lying no more. Just woke up one day and wanted to undo every lie I had done ever told myself. Maybe it was I had just realized that my momma wasn't never coming back to herself or maybe it was that things was just now clicking for me at sixty stead of thirty, but I promised myself I was done lying to my own self.

For a long time, I told myself my kids was why I was still living in Momma house, but that ain't right. That ain't the truth. I wasn't built to live in a world outside of Momma's. Done come to terms with I'm gone always be here. Done stopped lying to myself about moving out. And I done come to realize ain't nothing wrong with that. Shit, I'm the only one left out of all her kids. All of them gone. Wayne, Ruby Nell, and Marie. But me, I'm still here. I did something right.

Seem like right then I started to understand me better. Seem like the sun started peeking out on me after all them years of living in my own lies. Living in darkness. So after that, I decided that the next step was to be honest with everybody else. Seem only natural that if the sun peek out if you do something halfway, it might shine its brightest if you do the whole damn job. This part more of a process. This part harder.

I push myself up off the bed and walk to the open door of the bedroom I done slept in my whole life. Momma and Homer room right across the hall, but I know Homer ain't in it. He ain't slept in there since Momma been in the hospital. He act like he waiting on her, like she coming back, like he can't live without her either. I want to ask him if he heard Dr. Kharkuli today. If he heard him tell us to contact the people we needed to contact. That there wasn't gone be no coming home for her.

Homer ain't nothing like Daddy was, but that ain't no bad thing. Ain't no good thing either. He just ain't nothing like Daddy was. He been here since he got here and he know how to be quiet and not get in the way. Homer was anything like Daddy, that shed wouldn't of stayed in that backyard and maybe everything be different.

I step out into the hallway and make my way to the bathroom. It seem even smaller than it did when we was kids. Ain't enough room for the sink, commode, and tub to all fit in there without almost touching. I lift my big T-shirt up and sit down on the toilet seat. When I let the piss go from inside of me, it kind of sting at first. I squint, clench myself down there, and try to let it come out slow. I know it ain't no soap irritation cause I ain't take no bath after Kenzy and Tricia yesterday. I ain't worried about Tricia, but I hope that man ain't gave me nothing. Men always giving me things I can't use. Like Dale and all his hope.

I wipe myself and get off the toilet. I hold down the handle and flush and then I turn on the faucet and let the water run over my fingers. I shut it off and avoid letting my eyes crawl up to the small window over the sink. I don't look at myself these days. I ain't been pretty since the days of Dale.

Tricia always place her hands on the small of my back and call herself ministering to me. I can't help but look her in them honey eyes set in that taupe skin — skin that I can't help but think would be less wrinkled if it was darker, and I laugh. She don't know nothing about being my kind of black. Last time we was together by ourselves, without Kenzy worrisome ass, I laughed at her when she got all serious about Momma and tried to be all encouraging to me. She want us to be serious. Want me to stop fucking her only when Kenzy around. She act like she don't understand how my life set up. How I can't be that way. I'm honest with her about that, but she think I'm lying to her and myself. I don't argue much about it. Don't tell her that I really am learning to separate all my truths from my lies. I know this much: I ain't gone never be what she want me to be. My life ain't never been set up like that.

I leave the bathroom and I'm about to turn into my room when Homer round the corner from the kitchen. He wearing the same clothes he been in all the day, like it's just starting and not ending.

"Need anything?" I ask, pausing at my bedroom door. "You need me to get you anything before I go back in here and go to sleep?"

I get paid as a home health aide to look after Momma during the day, but Medicare don't know I was doing it for free fore they started paying me. They don't know I was gone be here either way.

"I'm all right, Julie B. Think I just got a little heartburn," he say, clutching his chest. "That's what woke me up."

It make me feel some type of way that he do that cause maybe red chile enchiladas was too much on him. I know his heartburn all on me.

"I'm gone try the bed tonight. First time since your momma been gone," he say, like I don't know. Then he move his other hand

and push the small of his back. "Done got to be a old man on you," he say, offering a lazy smile. "Couch ain't a good idea for a back been through what mine been through."

Two days ago, when Momma carotid arteries finally gave up, Homer looked so scared and so lost that I almost cried for him. It was early in the morning, even before Momma get up and go sit on that porch with Punkin. They was still in they bedroom and I could hear Homer talking to her, like she got a mind, like he do every other morning. Momma and Homer took to keeping they bedroom door cracked open when Punkin moved out. I know they did it so I wouldn't be alone, even though they didn't never say it.

I heard Homer clear as day when he called out to me, shouted my name. I jumped out the bed and run straight across the hall and bust through they door, like I was some paramedic. Momma was lying cross the bed, kind of sliding off, and Homer was standing over her, trying to keep her from touching the ground.

Momma eyes looked fuller than they have in a long time. They was darting wild from me to him, like she was trying to say something.

70

When Homer looked up at me, his hands wrapped around my momma, his eyes was watering and all he could get out of his mouth was "Help."

Now, it's just me and him here. His mouth ain't saying it, but I can see he need my help in his eyes.

I nod and say, "Make sure you shower before you get in between them sheets, Homer. Okay?"

Homer nod and I feel bad about having to tell him that, but Momma always said he come from nasty folks. Say he won't bathe or wipe his ass right if he ain't made to do so by a woman he love. I used to think that was the mean talking through her, but after Momma mind started to slip, I started smelling odors come off him that made me know.

"Good night," I tell him, and take a step toward the room.

"You think she come back to all this after she done probably seen glory?" he ask, just kind of blurt out in a hurry.

I look at his face to see if he seriously asking me anything about glory, and it seem like he need something I ain't got in me to give him. I think about my brother and sisters and all what happened in this house. How don't none of it look nothing like glory. But I don't say nothing. I'm worried about my own stuff. About my kids and all the lies that stretch from Jerusalem to Dallas and getting myself right so I can be real and true about all of it. I ain't got nothing for Homer. I just leave him standing there and walk into my room.

He stand in the hallway a little while longer and then I hear his body moving again. I lay in my bed and look at the open doorway, but Homer don't go in the room across the hall. He go back the way he came. He go back and get on the couch.

It's stuff I probably ought to be able to tell him about Momma. Make him feel better about her not coming back. Could tell him that it's good she gone finally be free and that she ain't got to see no more pain. Could tell him about how all these years she ain't been herself, but tears still roll down her face when I bathe her, like she know things she ain't posed to. Like she got regrets, like all the rest of us.

But I don't say none of that. I go back to my room and pick up my phone. I search through the contacts for Alex name. When I find it, I just stare at it. I think about being his momma and who he wanted for a momma. "Shit," I say out loud.

He ain't like Lydia and Punkin. I can't

tell him over the phone. After everything that happened, I got to take it to him in person. I tell myself I'm fine with that the whole time I'm getting dressed. I tell myself I can do it. And I use the time and the quiet to practice all my truths, and the whole time I'm practicing and saying the stuff out loud, I feel like I'm becoming and that's gone make it all right.

4

ALEX

The quiet is an oasis and a killer. When I came in from my shift, I put my gun and holster on the counter and let myself fall down on the couch. We had a rough night out there. You never can really know what to expect when you respond to a 10-16. Could be anything. Parents fighting. Siblings fighting. Grandparents fighting. Anything. Last night, it was a couple. By the time we dropped them off at the station, my arm was scratched up from *her,* and my partner, Chavis, had a knot forming on his head from *him.* Nights like that nothing left to do but sit down.

Nights like last night, nights I come in late off the beat, I pull out the one photo that means anything to me. Grandmoan's eyes look empty and her white hair is cornrowed back. The little girl is on her lap and the boy is right beside her. Every face in the photo loved me back at some point, and I try to hold on to that.

Julie B. used to bring the kids and Grandmoan to see me on Wednesdays after she picked them up from school. Sometimes it felt like cheating, not only because it was against what everybody wanted, but because Grandmoan wasn't Grandmoan anymore. That was back before Jan suspected anything. It only lasted a year, but I felt like somebody again. Like I had a second chance.

I can't always sleep when I get in and the quiet don't help. Seems like my mind likes to race and remember more when everything's supposed to shut down than any other time. I don't drink or do drugs or anything of that nature. I don't even take over-the-counter medication. I want to be present for my actions. In as much control as I can be.

It was around three o'clock when I decided that a run would be better than laying up replaying the past. Didn't take me long to get dressed and get out here. I usually run in the early hours of the morning, but not this early. I brought my badge. Always carry my badge. Matters little that I live in a safe neighborhood. That crime is low out here and people do things like run any time they like. Seems that's the problem.

Sometimes they harass me about being out. Those times, I'm usually in street clothes. Seems like they forget people can live anywhere they want these days. That there are no longer ordinances to keep some of us hidden in the Flats. That we are entitled to the vibrant side of town.

I run by restaurants and eateries and even our only mall. Everything is within arm's reach. Most things are dark and closed, until the sun rises, but there's a spirit of life — of prosperity in everything I pass.

When I was a boy, we didn't come to this side of town much. Back then, there were enough businesses to keep us contained on the east side. There was a Levine's, which most of us could only afford at Christmas and on birthdays, a small flea market complex, countless burger stands, clinics and public service buildings, and enough grocery stores to keep us on our side of town. We had Solar Roller Skating Rink and Mr. Fairs Pleasure Gardens, a make-out point in the '40s, '50s, and '60s turned into a small drive-in movie theater in the '70s. We had everything we needed. Bus routes didn't come all the way to the east side back then, so because we didn't know what we didn't have access to, we didn't feel it. We didn't feel stuck.

I suck air into my lungs and push it out, paying attention to my pacing. I concentrate on my form and make sure that life is moving through me as it should. Most times I run for seven or eight miles before I'm tired, but I've only gone about three miles when I decide to head back in. I'm not tired; my heart's just not in it. I'm consumed by what's going on between me and Veola. What it means when I place that up against what happened with Samra, the girl upstairs.

I tug at my ear buds, causing them to fall from my ears onto my shoulders. Bun B and Pimp C did nothing for me tonight. Might be time to change my playlist. Julie B. once told me that Dale used to be a runner. I wish I had found running when I was still living on the east side. It's therapeutic in a way that I think really would have helped me back then. Instead, I found it too late, at the boys' ranch, a place where folks sent their kids when they felt like there was nowhere else for them. One boy, Big Alfred, was there because his momma remarried and his stepdaddy didn't want him around no more. He had three sisters that the stepdaddy let stay, but Big Alfred couldn't and that broke that boy's heart. Another boy, Quintan, his parents were addicts and his grandparents, a pastor and his wife, were too old to handle him. Then there were boys that were there because they had drug problems and robbing problems and staying-in-line problems.

It was a whole mix of us. None of us had been caught by the law for anything, which is why we were even able to come to the ranch. It was a word-of-mouth place. No systems. A resource for black folks by black folks. There were six rooms and twelve beds at the ranch for us boys. They were always full, unless someone aged out. That happened, the bed would fill up in a matter of days. Guess folks dropped their kids off there and hoped they wouldn't see them on the news years later.

The ranch wasn't that bad. Two hundred acres, and it was a real live working ranch. There was so much land, I'm sure I never saw the half of it. It wasn't nothing like Grandmoan and them hog pen. It was the real thing. They had so many sheep and cattle and goats and pigs that it was impossible to count them. They even had a few horses. It was considered a small ranch, but none of us there saw it that way.

The folks that ran it were good people. A husband and wife. They had a fair system. Made sure we did no harm and none came to us. Shoot, if I'd have had Mr. Lewis and his wife in my life from the start, I could've been anything. They created an order for all of us. The whole place was built around three rules. The first one was do no harm. Lewis was serious about that too. It wasn't just us and them they expected us to avoid harming either. We couldn't treat the animals in ways that didn't serve the earth. We had to be good to them. Listen to them. They taught us how to catch rats and skunks and anything else I'd have killed back home and release them safely back into the wild. Guess that kind of fed into the second rule: Work, take care of, and respect the land. It didn't matter how old or how young we were. We all contributed. We all followed a schedule. We all did our schoolwork. Our chores. There were always animals to feed. To learn to ride if we followed the rules. There were barns to clean. Pastures to tend to. And we all ate from the fat of the land.

No matter how fat the land was, though, there was no getting past the pain and loneliness of losing my family. The third rule made this harder. Face your truth. My truth came to be that I put myself away from my family. There was something broken in me. Something that no one could love.

Going through my formative years without

my family made me value them even more. During those years, when a lot of teenagers got people loving on them so hard it's suffocating, I longed for it. Mr. and Mrs. Lewis, they were good to us. I can't ever fix my mouth to say otherwise. But they didn't love us. Theirs was a system held together by rules. I witnessed a few boys break small rules that got them put off the ranch. I never wanted to be put away from anywhere again. It was there on that ranch that I learned to be a good boy. To follow spoken and unspoken rules. Sometimes, though, when whoever I was bunking with at the ranch was sleeping, I cried for home.

It seems like that longing — that missing home — has persisted since I was a kid at the ranch. Movement like this, like running, it usually helps. I stop running when I make it back to my complex. It's late, and I know everyone is sleeping. I don't want to wake them with my feet against the pavement. They all seem to wake so easily.

When I stick my key in the door, I'm startled by her raspy voice. "Coming in late, Mr. Officer. Coming in real late," she says, making her way to the stairway nearby.

I stop with the key and look back at her. "Samra," I say, looking around, as if anyone else in Briarstone Apartment Homes would be out this time of night. The complex consists of twelve units. Most of the people here are quiet. Mostly old with no frequent visitors. Mostly forgotten or set-aside folks. Samra moved upstairs about six months ago. She's Pakistani — Muslim, I think. Not traditional, though. Not anymore anyway. Her parents helped her move in. She and her mother both wore hijabs. She was quiet and polite that day. Her parents seemed pleased when they saw me heading to my apartment in my uniform. She seemed pleased that they were pleased. After that day, she wasn't Muslim anymore, I guess. After that day, she let her wild side out. Now she smokes and drinks and, for a while there, took a lot of company. I haven't seen her with her head covered ever since that first day.

She nods and sits down on one of the steps. It seems that she has sat directly under a spotlight, the moonlight, and the way her face illuminates makes me think of all the images of Vishnu I've seen. Her hair is full, dark, and long. Her skin is even darker than I originally thought. It's cinnamon and, to me, she looks like a light-skinned black girl.

She brings a lit cigarette to her lips and sucks it in. When she exhales the smoke, I think about running and how the inhale and exhale is almost the same.

"So," she begins, resting her elbow on her knee and the side of her face on her fist. She casually flips her hair and it all tumbles to one side. The way she sits there with her hair like that makes her look weighed down by it. Makes her head look heavy. "Guess I have to take three a.m. smokes to even get a glimpse of you," she says before bringing the cigarette to her lips again.

I think about joining her on the step, making up an excuse, but I don't want to smell like cigarettes and I don't want to be close to her. I lean against my door and shrug.

"I — I've been working. Busy. Been meaning to stop by. I just —"

"Haven't seen you since that day," she says, cutting me off. She pats the concrete space on the step beside her. "You can sit down. I won't bite."

I take a few steps and lean the side of my body against the railing and say, "Naw, can't sit after running like that."

After she moved in, I could tell she was lonely, and I understood that. She would knock on my door and ask for help with things. Bring food. Chicken biryani and samosas and stuff like that. Samra's just a young college girl. Grad school. Barely in

82

her early twenties. Second-generation immigrant from a family settled in Houston. She missed her family and she didn't. She missed the company but not the pressure.

I can't remember the exact moment when I started to be okay with her knocking on my door. Stopped stepping outside of it and started letting her in, but eventually we eased into that and then into my leaving the door unlocked and her just walking in.

I want to tell her that what happened shouldn't have happened. That I shouldn't have let it, but that because I did, we can't be anything anymore. But I don't want to hear her whining. She did that day. *I know what I'm doing. We're two consenting adults,* she said. But all I could see was my sister in her eyes. All I could see was Jan.

She repositions herself, letting her elbows rest on the step behind her. "I know you've been avoiding me, Alex," she says. "I just want you to know that I'm sorry. If I offended you, if I overstepped. I just thought . . ."

I don't say anything. I think about Veola, a woman closer to my age. I'm lucky to have her, at least Chavis thinks so. *She bad,* he says when I mention her or we run into her during our shift.

"Shit," Samra says in a voice so raspy it

83

sounds like a whisper. "I thought we were both feeling something, you know?" she asks, looking up at me. Her young, wide eyes expect an answer that I can't give. I'm not sure I understand the question.

She sighs and looks out into the courtyard.

My mind wanders back to that night. Before that night, I liked to think she was teaching me to be a big brother until we crossed that invisible line. I liked telling her to be careful with the men she brought home. I liked walking past them in the breezeway, wearing my uniform, letting them know that no harm should come to her.

The night it happened, she walked into my apartment and I thought I'd get to be her brother. I hadn't expected her to slide her small hands around my waist and turn me toward her, to get on her tiptoes and bring her lips to mine. I hadn't expected to like it. I hadn't prepared myself for how hard it would be to stop the kiss after it started. In the end, stopping it just didn't feel like enough. Pushing her away — asking her to leave. That wasn't enough either. In that moment, when our lips touched, I liked it. I liked her lips touching mine and that's what bothers me the most. That's why I can't be anything to her anymore.

"You don't know me, Samra," I say, pushing myself away from the rail. "You don't know me and you should stay away from me."

Her eyes are wide. Looks like she wants to say something, but I don't wait for her to speak. I take the few steps to my door and insert my key. "Good night," I say, without turning to her. "Be safe out here," I add. And I disappear into the darkness of my apartment, knowing that her eyes are still on my back.

After my run, after leaving Samra on the stairs outside of my apartment, sleep finally caught me, but it wasn't the good kind. There's this recurring nightmare I have. In the nightmare, I'm five years old, walking home from my half-day pre-K class. It's not cold outside, but it's chilly. Chilly enough to cause me to have my tiny hands shoved in the pockets of my corduroy jacket and my shoulders stretched up to my ears. As much as I'd like to hop in a warm car with someone, I'm doing like Grandmoan and Julie B. told me the first time I walked at the beginning of the year: *Do not talk to strangers and come straight home.* But then a black Chevy pulls up close to the curb beside me, and I stop because the driver isn't a stranger. It's Uncle Wayne, and whenever he comes to Grandmoan's he's the cowboy I want to be. His eyes are hard and his words are always short.

From the driver's seat of his truck, his cowboy hat is huge and his gold-plated front tooth twinkles at me like magic. He's smiling and his eyes are lazy, but he's Uncle Wayne, so I trust him and climb into the passenger seat of his truck. The truck smells of something stale, like Granddaddy's hog pen shoes or Grandmoan and Julie B. cleaning chitterlings in the kitchen sink on Christmas Eve.

"I'm gone take you home, Alex, but first we gone stop by my house," he says, after asking me about school and Grandmoan and Julie B. And I just nod and get in because I have no reason to distrust Uncle Wayne.

We get to his house and the stale smell from the truck greets us inside. I follow Uncle Wayne into a room that holds a couch, a chair, and what looks to be a thousand pictures on one of the walls. It looks like a bedroom that has been turned into a den. The shag carpet on the floor is thick and I feel like I'm floating when I step on it. The nasty smell from the truck is heaviest in here.

"Sit down, Alex," he says, and pats the seat beside him on the couch. And then he places a smoker's pipe on the small round table next to the couch. "Every man need his own room. You hear me?" he asks, placing his heavy arm around my shoulder. "And every man need to know how to keep a secret." He points his finger toward the door and pulls my body close to his. "Close the door, nephew." And I do as I am told.

When I make it back to the couch, he points to a picture on the wall. "Me and your daddy. We was cool before he started up with your momma. I know your daddy. You know that?" I shake my head no and move my eyes from the wall to his. There is something wrong in them and it scares me. Still, I want to ask him questions about my father. Julie B. doesn't talk about him and Grandmoan curses when he's mentioned, but Uncle Wayne has this picture of him and I almost can't remember his face.

I walk over to the wall to get a closer look at the picture. I have to look up just a little to see myself in the stranger's face. Looks like a family shot Julie B. never knew was taken. It was from a time I couldn't recall. I look younger than a year old, and my father is holding me against his chest, looking down at my head, like he's proud. Julie B.'s

87

staring up at him, like she's lost in time and space, and my innocent face stares straight ahead — at the camera — with spit dribbling down my chin.

"I took that picture right after I bought this house," Uncle Wayne says. At this point, he's standing right behind me. Towering over me. So close I can almost feel his skin. "I know where your daddy at," he whispers, throaty-like in a voice I don't really recognize. "That's me and his secret." And I twist my head to look up at him.

"Can I see him, Uncle Wayne?" I ask.

He nods his head and smiles. "Go lay on your belly on the couch. We got to learn to trust each other before I share me and your daddy secret."

I obey him, and when he undresses me, I don't cry. When I feel the first cold and then warm oil on my bottom, I don't say a word. When he lifts my hips slightly and pulls me closer to him, I put my face in the couch. When he cups my front in his palm and enters me from behind, I grunt, and I bite the cushion as he moves in and out of me. But I never scream. I never cry. Not even when he drops me off at the corner of Colgate Street and I feel the wet in my pants. Not even when Grandmoan whops me for being late and shitting myself. I let the silent tears roll because I want to see my father. I want to see myself.

That's where I was when Julie B. knocked on my door. A small kid again. Living like that again.

To me, Julie B. is usually like a mosquito. She buzzes and speaks, and sometimes she tries to caress me, but she's been mostly useless my whole life. Her love, her faith, her protection, it has all equaled shit. But I am grateful for her knock this morning. She roused me from my sleep right when I was looking at Uncle Wayne's wall of photos. Right before that moment I can't make myself forget.

She was jiggling the door handle by the time I made it to the small living area of my apartment, like she was prepared to force her way through, and when I opened the door she just fell into me, like she could go no further.

And now, after the strangeness of that moment, she's sitting on my couch sniffling, trying to stop crying like a child would after a spanking that hurt her feelings. Julie B.'s never been a drug addict, but she looks the part. Everything from her frail body to her missing teeth to the way she dresses says she is and always has been a drug addict. But she isn't. She's just been beaten down by life and by people, and now she's basically nothing.

I go to the kitchen and fill a glass with tap water, and when I return it appears that she's caught her breath. She's looking down at her hand, but like she has eyes in the top of her head, she reaches up for the glass. She just holds on to it, though. She doesn't drink.

She clears her throat and says, "I did the best I could with y'all." She sighs and then looks up at me. I'm standing in front of her, trying to figure out the source of her tears.

"I just . . ."

I exhale. "You come here at five in the morning to tell me that?" I ask. "All the way —"

"Just let me talk," she yells, and I take a step back. I've never heard her raise her voice to anyone or anything. "Nobody ever let me say shit." She tilts her head and waits for me to reply and when I don't, she goes on.

"I . . ." she starts, and stops again. And then she closes her eyes. "I was there when Momma built that shed. She built it for him. She put him out there to give up on him —"

I hold up my hand to stop her. I don't want to talk about that with her. Not the shed. Not who I think she's referring to. She's not the one this conversation is for. She is not fit for this. "What are you talking about, Julie B.? Why are you here?" I hear my voice raise. There are cracks in it.

She shakes her head, purses her lips together, and closes her eyes. "She dying, Alex. Grandmoan in the hospital and she ain't gone make it."

"Wait — what?" I say, letting my hand slide down my face.

"My momma. Doctor say this it," she say in almost a whisper.

I feel like she's kicked me in the stomach or like Uncle Wayne is entering me again for the first time. I don't say anything. I don't know what to say. And I feel my legs weaken. I need to sit down, but the couch is all I got in the room and I don't want to sit next to her. I lean on the closest wall and let my body slide down to the floor.

"H-how did . . ."

Her mouth drops open, like she wants to say something else. Like she has more than that inside her. But she closes it and shakes her head and waves both hands in the air as if she surrenders. She places the glass on the floor, stands up, clears her throat, and tilts her head. "That's all I wanted to say. That's why I came. Thought of all people, you'd want to know."

From the floor, I watch her walk to the door. Her body is wavering like a desert mirage and I wonder if this moment is real. I want to call out to her. To ask her what she wants me to do, but I already know. I've known my place for a long time now and all I can do is put my face in my hands.

HELEN JEAN
1961

Some mornings she'd wake up and remind herself who she was. *You Helen Jean. Your momma was Dimple Mae. She wasn't right in the mind and you was just a girl when she left you here to take her place in the rot that was her life.*

Helen Jean knew one day she'd wake up and all of that would be gone. She knew she wouldn't remember who she was or how she became that person and that it would leave her in pieces, like chipped nail polish or cracker crumbs in shag carpet. She imagined that some of the pieces would fall and she would never find them in the carpet of the world. And to her, that would be heaven.

But she meant to always remember the day she knew where she was headed. The day she looked at her father standing there, half naked, speaking to the dead. The day she felt cheated because he couldn't remember it all as it had been. How he had rotted them all. She meant to remember the day that she realized that she would one day be him and she still saved his life. She wanted to hold that day in her head so that she could remind her maker of the right she had done if she ever met him.

Helen Jean had juked with her brother, Bacon, the entire night before that day. When they pulled up to the curb of her husband's house in the truck her brother had borrowed from one of his girlfriend's neighbors, the street was dark and quiet. Helen Jean could hear the crickets singing along with all the other night sounds. She wanted to go inside, but Bacon was trying to push her to let him come in, too.

He wanted to sleep on the couch, but she couldn't let him in. He wasn't welcome in Jessie B.'s house. Bacon would've remembered that if he wasn't such a lousy drunk. And to Jessie B.'s credit, Bacon *was* a nuisance, a violent drunk even, but he was her brother. The only one she had left, and that meant something to her. She had the memories to prove it. From when their mother was alive. When they thought she was well. When Bacon and Dennis would ball their fists up at night as they listened to their mother's screams on the other side of

94

the wall. On those mornings after, their mother would make them corn cakes and smother them in maple syrup. She would kiss them each on the head and say *Ain't no love out there like a momma's. It go big and wide and far and always. Member that.*

Back then, there were no chores outside of chasing each other on the country plot of land they lived on. Helen Jean and her brothers Bacon and Dennis loved each other with words back then. *Love you,* they'd say when they parted for school or dozed off to sleep. *Love you,* they'd whisper on those nights their mother screamed. *Love you,* they'd say right before their father came in from work and the house went silent. And they helped their mother look after the youngest brother, the one who wasn't whole, Herbert Lee. They learned to understand his hungry moans from his lonely moans from his wet moans. They all determined, without saying it, that as long as they lived, they would have a home in one another. *Love you* is what they meant by that.

But Helen Jean's husband didn't know all of that. Jessie B. might've been ignorant to it, but adulthood hadn't erased it in Helen Jean's mind that even though, after her mother was gone, she grew up the only girl in a house of men, she wasn't the only one to suffer. They had all suffered their father's ways. His touches. The silent horrors that sat between them. The ones they could never speak out loud.

Her brother was a big baby when he was drunk. He'd do anything. Beg, cry, and sometimes become their father. Sometimes, Bacon would forget that his sister was all he had in the world. Forget that she was more than just a thing to remind him of how their father loved. And he would haul off and strike her, and she knew it was because he had never been able to strike their father. To fight him off them. When he became a baby like that, she became the person to take care of him. To make him feel like he had power enough to be a man in the world. She thought her big brother was at least worth that.

So that night, she decided to let him sleep a little of it off in that truck. She planned to let him fall asleep, after which she would sneak out and go inside. But she dozed off too. Woke up to a door slamming. To seeing her father making his way to her husband's porch. He'd bought the house next door three years earlier and she was sure he did it to torture her. Helen Jean woke up to seeing him walk the path he'd created between her husband's house and his, and she listened to the scraping metal from his chair being dragged across hard dirt and then the cement under the carport.

She thought he'd wake up the whole neighborhood, especially when that mutt Jessie B. bought the boy popped her head up from her paws and started barking.

And when her father made it to the porch with his chair, he stood there for a long while, like he was sending some type of telepathic message to the truck before slowly easing his body into the chair and mumbling something she couldn't make out.

He told the dog to shut up and Helen Jean looked over at Bacon, who was rubbing his naked eye with his index finger and had his other index finger stuck under the black patch he'd worn on the other eye since the year their mother died. Helen Jean watched him for a moment before turning her head back to the window.

Helen Jean hated the boy's dog for reasons that all turned back to the things she lost long before the boy and his dog entered her world. Those things were things she couldn't imagine ever forgetting, but she always welcomed the idea as an undeserved blessing. The dog was something filthy to Helen

Jean. And the boy loved her. Didn't care that she was ugly. Didn't care about her long body or that she was covered with stringy, matted black fur. He was unbothered by her one eye that was coated over with a milky glaze or that her teeth protruded out of her mouth, like a bucktoothed child's. He loved her and Helen Jean hated that.

The dog, Black Gal, hushed barking when the boy walked out of the front door of the house. He moved quiet and sneaky, and like her father, he wore only his underwear. Helen Jean knew without being told that he'd probably pissed the bed. She would beat him later on that morning. Had told him the day before that he was too old to be pissing his bed, but she'd been too hungover to beat him then. To bruise him in the way that she'd done the day before that. She'd threatened, though. *Do it again. Let me find piss in your bed tomorrow. Just let me.* She couldn't not do it. All of the boy's ways had to be kept in check.

Bacon asked her if she planned to get out of the car. "Need to get this pickup back to Vera so she can get it to Roy Lee before he got to leave for work," he said to her.

She closed her eyes and thought about getting out of the truck, passing her father and the boy before making it into the house.

She shook her head and asked her brother to give her a minute.

And then she felt his warm hand on top of hers. She heard his lips smack and he whispered, "Okay, sister. Okay."

And they sat in the silence of the truck with the windows cracked a bit. Helen Jean heard the boy call out to his dog. Ask her if she was waiting for him. His sound was strong like her husband's and that almost made her feel right, like the boy might be okay.

But then her father said, "What you doing out here, boy? Fooling with that old hound. Go on, now. Gone to bed." And Helen Jean could feel the sides of her lips twitch.

She forced herself to peer through the darkness at him, sitting with both hands resting on the head of the cane that stood between his spread legs. Besides his underwear, he wore a Panama hat — his daily uniform. Had been since he moved into the house next door. Helen Jean didn't bother with trying to figure out how long he'd been behaving that way. When she left him in the Flats all those years ago, he didn't go out in his underwear. Back then, he had so much dignity and pride that he forgot to have shame. Now he walked around the neighborhood in his skivvies and talked to the dead, forgetting the things about himself that Helen Jean and Bacon couldn't.

"What you want with me, Herbert Lee?" She heard him hiss her dead brother's name at the boy, and the boy simply stared at the old man in the weird way he was prone to stare. "Sit down somewhere. Dimple Mae bout to bring the sun," he finally commanded.

The boy's body dropped into the iron chair on the porch, causing it to scrape against the cement. Helen Jean gritted her teeth and cringed at the sound. The chair was one of four that she bought on credit from the Watkins truck. Her father never used her chairs. Each summer morning he'd bring his own and sit quietly until breakfast, during which he'd leave and return after, until lunch, during which he'd leave and return after, until supper when he'd retire for the evening.

He didn't say much of anything that made sense while he was out there. He watched the children play, frowning every now and then, and commanded the dog to shut up, to stop chasing the mailman, and to die. When he was there, her husband fussed and complained and told the old man to leave his kids and the dog alone, and Helen Jean stayed inside. Some days, just after supper, Bacon would pull up in a borrowed car or truck, and she'd emerge dressed for juke jointing, trying hard not to make eye contact with any of them, trying hard not to be part of her own life.

Since that night in the outhouse, that night the turpentine failed her, she'd tried. Tried at being a wife and mother, and even though she still gave life as promised, as required by Jessie B., some of that trying just didn't stick and Jessie B. let her be who she was.

In fact, they made a silent arrangement before the second child, Julie B., was born. The arrangement: Jessie B. would love, nurture, and provide for the children. Helen Jean would stay with them during the day while her husband worked and she'd respect him by making sure that each child born had his blood coursing through its veins. There was never a verbal discussion regarding the so-called arrangement, but they both knew to live by it. To Helen Jean, Jessie B. slipped into his part with ease. Herself, not so much.

Two things happened to set the arrangement in place. The first thing: When the boy was still an infant, Jessie B. came home from the garage midday for dinner to find his wife still in bed while the hungry, soiled child screamed at the top of his lungs. Since this wasn't the first time, it became clear to him that Helen Jean would not care for the boy. Still, Jessie B. didn't commence to beating her, like other men in town might've done. He tended to the boy's needs and stayed with him for the rest of the day. After that day, she'd wake up at noon to find that Jessie B. had taken the boy with him, which he continued to do until the child was old enough to care for himself in small ways, like going to the toilet and pouring his own cereal.

The second thing happened about four months before the birth of the second child. It took Helen Jean a while to figure out that Jessie B. had figured about the man she'd taken up with. It was Ernestine who told her that Jessie B. had taken care of it. That he had beat the man badly with the butt of his pistol, almost to the end of his life, and that the man was long gone. After Jessie B. ran him out of town, he never asked Helen Jean about the baby she carried, the one she named Julie B. after him, but she knew that they best be his after that.

For Jessie B.'s part, he seemed to know all there was to know about why his wife struggled to love her son — to even look at him — and why she hated her father. She was grateful that he'd never made her speak about it. That he seemed to understand that some things could not be put together with words without taking the soul apart. As he'd promised her in the café that night, he took on the responsibility of the cause and condition in which he found her and satisfied his own search for purpose in that and all that would come from them.

And now, she listened to her father tell the boy to look at something and watched him point his finger toward the sky. "Sun turning the sky pink, boy. You see it?" he asked the boy.

The boy was quiet and that seemed to unnerve her father.

"What? What, boy? You sit up there with your fool self, staring at me. I'm trying to show you one real thing," he said. He smacked his lips and shifted his body in the chair. "What you know about anything, boy?" he said. "Bet you can't even use no knife. Can you?" he asked.

And still, the boy didn't answer.

There was silence for a while and then her father spoke again. He said, "Kay, boy. My papa showed me. I'm gone show you. This how you do it."

Helen Jean's eyes widened, like that would

103

change what she was watching. She watched him try to teach the boy and thought about all the childish lessons passed between him, her, and all three of her brothers. She told herself to step out of the truck and put an end to it. That the monster who was her father should teach nothing to the monster who was her son. That nothing else should pass between them because the blood was already too thick, but she stayed still and listened. When she looked over at Bacon, he was still, too. His eye was focused on the darkness of his lap.

By the time she finally said yes to Jessie B. and left her father's house, her youngest brother had died in a filthy home for imbeciles and both of her remaining brothers had seen opportunity in Korea. They ran away to war with no plans of returning home after. Dennis died in Korea, and Bacon, remembering his sister long after the war had ended, returned to Jerusalem to find her married.

The first time Bacon saw the boy, he broke down crying and she knew he knew how the thing had come to be. She knew her brother felt guilty for leaving her — for being the oldest and not being able to protect any of them. Sometimes that guilt came out as extra care toward his sister, but sometimes it was something else. Something dark. Something mean. She never told Jessie B. about the times her brother hit or cursed her, but she learned to expect it when his good eye was coated in a sadness that kept him from seeing who she was.

"He should've died instead of Momma," Bacon said. His words were slow but they didn't crash into each other the same way they had before he and Helen Jean dozed off in the truck. "Herbert Lee and Dennis might still be here," he said, his voice cracking.

Although she was thinking of her mother's uselessness, how she'd voluntarily left them to a father that she knew herself was a monster, Helen Jean nodded. Bacon was right. If her father had died instead of their mother, the boy would not exist and all of her brothers would likely be alive and be whole. But her father had been as bad a husband as he was a father and had chased their mother right to her grave.

"Member that time she took us to Reno? Thought it was a doctor out there what could help Herbert Lee. Make him right." Bacon smiled. "Stopped at Hoover Dam on the way back. Member that, sis?"

Helen Jean nodded, but remained silent.

"Momma showed us a good time. Every

night in a different state on the way and back." Bacon chuckled. "Member Dennis disappeared in Albuquerque? Momma had us searching all over that motel for him. I ain't never tell her I found him. Nigga was balled up sleep behind some old pickup with some nasty-looking gal." He laughed.

Helen Jean's eyes widened as that night came back to her. Her mother was so afraid. Almost in tears as they searched for Dennis. She held Herbert Lee's hand and gently dragged him around the property. Her voice was soft, like cotton to an ear. Helen Jean could remember her comforting whisper to him. *Come on, baby. Momma got you. Momma gone always have you. Got to make sure I have Dennis too.*

Helen Jean remembered watching them and believing her mother and loving her harder for saying that.

And then she was gone.

"Slice it just like that," her father continued, waving the knife through the air. "That's how you fix things done messed up fore somebody else come to fix it for you," he said, and she could hear the smile in his voice. "Yep. Fix things right on up."

After a while, Helen Jean let her head fall back against the window, everything went silent, and she drifted off into an uncomfortable sleep.

When she opened her eyes an hour later, the porch was empty. All of the chairs were still there, including her father's. She opened the door of the truck and looked over at Bacon. His head rested against his own window, but he was not asleep. His eye was open and glazed over as if he were caught in a waking dream.

The door creaked open and he raised his head from the window and sighed. "I'm gone have to whup Vera ass. She gone try me for being this late."

"Don't come get me tonight, Bacon," Helen Jean told him, as she steadied herself on the ground.

"Be at you tonight," Bacon said, as if she hadn't said a word. He turned the key to start the truck. The engine was loud when it erupted and he yelled to speak over it. "Bring some extra money with you. Might have to bring Vera ass with me." The truck moved away from the curb and she watched it until it disappeared.

An hour later, Helen Jean was inside and her father was back on the porch with the boy. The morning sun was high in the sky and Jessie B.'s legs stuck out from underneath the front of the Buick Super he was forever working on and Black Gal chased

Julie B. around the front yard. She was giggling, and Helen Jean tried to remember
herself that way. Every now and then the
dog would catch her by the trim of her panties, and Helen Jean almost laughed out loud
because it was almost cute. The baby's cloth
diaper was brown with dirt. She sat on a
grassless corner of the yard, banging on a
colorful xylophone.

Helen Jean sat on the couch, peeking out
from behind the curtains. She could see
everything from that spot. The boy was sitting next to her father, mimicking him, trying to be like him. The old man coughed
and the boy coughed. The old man yelled at
Black Gal and the boy did the same. Something inside of her knew she needed to go
out to him, snatch him up from the chair,
and shake everything in him out. To let him
know that her father was the last person he
had to mimic. The last person he had to
ever try to be. That he was already him. But
she didn't. She sat there, her face half hidden behind the curtain, and watched the
boy try to be her father.

Her headache was lifting. The strong black
coffee Jessie B. handed her when she got
out of the shower was helping. He didn't
say much when she walked into the bedroom after sunrise, wearing the same clothes

from the night before. He didn't look up from the edge of the bed, where he sat with his body bent, tying his work boots. When she tried to explain that she'd been out front, he simply held up his hand, like a stop sign. She knew they were okay when he handed her the coffee later. Knew all would be well by nightfall.

She continued to watch the boy and her father. She watched both sets of eyes travel to Mr. Roth, the sometimes substitute mailman, slowly pulling his mail cart behind him. Mail was early that day. When Mr. Roth delivered, it was usually early. On normal days, mail came long after Jessie B. had gone to work, but on Mr. Roth's days, things were usually a little different. A little tense. Mr. Roth was a few houses away, but Helen Jean could see him stealing nervous glances in the direction of her husband's house.

"Get your dog, boy," her father commanded through gritted teeth. "White man come and get you. Put you in that place."

The old man stood and waved for the boy to stand, too. When he did, the old man gave him a light shove forward. "Gone. Get her."

Helen Jean cringed. Maybe it was her father's hands on the boy and maybe it was that the dog had a history — a special relationship with mailmen — but something in her knew that something outside of her was about to happen. Something in her knew that it was out of her control.

The regular mailman, Mr. M.J., was from the east side. He was the first black postal worker in the whole city, but he only delivered to the Flats, Little Guadalupe, Chapman Park, black and Hispanic neighborhoods on the east side. A few years after Helen Jean's family moved to Parkley, Mr. M.J. was assigned that neighborhood, too.

On normal days, when Mr. M.J. was delivering, Black Gal would bark viciously and take off after him, threatening to attack by showing her bucked teeth. Mr. M.J. would laugh and stomp a foot at the dog or kick her if she got too close. *Gone now, Black Gal,* he'd say. *Got too much work to fool with you today.* Black Gal would stand there and continue to bark, but there was no fun in Mr. M.J.'s bravery, so she never did much more than that.

When Mr. Roth hesitantly pulled his cart to the sidewalk in front of their house, the boy stood and the dog stopped chasing Julie B. and looked in the boy's direction. The boy looked like he wanted to say something to the dog — like he was just about to — but Mr. Roth spoke instead.

"You people need to secure that animal if I'm to deliver to you today," he said with the authority that most white folks spoke with, and that's when he got the dog's attention. She looked from Mr. Roth to the boy and back to Mr. Roth, like she was asking for the boy's permission to chase him.

"Come here, girl," the boy said. He kneeled to the ground and patted it, but the dog didn't come to him. Instead, the dog barked, like she was telling Mr. Roth to run and play the game with her, and Mr. Roth's eyes got wide and he stuttered, "W-wait, now, dog." He fiddled with his pocket before deciding to just run.

Helen Jean watched Jessie B. push his creeper from underneath the car and sit up. He looked toward the porch at the boy and her father and then in the direction where the dog had run. "Shit. Not today," he said, frowning and dropping his wrench to the ground. He jumped to his feet and went after the dog.

Helen Jean stood up and tried to get a better view. The boy had left the porch and was running barefoot behind Jessie B.

She couldn't see much. They were several houses down the block, but she could hear Jessie B. He shouted, "Black Gal! Down."

Then she heard him holler, "Get her home, Wayne! Get her home, now!"

Jessie B.'s words became mumbles as he spoke to Mr. Roth. And when the boy approached the yard, she watched both him and the old man stand there, each in his skivvies, the latter with his cane in one hand and his other hand on his hip.

"Told you to get that dog," her father said, as the boy let the dog go and headed back to the porch.

The boy sat down in the same chair her father dragged to the house with him. Black Gal stood on her hind legs and put her front paws on his legs and began to sniff.

When the old man walked up, he stood in front of the boy and waited for him to move. The boy sat still, looking in the other direction, pretending not to see the old man standing there. When the old man reached out to move the boy, Black Gal growled and snapped at his fingers.

"Black Gal," she heard the boy say. "Be nice to Pop Albert —"

But her father's quick movement cut the boy's words in half. He grabbed the dog and gripped her neck in the palm of his hand. The boy screamed and the dog wiggled to free herself and for a minute Helen Jean felt like a mother who needed to protect her child from the thing that got her.

The old man's cane fell, but he didn't lose his balance. The corners of his mouth twitched at the sight of the struggling dog, like he wanted to smile.

Helen Jean watched Jessie B. and the mailman approach. Her father had the boy's full attention.

"You don't snap at me. Bring trouble to this house," the old man said, reaching into the waistband of his skivvies with his free hand. He brought the dog close to him, fastening her between his arm and upper waist.

Jessie B. called to the old man's back. Asked him what he was doing.

Her father's eyes stayed on the boy as he took the blade from the knife. "Member what I told you, boy. Got to fix it yourself."

The boy stared back but didn't make a sound. The dog let out a final whimper when the old man made the quick slice across her neck, and the blood splattered in the boy's face. The old man released the dog, letting her drop to the ground, and her body vibrated for a few seconds before she went completely still.

Helen Jean clasped her hand over her mouth and gasped.

The boy screamed again and dropped to the ground next to the dog. Jessie B. walked toward the baby, who was still sitting in the corner of the yard, and yelled for Julie B. to follow them into the house.

And Helen Jean watched the front door. When her husband walked through it, she followed him and the girls to the back, where he sat the baby on the carpet of the girls' bedroom floor and told Julie B. to stay there until he came back, before closing the door on them.

She asked him, "What you gone do?" as he headed to the master bedroom.

He opened the door to the closet and when he reached up toward the top, her heart sped up because she knew.

"Not like this," she said, stepping out of the way to let him pass with the Winchester tight in his hand.

Helen Jean followed Jessie B. out to where her father was now sitting down in his chair. Mr. Roth watched in horror from the sidewalk, until her father tipped the Panama hat and waved in his direction. Mr. Roth grabbed his cart with a shaky hand and rolled it away, looking back with disbelief and disgust on his face.

The boy hovered over the dog in tears. He kept telling her to get up. It dawned on

Helen Jean that a mother, one who had hope in the future of her son, would go to him and explain why the dog would not, could not get up. But she did not go to him. She turned her eyes to Jessie B.

"Go inside, Wayne," Jessie B. said, and the boy stood to his feet and watched his father approach the old man and point the gun at him.

Jessie B. didn't say a word to the old man when he cocked the gun and perfected his aim, but Helen Jean, standing behind him, could see the anger in her husband's eyes. And she wanted to be silent and still and let him do what he needed to, but he was her father and that had to count for something.

"Momma, you letting Papa hurt me?" her father asked with his eyes on her. "I'm tired of him killing me."

And she jumped, surprised because she'd never considered her father someone's son. She let her eyes roam over him, like she was seeing him for the first time. He was old. She knew he was losing his mind, suffering what all old folks suffer. And she thought about herself. It wasn't fair that he should forget. That he should not live with the monster he made. Forgetting and dying seemed like gifts. She looked at the dull gold that stained his skivvies. Stains on top of stains that had not been properly cleaned. He was suffering in his old age. He needed to live for that.

"Boy," Jessie B. said. "Go inside," he commanded the boy again.

But the boy remained frozen, and though Helen Jean was always eager for a reason to correct him, she was frozen, too.

"Jessie B.," she finally said, turning her attention to her husband. "Don't do this. You do this, what's gone happen to me and these kids?"

Jessie B. broke his stare with the old man and looked at her. He nodded in the direction of the old man. "He ain't gone never hurt you no more. Ain't gone never hurt my children. Never."

"You got to be here to make sure of that," Helen Jean said in the softest voice she could muster.

Jessie B. turned his head toward her and she could tell he was considering her words. He looked at the boy and then at the house before placing the gun on the ground.

He grunted and opened his arms to his wife, waving his hand inward to let her know that he wanted her to fall into him, but she didn't move. She stood there, looking at the triangle the boy and the men made with the space they took up.

Jessie B. finally lowered his arms and looked at the old man and grunted again. "Well, go on now. Get on out of here, Albert Pines. You ain't holding up my porch today," he said, waving a lazy hand in the direction of the house next door.

The old man looked over at the boy, and she thought about picking up the gun and shooting them both. Doing what needed to be done. And then she thought about the night in the outhouse and the covenant she'd made for her life. *Bear it or perish yourself.*

Her father steadied himself with the cane, and then he grabbed the back of his chair and began to drag it back the way he'd come so many hours earlier.

5
LYDIA

I end up taking a red-eye but when my plane lands — and even after I shuttle over to the car rental terminal — the sun still hasn't risen. It's too early to drive straight to the hospital. To just show up there, like some long-lost relative. Anyway, I need to prepare for that. After seeing Mother, I'd rushed home, packed, and just left. So I'm still wearing the sneakers and sweats from when I drove to Fort Worth to see her last night and that's no way to look the first time I see my family in years. So I check into a hotel near the medical plaza to clean up a little, take a shower, and change clothes.

My hotel room is stuffy, but everything in it is pristine. The white of the duvet shines. The plushness of it is inviting, considering that I have had little sleep over the past few weeks. And the empty bed serves as a reminder of what my life has been at home. I sit down on it and let my mind wander to my husband. Walter moved out of the house a few weeks ago, but he moved out of my bed months earlier. Or, rather, I guess he would say that I moved out of his.

Our problems started long before we lost the last baby. Even before we lost the first one. They started when I began believing what my mother believes. *Some people can't have children for a reason.* If I had to choose when, I'd say I was twelve or thirteen the first time the thought occurred to me. I'd gone to see the palm reader, the one everyone called a witch, who lived in the apartment complex Mother and I finally settled in, in Dallas. Some folks might say that lady cursed me but I think she just told me who I was.

Walter traces our problems back to when we left the hospital last year. He's given me space for as long as I've known him. Space for everything. Time for everything. He's always been patient but after the hospital last year, it's like his reservoir of patience just dried up. He expected us to try again, just like we had after all the others. But I was done. I was done taking my temperature and peeing in cups. And when he didn't take my no for an answer, I decided I was also done with letting him touch me.

In the hotel room, I get up from the bed

and begin unpacking my one small suitcase. For a long while, I stare at the tweed suit I brought. It's all wrong — for the weather, for the occasion. Mother never taught me how to dress. Most of the time, she didn't even have it in her to dress herself.

But Julie B. could've taught me. She always kept Jan's hair combed. Her clothes pressed. My aunt never even tried to talk to me about clothes or makeup, never once showed me how to do my hair, and for the first time I feel angry about that as I look down at my old, ugly suit. Aunt Julie B. should've known that Mother wouldn't be able to teach me any of those womanly mysteries. More than that, she should've known that Mother wouldn't be able to take care of me much at all.

I can't imagine how they all allowed her to move a child more than three hundred miles away from them, but they did. And they never called. I rarely saw them, at least not until after Alex was gone. The summertime visits began with Jan's eleventh birthday. Aunt Julie B. met Cousin Joy, one of Aunt Ernestine's daughters that I had not seen since Mother and I lived with them, in Grandmoan's blue Buick, like it was an everyday thing. I hadn't seen them in years, so when my aunt called, I was shocked and excited about seeing them again. She didn't ask about Mother. Didn't ask me to ask her if I could come. Simply said, *Talked to Ernestine daughter, Cousin Joy. Member her? She'll pick you up fore day in the morning. She gone meet us halfway. Be ready.*

When I told Mother, she nodded and told me a story about Soweo. I was up all night. I couldn't wait to finally see Jan again. I wondered how she'd changed. She'd always been so pretty. I wondered how Aunt Julie B. now styled her hair and if she would style mine that way too. And that very first reunion was everything I thought it would be. When we connected in the back seat of that Buick, it was as if I'd never left Jerusalem. Jan was even more beautiful than I remembered. I'll never forget how neatly the edges of her hair were slicked down. How she had a shine — a glow to her skin, like someone with a mother. I was embarrassed sitting next to her in the back seat of that car. She was so much better than me. My hair was brittle and had not been combed since our neighbor's arthritis flare-up. It was during those middle school days, when I was learning to be ashamed, when I was learning what it meant to have my mother as a mother. In the car, I caught

Aunt Julie B.'s eyes on me in the rearview mirror. *Damn my momma. Can't nothing good come from none of us,* she mumbled, shifting her eyes to the road. And the knowing look in her eyes made me think about the palm reader from our complex and how I figured she was probably telling the truth.

But Jan didn't care about my hair or my clothes. She grabbed my hands and told me she thought she'd have to miss me forever. And then she smiled sadly and said, *You all I have left now, you know?* I wouldn't find out what that meant until Aunt Julie B. took us to the ranch to see Alex the next day, but I could tell it was something like bondage and freedom by the look in my cousin's eyes.

We didn't worry about any of that during the car ride or my first night at Grandmoan's. We built a tent on the floor of the room Jan shared with her mother and we shared our lives with each other all night. I told her about the friends I had met and she told me about some girl named Keesha. We didn't talk about Mother or Soweo or any of the things that tore us apart. We talked about missing each other and growing up so that we could be roommates until we died.

When Grandmoan came through the kitchen the next morning and saw us making breakfast for the whole house, we went quiet. We didn't know if she'd be cross with us for using her eggs and bacon. For using her things. But she made her coffee and slid out of the kitchen on her slippers the same way she'd slid in. When she yelled down the hallway, *Fry my eggs hard!* Jan and I erupted in laughter.

Later that day, after Granddaddy and Grandmoan left for the hog pen, Julie B. put us in the Buick and rode us past everything. When she parked the car, she turned to us in the back seat and said, *This where Alex live. We gone go in there and see him. Take him a little care package and then we —*

I don't want to go in there, Momma, Jan said, shaking her head. *I'm not going in there,* she said sternly.

I'd been looking out at what appeared to be cornstalks, trying to set my eyes on a house — a place where Alex could be living — but I couldn't see anything from where we were parked. And then I remembered. I put my hand on her shoulder and said, *I can stay out here with her, Aunt Julie B.,* I said. *You can take his care package and I can stay with Jan.*

Aunt Julie B. smacked her lips. *He your brother, January. He ain't got nobody but us.*

Why you just can't . . .

She let her words go and opened the door of the car and got out. *Don't open this door for nobody. Keep it locked, y'all hear?*

We both nodded. But all of it made me feel so awkward, so out of place. I needed to let Aunt Julie B. know that I was grateful. That I appreciated her getting me to Jerusalem. That I was worthy of being saved and that I recognized that she had been my savior. I needed to give her just a bit of what she was asking Jan for.

When she turned to walk away, I called out to her and she stopped and turned to face me.

Tell him I said hi, Aunt Julie B. She smiled and came back to the car. Put her soft palm on my cheek and said, *Maybe the hope was in you all along.* And I couldn't help but smile at her words.

Jan didn't have many words for me after her mother left us in that car. She didn't want to look at me either. When I asked her what was wrong, she shrugged and said, *Nobody ever pick me. You picked Alex when you said hi and Momma picked you cause you did that.*

I didn't know what to say but I don't know why I said this: *He's your brother, Jan.*

124

It's not a competition. People can love both of y'all.

Her eyes widened with horror and I saw more than just legs dangling from a bed. I saw something so much bigger than me. It made me wish I hadn't opened my mouth at all.

By the third year, my little cousin could hardly stand me. So many minor infractions on top of that day at the ranch had wounded us.

We did that, the three of us — met up halfway to Jerusalem — three years in a row, but I knew before my return from that last visit that Jan was lost to me. Whatever was broken between us, it never healed.

And everyone knew Mother was unfit. Had known since the year my father was put away. But no one came to rescue me. I figured out all the things that I'd missed for myself. Mother never taught me about dressing. Now that I know more about her illness, at times I think she was away from me more than she was with me. Most of the time, she really didn't have it in her to dress herself. Keeping up with the latest trends wasn't a big deal before middle school. That's where I learned to be ashamed of my overworn thrift store things. I learned to comb my hair from the senile woman who lived next door to us, and I learned to shoplift by following the popular girls to the mall.

The first time I followed them, I thought I was in for it when they figured me out. I'd stalked the leader, a tall, loud girl who lived in my apartment complex, from her apartment to the bus stop, where she met the others. I let a group of boys get in between us and climbed on the bus and sat close to the front. I thought I was being real sneaky. I was desperate by then. I was tired of being laughed at because my clothes didn't match or fit.

They didn't beat me up, though. They recruited me and made me over. Made me their mule. That first time, they stuffed my bag with so many clothes that I was sure I'd get stopped and in trouble. We didn't get caught, and I walked away from it with only a shirt, but that didn't matter to me. Not when the leader knocked on my door the next day, gold hoops dangling from her ears, red lipstick popping, and microwave ponytail sitting perfect.

I'd never had friends, so I was taken by their acceptance. It didn't matter that they were using me. I understood that part. I was just tired of being alone. Carrying the weight of all their clothes and things made me in so many ways. By the time I was in high school, I was the biggest shoplifter there. Everyone, even the crew that I started with, bought their clothes from me. I boosted high-end — at least high to us — clothing. I'd go to North Park and the Galleria with a special tool for popping sensors and fill my bags many times over.

And then one day I got caught. Over the years, I'd learned who had no-chase policies, dressing room counts, and loss prevention, so I'd never been caught before. One of the football jocks wanted some cologne from a store I'd never tried and I didn't do my research. When I walked out of the store, a cute guy stopped me to chat me up and then someone else came, claiming they were loss prevention.

The police were called and I was loaded into a shuttle, which was supposed to take me to a squad car. I was in tears, thinking about my record and how I wasn't sure if my mother would be who she was supposed to be — if she would be in her right mind — if I called her. When two guys ran past the shuttle, both carrying several boxes of shoes, the driver turned to me and looked back at them before quickly telling me to get off his shuttle and never visit the mall again. It took me a moment to realize that

I'd been caught and let go, and that was enough to end my boosting career.

In the hotel room, I finger the selenite crystal that dangles from the only necklace I ever wear. I close my eyes and take a deep breath. The only outfits I really brought to wear are my suit and a couple of jumpsuits. But though these people are my family, I don't feel comfortable-jumpsuit casual with them. Not that fold-up-my-legs-on-the-chaise-lounge-and-talk comfortable that I imagine a close family being. I've not been that way with anyone in a long time. I try to imagine myself throwing my head back in casual laughter with Jan. Aunt Julie B. I can't.

I open my eyes, and I decide to wear the tweed suit.

After a shower, I wrap one towel around myself and another around my head. I don't know why I do that. I don't have much hair these days. After years of growing it out, I cut it a few months after I lost the last baby. In an African movie I once watched, a village woman mourning the loss of her husband allowed other widows to scrape her hair off with what looked like broken glass. That stood out to me. I didn't scrape mine with broken glass. I went to my regular styl-

128

ist, who pouted the whole time, saying things like "I can't believe you throwing away such beautiful hair."

Walter didn't panic when he saw my hair. He didn't yell or get upset. He smiled and leaned his head to the side a bit, as if he were adjusting himself to find me. *I just want you healthy, baby,* he said. *You're beautiful no matter what. I just want you healthy.* And I believe he meant that. I believe he cares for me deeply, but I also know that this baby thing is important to him.

He must've thought it was still important to me, too. I mean, it had been in the beginning. I never told him how disappointed I was when we found out that the last baby was a girl. Never told him that losing her wasn't as hard as the other two, but there was a moment after everything — a quiet moment in the hospital — when some revelatory thing passed between us, and that's the moment when I knew that this one was not the same as the others. I think that's the moment he knew too.

That day, Walter reclined in a chair beside the hospital bed, his eyes focused on the wall-mounted television. My head rested on the pillow and he caught my gaze on him, tilted his head, and offered me a weak and sympathetic smile.

129

"We'll get through this, baby," he said. "The next one will make it."

I shook my head and exhaled, before letting it rest on the pillow behind me. I felt a smile — a wide one — spread across my lips, and my hand flew up to cover it. I watched his eyes as they widened and his lips as they straightened. And I think we both felt the shift between us.

Much later, right before he moved out of the bedroom we shared, Walter and I had one of the best days we'd had since before the last baby. We had dinner at this cute Mediterranean restaurant in the Art District that we'd talked about visiting before the last pregnancy. Over dinner, we smiled and flirted and it seemed like we were healing from that last blow. After the waiters had taken our plates, while we waited on our desserts, Walter reached across the table and placed his hand on top of mine. He'd looked into my eyes and said, *There is no other human I'd rather do this with, baby.*

On the ride home, he rested his hand on my leg and his touch made me feel like we could get through anything. At end of the night, when we were back home, I stood in the walk-in closet, undressing and half watching a couple flip a house on the mounted TV. I didn't hear Walter come up

130

behind me, but when I felt his body fold around me, I couldn't help but sink into his embrace. I couldn't help but close my eyes and moan from his touch. His lips were soft on my naked shoulders and then my neck and I could feel all of his love — all of his passion seeping through my skin. And I pulled away.

I hadn't meant to push and pull at the same time. I hadn't meant for him to stumble over the shoes I'd just taken off. I hadn't meant for him to have to catch himself in that way. But that's what happened.

The whole time, his face was coated in confusion and questions, and I wanted to reach out and grab him, hold him, give him what he needed. But I didn't. I stood there and watched him gather himself. His chest, rising and falling rapidly. His teeth clenched. When he yelled, *What is it, Lydia? Why in the hell can't I touch my wife?* I wasn't frightened by his voice. I knew he wouldn't hurt me, but I jumped anyway, and his eyes turned down, like two sad moons, as if he were more hurt by that than anything.

I probably should've said something then. It had been half a year since the baby. Longer than that since I'd let him touch me. I should've told him about me. About

131

the palm reader. About what she said to me all those years ago. About how I went to her to ask about Mother, about her healing, but I found out about myself. I should've told him about what I saw pass through her eyes when her gaze shifted from my palm to my face. When she said, *The fruit of your women-folk is tarnished, little girl. Nothing gone live outside yours. Nothing ever should.* I should've told him that. I should've told him I've held on to her words — that I'd lost my way and forgot how real they were — but that they had always been with me. I should've told him that's why the babies won't stick. And I certainly should've run to him and told him that I didn't mean to pull away so hard. I didn't mean to push.

But I didn't. I stood there and didn't say a word.

And even after I stood there silently, even when he begged me to talk to him, I didn't open my mouth. *I'm trying here, baby,* he'd said softly. *But I can't do this alone. I need you to give me something.*

He took a step toward me and I backed away. He exhaled and kneeled down on one knee. *I love you,* he said. *But I need more than this.* And when he stood and walked out of the closet, I broke down and cried.

When I woke up that night, panting and

breathing from a nightmare I often have about me becoming my mother, I moved my body near his. Since the beginning of us, he'd opened himself up and received me. Comforted me. Asked me to talk about my nightmares. But that night, he stiffened under my touch. Scooted away and turned his back to me. We lay with our backs to each other, a thick silence marking the space between us, until he finally stretched out his arm and placed his palm on my back and whispered, *You can talk to me, Lydia. Tell me where you are with all of this. I love you. I'm here.*

I could hear in his voice that he meant it, but I recoiled from his touch. Slid my body as close to the edge of the bed as I could without falling off, and I exhaled in a way that said *Leave me alone. I'm tired of this. I'm tired of you.*

He moved out of our bedroom the next day and I'm certain that's when he gave up on us. I didn't know it could get worse than that, until two weeks ago. Until he walked out on me.

After Walter moved out of our bedroom, I developed this habit of sneaking into the bathroom of the guest room and silently watching him shower. It was a habit that reminded me of Mother. She took to doing a lot of strange things after my father left. She would sit outside of the house he grew up in for hours at time, which by then had long been occupied by the strangers who bought it. Sometimes we'd have popcorn and movie snacks. Other times, there was only my silence and her tears. I never understood it then — her obsession with my father — but that habit of mine made us similar in the way we love. I like to tell myself that our similarities end there.

Those nights I spied on Walter in the shower, I'd come down right before I knew he'd get in and stand just outside the bedroom door. There was usually a sad, quiet energy about him as he moved through the room alone. Before our life fell apart, he would sing as he prepared to shower. He would sing in the shower. And he would sing after his shower. My husband is a playful man. A happy one. As I listened to him ready himself for the shower those nights, it was almost as if he couldn't be whole — couldn't be himself with things so tumultuous between us. I don't know why that comforted me, but it did.

The night he walked out on me, I stood there listening for that comforting quiet. Instead of quiet, he softly called out my name, as if he knew I was standing just outside the door. As if he knew I was spying. I stepped hesitantly through the cracked door to reveal myself to him, but I could not contain my gasp — the shock and alarm of finding him bent over the bed, folding his underwear into a suitcase. I cleared my throat and asked him if he was traveling for work.

He dropped his head and looked at the floor. *It's not work,* he mumbled. He lifted his eyes and looked into mine. The dark of his pupils against the whites of his eyeballs against the darkness of his skin, the way the corners of his eyes turned down toward his cheeks startled me.

More boldly and somewhat defiantly, he said, *It's not work. I just — I just need some time.*

I cleared my throat again and nodded. *If it's what you think you need.*

He shook his head. *It's not what I need, Lydia. You know that.* He sighed. *You know what I need. And you won't even let me touch you.* There was so much sadness in his voice.

I need time, he said again, and an hour later he was gone.

135

6

JAN

I push the palms of my hands flat against the bed and slide toward the edge. My eyes gazing around the room and it seem like I'm about to panic before I spot my phone on the floor. Omar make sure my phone bill paid — make sure he can always reach us. I appreciate him for being like that. For being reliable even after we ain't fornicating no more.

Sometimes I think I made the wrong decision with him. He was something to me ain't nobody never been. A sweetness in the gut — the core of me. Omar look at me in ways nobody else ever have. He the one what noticed how I get anxious round a whole lot of folks.

We was still new when I flipped out at the county fair right before our son was born. Walking through them crowds of folks and flashing lights had my head spinning. The whole while I was thinking about somebody

136

nasty hands accidentally touching me, about me taking in they germs, they spirits. I was doing my best to squeeze myself into Omar and let him shield me from all the folks, and the whole while the smell of popcorn and smoked meat was reminding me we was there. Every once in a while, Omar squeeze my hand, which he made sure was gripped tight in his. We had been messing around awhile, so he'd noticed how nervous I'd get in malls and restaurants, but he'd never seen me bug out the way I did that night. Somehow, he lost his grip and we lost each other in the crowd right outside the mirror maze. When he found me, I was in the exact spot where our hands had broke, crying like a two-year-old who'd lost a good mother. That man scooped me up, cradled me just like a little baby, like he was some kind of superhero and got me out that place without stopping, the whole time whispering to me, *I got you, baby. I'm here.* And that's when I knew he knew me in a way that nobody else was gone know me. That's when I knew I had the right man.

Sometimes I wish I could've let go of myself and give what I got left to him cause sometimes I do believe in love and in him. Other times, I feel like we'd of outgrowed each other anyway. I dial his number without even paying no real attention to the time. The phone ring three times before I hear his groggy voice on the other end.

"January," he say, smacking his tongue around his mouth, like he trying to moist out all the dry. "What's wrong? Y'all all right?"

"You up? Can you talk?" I ask, in a whisper, like he sitting beside me instead of on another side of town.

"Huh," he say. "Yeah. Yeah, man, of course." And I hear him exhale, like he readying himself for something he used to, like he welcoming it and he ain't.

"I'm sorry, Omar. I don't mean to call you like this. I hate to, but I ain't got nobody else." Omar is all I really got and sometimes that would be fine but I know as good as he is, he got a motive. Omar think if he stay being good to me, stay loving me, we gone be us again. He think we gone be something we never should've been in the first place. Something where he always looking out for me, taking care of me and trying to calm my mind. Something where he love me but got to look away sometimes cause that's the way his people is. Cause his daddy made him when he was looking away from a woman he say he loved, too.

When I first found God, I told Omar

138

wasn't gone be no more sex without marriage. He looked at me crazy and tried to wrap his self around me that very night. I tried to explain to him that what the seahorses got is much better than what the sockeye salmon got. One love each other for life and the other love each other to death. I think that went over his head cause I was talking about love and he wanted what he only thought love was. That's when I understood what Paul meant when he said the spirit is willing but the flesh is weak. After that, I told him he couldn't sleep with me no more. After that, he started looking away to some cashier at the car wash. I started wondering if I should gone and give him what I had been giving him for years already, and God answered me quick with thyroid problems.

I told him he had to go after that. Told him wasn't gone be no more shacking. No more sinning. Gave him two weeks to find a place on his own. Gave him a clean break and didn't hold no grudge about the cashier or any of the women before or after her. Sometimes it make me feel some kind of way that he ain't do nothing to stay with me. Ask me to marry him or even just agree to keep his hands off me. Stop tempting me. Anything to show me he choose me first.

Other times, I hold on to the focus I know come with cutting a dead thing away. When Grandmoan made Alex leave, seem like my mind opened up. I could focus in school. I learned that I liked to read about animals. About how they is with they young and each other. I started reading all that and trying to connect it with who we is. Instead of trying to keep up with folks moving lips — follow along with what they was trying to say — I could actually hear what people was saying to me when they talked to me. And I could be free in that house. I could be normal as long as I didn't think about it. About him. Sometimes Alex ghost rear his head and remind me that I ain't nobody first choice. Like with Lil, when she come to visit and Momma took us to see him. Lil volunteered to stay in the car with me, but it made me feel some kind of way that she could divide herself between me and him. For me, it was like she chose God and the devil. Like being lukewarm, so I spewed her out.

It didn't sit right with me cause I always chose Lil first when we was young. Always acted to protect her from my brother. Like the time I got sent inside to take a nap on purpose cause I didn't want for her what was already happening to me.

I don't remember if it was cold or hot that day. Summer or winter. If the sky was blue or pink. All I know is that we wasn't supposed to be out there on that hog pen truck. Grandmoan had already told us no. Ain't nobody have time for our help. We'd only get in the way. But we loved Granddaddy. Wanted to surprise him by having the barrels full of water when he got in from work. We was just little girls. I couldn't have been more than seven.

Lil climbed up first cause her legs was longer. She'd already pulled me up by the time we realized we forgot to turn on the water and wasn't nothing coming out of the hose we'd pulled and draped over the bed of the truck. Lil wanted to stay on the truck to help me back up once we turned the water on.

Whoever get caught on this truck getting a whooping, Lil said. *That's dangerous. I'm the oldest. I'll take it.*

I knew better, though. Grandmoan was watching *Guiding Light.* Wasn't gone be no whoopings during her stories. Whoever got caught was taking a nap. I didn't want that for Lil, especially that day. Alex was home. Had been inside laying down all day cause his stomach was messed up.

I remember hugging her. Holding her

141

hand as she climbed down and knowing in my gut that Grandmoan was gone walk out that house or come to that window and see me on that truck before Lil feet ever touched the yard. I remember choosing her over myself that day. Feeling good about that part cause it felt like love. I knew what was gone happen before Grandmoan opened her mouth to let me know I was caught.

"You was on my mind, Omar. I really just wanted to hear your voice, you know?" I say.

He sigh, like he want to say something. But he know I already know everything he want to say. He want to tell me I should let him come home. He want to remind me that we got a family. He want me to know that his not being with us make both us look bad.

"Remember that time we drove to Mexico?" I ask him. "Them federales pulled us over?" I chuckle a little and can feel myself trying to be back in that moment, instead of here.

"Yeah, man," he say, and I can hear the smile in his voice as he let his words roll out slow. "You was shaking like a leaf on a fucking tree. Talking bout, 'The cartel gone get us, O.' "

I cringe at his cussing, but I don't correct

142

him. The Word say *Be ye holy; for I am holy.* I choose that way with Omar. Maybe one day, he'll hear all the things I don't say.

Instead of correcting him on his cussing, I say, "Yeah, but you made me feel all right about everything. Remember? You just put your hand on top of mine and rubbed it until we was good."

He laugh. "Them federales was tripping for real, though. Crazy as them Mexicans drive, they gone pull us over. Can't be black nowhere, man," he say.

We go quiet and then I swallow and say, "Sometimes I think I'm gone call and you ain't gone be able to talk to me. To hear me, O. Sometimes, that scare me."

He make a smacking sound and say, "I'll never be in a place where I can't at least hear you, January. Not unless I'm dead. And even then, I'm gone listen to you. You the love of my life. You know that."

I nod and think about how hard he work in the college dining hall during the day and at the taco stand some nights. I think about him handing over money for the kids and how even though it ain't a lot to people money come to easy, it's a lot to us. And I believe I am the love of his life and maybe he the love of mine, but he ain't never asked me to marry him and I ain't never pressured him to do it. I ain't never been sure if we can make it for real. Not like that. Not all official. And for me that mean we can't be together cause God's word is clear. It's better to marry than to burn with desire. Omar always burning. Always gone burn.

"January," he say after a while. "If you ever really want to talk to me, you can. Baby, you always can."

I nod, knowing he can't see it but also knowing he know I'm doing it.

He exhale again and say, "Saw your momma. She told me about your grandmomma. Sorry to hear it. You need anything, I —"

"Thank you, Omar, but I'm fine. We ain't close no way," I say. And I know he don't understand that. His grandmother, who the whole neighborhood call Momma Mae, is a good woman. Make the best pound cake in town. Every time somebody die, she call Omar to go to the store to get her ingredients. Bake two cakes for the grieving family and make her grandson drive her to deliver the desserts personally. She a good woman. Woman of God. Grandmothers something special to Omar. I know he don't understand nothing that go on between me and mine.

"I know. I know. But still, I'm here for

you. You ought to know that."

I smile, even though I know he can't see me. And then I hang up the phone without saying another word.

I lay back down and wonder what the world gone be without Grandmoan. She always been something so strange and so strong to me. We ain't really close, but I'm smart enough to know that she wrapped around everything. I done spent a year trying to know her — trying to see if she gone know herself again.

I take pills to help me sleep cause my biggest fears always with me. A lot of times, I lay up at night and think about them fears. Bind them demons. Scariest things in the world is the things you can't come back from. That's the kind of mess that keep me up at night. And I know that's bad on me. On my relationship with God. You ain't supposed to fear nothing but him, but I don't know what else to do.

I took a few pills after what happened with the kids last night. I appreciate that drowsy feeling I get and the way everything clouding my mind get heavy with my eyelids and it just drown all out and I go to sleep. Problem is it don't hold through the night and I wake up and all that stuff be right

145

back where it was. Sometimes I take a couple more and that hold me over till morning, but that's all I want is to sleep through the night.

When I was younger, in my twenties, before I had my daughter, I had a scare that make me real careful about who know I take pills. These days, I drive to other side of town to buy my pills, even though they sell them right over the counter. I don't want nobody seeing me buy no PMs, not since Omar caught me shaking a handful into my palm all them years ago. I'll never forget that night. I don't blame him none for calling the police, specially cause of how his eyes was all welled up with tears. He wasn't being ugly. He thought I meant to hurt myself, so I went on with them officers and let them take me to the twenty-four-hour mental facility across town. When it was my turn to be assessed and talk to the doctor on the little computer tablet, they ain't want to keep me. They understood it wasn't suicide ideation or nothing like that.

And Pastor Haynes say when the Lord got you up at night that mean he want you praying. So I'm lying up here trying to pray for Grandmoan but my mind keep slipping back to Dallas. I been fighting it for a hour and I'm thinking about giving up and taking my pills when I hear screaming coming from the kids' rooms.

I jump to my feet and hurry to Jazera room. When I stick my head in the door, she sound asleep. I go into Javon room and he tossing and turning and moaning "Stop" and "Don't" in his sleep, so I reach out and shake him until he awake.

For a minute, I think about the day Jazera say they was with my brother. My momma waved her hand and said, *Oh, Jan. That girl confused. I told them who Alex was — what he did for a living. We saw a police at the store and I guess she connecting all that.* I can't prove she lying, but I know my momma. My baby called him uncle and everything, but Javon say he didn't know what she was talking about neither.

I let Momma off without drama, but that's in my head when I feel how sweaty my baby is underneath my hands.

"You dreaming, baby," I say when he get to looking around, trying to place hisself in the world.

"Oh," he say, and I tell him I'll be back with a cup of water.

I make my way to the kitchen and don't even turn on the lights or nothing when I get there. I know where everything at and the night-light I keep by the microwave is enough to guide me if I need it. I reach up toward the cup cabinet with both hands, one to open it and the other to grab a cup, but standing there like that remind me of what Pastor say about supplication and prayer. *Ain't never no wrong time to call on the Lord,* he like to say when he making his altar call. *He everywhere all the time. All you got to do is reach for him.*

I stand there for a moment with my hands outstretched and I can hear hoarse in my voice when I say, "Lord, please let my son be whole. Let nothing be done touched him in a way I can't fix. Let me be wrong about my momma having them around Alex. Let him be good and innocent and free."

I continue about my business of getting his water, but I know God done heard me. I want to believe I know it. Faith is the most important part.

I've been watching the kids since I found out my momma was taking them around my brother. Watching for signs of broken-ness. Watching for nightmares and anger and sadness. Watching for me.

Javon sitting up waiting for me when I get back with his water. "You gone have to get up and change your clothes, Javon. You soaked," I tell him when I hand him his cup. "What was you dreaming about anyway?" I ask, making my way to his dresser to get the change of clothes. I hold my breath a little cause I'm scared of what his dream gone reveal to me.

I go through the top drawer — his pajama drawer — and I see myself in how everything is. Everything folded up so neat I can almost see the wood of the drawer. Ain't nothing out of place. Everything where it's posed to be.

Javon take a big gulp of the water and swallow so hard he got to open his eyes wide and take a moment to catch his breath. I sit down beside him and help him get out his shirt.

"A monster truck was chasing me," he say, like he all excited about it. "It had a mouth and eyes and said, 'I'm gone eat you up, Javon,' " he say.

I smile at him and tell him it was just a dream as he hand his wet clothes to me. Then I say, "Go back to sleep, baby. Don't want you tired when I wake you up for school in a few hours."

"Can you leave the bathroom light on, Momma?" he ask in a rushed voice.

"Yeah, scaredy-cat," I say, and smile real big to let him know I'm teasing him before I turn off the light in his room. All the weight that's been on my shoulders since he first screamed out lift from me. I'm relieved. Real relieved. Everything is how it should be. My momma can't never get my kids no more.

I flip the light switch on in the bathroom and wonder what my babies would think if they knew I sleep with my bathroom light on, too. If they knew I have nightmares. Can't sleep without pills.

When I'm back in my room, I sit on my bed and open the nightstand drawer next to it. I take out the big bottle of store-brand nighttime pain relief and I shake four of the blue pills into my palm. I look at them for a minute. I feel guilty about taking them. About needing them all these years. Omar the only person who ever knew I was taking them, and even he don't know I still do. I'm gone stop taking them and go to sleep like normal folks one day. I keep telling myself that. I tell myself that when I throw my head back and toss the pills in my mouth.

HELEN JEAN
1968

When the nursing home called to tell her that her father was dead back in '63, Helen Jean finished her cigarette and cup of gin, took a nap, and beat Wayne for half mowing the lawn before calling the shop and telling Jessie B. that her father had finally passed away. She told her husband that there was no need for him to leave work early that day. She let him know that she would be fine. That afternoon, she prepared a meal fit for a king. It tickled her how that confused the children. They didn't know what to think about the meaty oxtails and beans she'd boiled all day. She smiled inside when they moaned at the goodness of her corn-bread. She knew it was perfectly moist and just sweet enough for them to feel like they were eating butter cake. She was good at it, but she never really cooked for them be-cause it reminded her too much of being in her father's house.

151

Later that evening, after Jessie B. put the children down, she dressed for juking and told him she was going out. Bacon picked her up and drove out to Don Earl's hog pen. Helen Jean haggled with the man until they came to an agreement on the price of a hog. Bacon didn't say a word when she came back pulling the hog by a rope. He emerged from the truck, opened the bed, and helped her push the animal up the wooden make-shift ramp. Her brother didn't ask questions when she told him to drive out past every-thing, when she told him to stay back at the pickup while she pulled the hog out into the wilderness. She was grateful for that. And when she came back to the car an hour later without that hog and slid in the car beside him, he put his hands on the wheel and exhaled in a way that was meant to let the air out of his lungs. Then he looked at her and asked, *So it's finished*? And she nod-ded. He dropped her off at home that night and the two never spoke of their father again.

Back at the house, Jessie B. must have warned the children that she would be delicate because the following day they walked around like frightened mice, and Wayne stayed completely out of her way. Helen Jean considered all the things her father's death might mean for Wayne. She considered that perhaps he might be better for it, that he might actually be all right, all the while tapering her hope that the boy's being all right was even a real possibility. Jessie B. must've thought she'd lost her mind when she suggested that they all pile in the car and head to the Lone Star Drive-In. Though it was a Friday night ritual for him and the kids, she never went along with them. Once there, it was as if she'd always been part of their movie outings. She rallied for snacks from the concession stand and let them drink as much soda as they wanted, even Wayne. And she noticed the surprise in all of their eyes when she laughed louder than any of them during the movie.

When her father died, she needed to prove to herself and everybody else that nothing had changed — that she was still her — still able to live — to be the life of things. She didn't want to rebuild him as good with grief in the way that people manage to do when evil men die, so she made it a point not to grieve him or anything he'd ever done.

When Jessie B. died in '67, things were different.

She had never lived not being a man's daughter or wife, so she didn't know what life would be like after Jessie B. died. She almost mistook her grief for love. There were many reasons she made this mistake. Three years after Julie B. was born, when she was pregnant with Ruby Nell, he painted the walls a dark wine color and draped the windows with dark curtains. He never said he was doing it so that she could have her dark days, but she knew it was his way of making room for who she was. And there were other things too. He never once put his hands on her without asking, not even to remove a piece of lint from her hair. He was a man — a ruler — but he was just.

In her husband's last days, she and Jessie B. fought. He reset his expectations of her. Tossed their arrangement and told her it was time to give back. But he was too weak for anything other than weak words. He repeated them to her like a song: *I ain't long for this earth, gal. I need you to do right. You gone be they only thing from here on out.*

But during his illness she kept partying, kept on drinking, kept being with other men, and kept ignoring her children right up until the end. Even after he was admitted into the hospital, she refused to slow down. She let Wayne, the oldest of them, pick up the slack, and she went on living her life.

Despite Jessie B.'s drawn-out illness and the preparations he tried to make, his death took Helen Jean by surprise. So she grieved.

Six months after Jessie B.'s death, Bacon knocked on her door carrying one oversized suitcase and a hatbox. *Moving in, little sis,* he told her. *Woman always need to be covered by a man.* And she'd wanted to tell him that her and the children were fine, he needn't worry. But he squeezed through the door and walked past her, taking his belongings to Wayne's room.

She knew that Bacon knew everything about the evil that lived inside Wayne, and unlike Jessie B., who was always gentle and kind and soft when it came to the boy, Bacon was hard on him. He watched over him, watched *out* for him. He didn't let him get away with a single thing. Helen Jean watched her brother punish Wayne for all of his childish mistakes. Spilling or wasting food, staring at someone or something too long and too hard, making his sisters cry, or any other infraction he wanted to punish him for. He had always been watchful of the boy. Looking for signs of their father's evil in his every move, but he had not been able to have his way, not with Jessie B. around to guard and protect the boy. After Jessie B. was gone, Bacon beat the boy when

155

he felt he needed to, locked him away in his room for days at a time, and made sure that he understood that he had no guaranteed place in his mother's home.

Something in Helen Jean thought these things could — wanted them to help the boy be better than what made him, so she let her brother stay. Bacon had always been as good to her as he could, and because she secretly hoped that he could change the thing inside — the thing that made her son — she allowed Bacon's disciplinary measures without protest. There were times that she thought the lessons were too tough, but she didn't open her mouth to stop them. After all, he knew all there was to know about the boy. All there was to fear.

On the first anniversary of her husband's death, though, everything changed. It had taken Helen Jean that long to realize that Bacon's being there — her letting him be there — had been a mistake. It had taken what she'd witnessed the night before while having her cigarette out on the porch.

Bacon had been gathering wood for months for a project that made her somewhat uneasy. He brought the drawing to her a few weeks after his arrival and she couldn't help but think of the old outhouse on Ernestine and her family's old land. His childish sketching was almost identical to that outhouse, except for the windows drawn on each side of the door.

Every backyard need a shed these days, Bacon said. *Don't know what the hell Jessie B. was thinking not building one in the first place.*

And so for months, Helen Jean watched her brother bring wooden planks through the house a little at a time, and for a while, she thought nothing of it. Or at least, she tried not to. But then the night before the anniversary of Jessie B.'s death, she'd been smoking a cigarette out on the porch when she'd caught something strange in the way Bacon was ordering Wayne around, commanding the boy to hand him tools, pass him the bucket of concrete, and do whatever it was he needed done. She might've missed it had she looked away for just a second, but she kept her eyes on the boy. So she was watching when Bacon told him, *Hand me that mallet, Wayne. I need to drive this in further.*

She could feel her own frown as she watched the boy retrieve the tool and pass it to her brother, but something familiar overcame her when Bacon put his hand on the boy's back. It was a touch that might've been mistaken by someone else as a warm gesture. A thank-you. It might've been taken for such a gesture by her had Wayne not jumped — trembled — when her brother's hand touched his back. Helen Jean knew enough about those kind of jumps, about how both she and Bacon had jumped like that under their father's touch, to know what was happening between the boy and her brother, to know to call her brother's woman and tell her it was time for him to go home.

Later that night, after she had made her call to Vera and arranged for her to come and collect her man, after the house went quiet, Helen Jean lay in bed thinking about what she'd seen. About the boy's trembling body under her brother's hand. She lay there straining to hear the boy's whimpers or cries. She lay there thinking that she knew all too well what was going on in the boy's room because she knew all too well who had made him. And when she never heard a cry or a scream, she thought it was because of one of two things: Bacon knew how to stop the boy's mouth, how to keep him from crying out (he had to know because their own father had always clasped his hand tightly over their mouths when he had his way with them).

She closed her eyes to the image of Bacon

stopping the boy's mouth with his hand. To her father stopping her mouth. Stopping Bacon's. She could feel the tears squeezing through her lashes as she thought about her mother leaving them unprotected. Leaving them to a ravenous wolf. Had she done the same thing to the boy? She shook her head and told herself this was different. Bacon was wrong; she had been wrong to allow him to stay, but this couldn't be on her. The boy's evil flowed because he existed at all. Bacon hadn't needed to stop the boy's mouth at all. Maybe it was what the boy wanted. Perhaps he was born *for* such things because he had been born *of* such things.

She'd spent the better part of the next day lying in bed, thinking about what she'd witnessed and practicing it — what she needed to say in her head over and over again. When she finally placed her hand flat against the bed and pushed her upper body to an upright position, she sat like that on the edge of the bed, looking at the pistol on the nightstand, trying to decide if she would use it. And then she heard her brother's voice boom down the hallway. "Wayne, come on. Time to get to work on this shed."

She closed her eyes and thought about keeping them closed until the world passed away. The conflict swirling inside her made her want to be sick all over everything until everything was nothing and she was gone. Bacon's betrayal was unexpected and the night before she had considered the cost of ignoring it, but as much as she hated how the boy came to be, he was hers and she could not allow Bacon to remain hers with what she now knew about him. She hadn't expected to mourn her brother before he was gone. She hadn't expected to have to kill the oldest living thing in her heart so soon. And for such a thing as this.

She cleared her throat, pushed her lower body up from the bed, gripped the pistol in her hands, and headed toward the door without bothering to grab her robe.

"Bacon," she called out, grabbing the handle of the door. "Bacon, wait."

She took a deep breath, pulled the bedroom door open, and emerged from the room with the gun behind her back. Bacon was standing at the end of the hallway, in the front room really, and Wayne stood a few feet away from him. Bacon's brows furrowed in that way they did when he was irritated and Wayne's eyes were on his feet, like there was nowhere else to put them.

They all looked toward the front room when they heard the screen door jiggle and open.

"Yoo-hoo?" Helen Jean heard, and almost sighed openly at the sound of Vera's voice.

When she stepped into the dim front room, Vera was standing there, Bacon beside her, waiting.

Vera seemed to be dressed for juking, in a shiny sequin-looking dress, matching purse, and feathered scarf. Her wig wasn't something Helen Jean would've worn but she wasn't as old as Vera either.

When he was alive, Jessie B. never allowed Vera in the house. Like with Bacon, it was something he drew a line about early on. He told her, *That woman is loose. Long as I live my children gone believe that their mother ain't that. They gone believe you is a mother and nothing else.*

Bacon's good eye was wide and darting back and forth between his sister and his woman. Helen Jean knew he was surprised by Vera's being there. After Bacon moved in, Helen Jean learned that it had been a great ordeal between the two of them when he announced that he was leaving to watch after his sister and the children for a while.

She hadn't told Bacon she'd called Vera. She couldn't bring herself to do that, but she had known Vera would be glad to come and claim him. Vera would open her mouth and command him to be where he needed

161

to be. She was not afraid of Bacon. She gave as good as she got.

"What you doing in work coveralls, Bacon?" Vera asked, waving her hands around his clothes with her nose scrunched up. "You posed to be ready?"

Helen Jean looked at Wayne. His eyes were set on her, like a pleading, a sort of begging. She knew that she was — she would be his choice at the end of everything. Choosing her, no matter how many times she couldn't choose him, had always come easy to the boy. He was like a deformed piglet set on choosing a sow that couldn't see past its deformity. One that would never allow him to suckle because of it. Helen Jean shifted her eyes from his pathetic face and said, "Go on, boy. Go to your room."

Bacon took a few steps back and leaned against the arm of the couch. The side of his mouth curled up and he looked at Vera, like she was something funny. Then he turned his gaze to his sister and asked, "What she talking about, Helen Jean?"

"Well," Helen Jean began. "Vera miss you, Bacon," she said. And he held up his hand to stop her.

His eyes were fixed on the other side of the room, on the record player. He headed in that direction. "Vera, baby, you want a

162

drink?" he asked. "I'll put on a record. Helen Jean, get her a drink," he said, without waiting for Vera to answer.

And Helen Jean almost moved her feet to fulfill his command, but she thought about how he'd looked at her the night before. How Wayne had jumped under the touch of his hand and how Bacon had turned and smiled at her, like that was okay. Like he knew she hated the boy, so anything was okay. And that made her angry. Her knowing what the boy was didn't give anyone a right to take from him.

She ended up just standing there, watching him make his way to the records, watching his feet move in the same drunk way they always moved, and she called out to him, "Bacon, watch my leopard." But it was too late. His foot crashed into one of the porcelain leopards that sat on the floor in front of the record table.

When she turned her attention to the leopard, it seemed that everything went quiet and she felt her mouth drop open to a tiny O. Her eyes watched the leopard tip forward and then rock a bit before the foot broke off and fell onto the shag carpet.

She looked at the paw on the floor. It had broken clean, not into bits and pieces, and she could tell the rest of the leopard was hollow. But she had always known that because of how light the leopards were to hold. It had been Jessie B.'s idea to decorate the family room like a jungle. The leopards were her favorite thing, but she never thanked him for them. She thought about his face the day he brought them home. *What you think, gal?* he asked, looking at her with eyes that were serious and playful at the same time. She didn't say anything. Just shrugged and walked away.

She let her eyes roam up to her brother's face. He stood fidgeting with the record player, like the leopard never existed. And something boiled inside of her enough to make her bold, to make her forget to care about who Bacon was and what he could do to her — what had been done to him.

"I'm gone kick your ass, nigger." She heard her own voice rip through the front room. "My husband bought me them porcelain leopards. Them beautiful statues. You done broke my goddamned leopard," she said, bringing the gun from behind her back and pointing it at him.

"Awh, Helen Jean. Shut that shit up. Ain't real no way," Bacon said, waving his hand at her, without turning around to look at her. "Damn things ain't nothing but ceramic. And you ain't cared nothing about no goddamn Jessie B. no way," he added, almost laughing at her.

"Momma," Wayne said from the doorway. "Momma, you —"

"And you better watch your mouth, Helen Jean," Bacon said, standing up straight. "You done forgot who you talking to. I'll —"

Then his eye focused on the gun and she knew he knew what it meant. "You done pulled it, now you got to use it," he said, and she couldn't hear a trace of fear in his voice.

"Boy, go to the back," she said to Wayne, without taking her eyes off her brother.

"Y'all wait. Wait now," Vera said, patting the air with her hands. "It's just a thing. A thing that can be mended."

Helen Jean felt tears in her eyes and her lips trembled. From the corner of her eyes, she could see that her daughters were standing in the hallway.

"I'm tired," she said, gripping the gun in both hands. "I'm tired of men deciding how I'm gone be. Breaking my things. Breaking me." And she felt herself crying. Felt snot on her face, and all the people, her brother, his woman, and her children, wavered through her tears.

She almost put the gun down. She almost

turned back into herself and then her brother smiled at her. Smiled and said, "Woman, you crazy." He waved his hand to dismiss her and said, "Wayne, come on out here and get your momma."

She looked over at that boy, standing in the doorway with his eyes on her. Eyes that were asking her for something. Had always been asking her for something. Something she thought she could not give. And Jessie B. was gone. He could no longer stand in the gap. Someone would have to stand in for the boy. She would. Her brother moved his lips again, and something in her saw red. She was on him before she could think about it. He stumbled and hit the carpet, landing on his back, and she straddled him, dropped the gun, and wrapped her hands tight around his neck. He was holding her arms with his hands, trying, struggling to push her off. But she gripped his neck tighter than she had ever gripped anything, like she meant to take his life right there.

Then she heard her daughter Ruby Nell's voice over her, screaming at her. "Momma, no! Don't kill him!" she said, and Helen Jean could hear the tears in her voice. "She gone kill him. Momma, don't kill him!"

And she let go of his neck. She saw Wayne sneak the gun away from her reach — away

166

from Bacon's — out of the corner of her eye. Vera cursed and along with her daughters struggled to lift Helen Jean's body off her brother's. And as soon as they had moved her, as soon as she thought she could crumple into a ball and cry, he came alive.

"You bitch," he said, coming for her. "I told you to use it. I told you."

And she felt the cold nose of the pistol being placed in her hands and she heard her daughters screaming and Vera calling her brother's name. When he reached her, when he was putting all his weight over her body, over to where she was still weak with exhaustion on the floor, she prepared herself for his blow, for his beating, by throwing her hands up with all the strength she had in her. And the butt of the gun connected with his head with a force she hadn't planned for, with a force that knocked him back on his ass. His eyes widened and he looked at her with shock all over his face, touching the spot on his head that the gun had hit. He looked at his hand and then back at her and she knew to rear her hand back with intention this time. When he came again, she was ready. When he came again, she knocked him out.

The girls stopped screaming and the whole room went quiet, until she looked across her body at her brother's feet and said, "We all right, y'all. We all right."

Vera called her brothers. Told them to come quick. To hurry. And they moved Bacon's unconscious body and his things away from Jessie B.'s house.

Before Vera slipped out the door behind Bacon and his things, she turned and hugged Helen Jean and said, "I'll take care of him." She nodded at the three children behind Helen Jean and said, "You take care of them."

Helen Jean sat on the steps of the back porch later that evening. She'd been there for hours smoking cigarette after cigarette with her eyes glued to the lumber in the right corner of the backyard, the lumber that Bacon had gathered to build his shed.

She knew her brother had suffered in their father's house, but she'd never expected him to become *that* — to become the cause of any child's tremble. She wondered how long he'd been touching the boy. How she'd missed it. She'd allowed him to be the leader of them and he'd made her live to regret it. Bacon had always been Bacon, but he'd never given her reason to believe that he would take from her in that way. She knew what her father had done to him because her father had done the same thing to her, but she thought that made her and her brother the same. She never imagined that he could be a monster too.

She called Wayne out to the back porch. She could tell he was nervous and unsure about what she wanted with him. She only ever called his name when he was in trouble.

"Ma'am," he said, looking down at her.

And she thought about that night in the outhouse, and she thought about her brother's hand on his back, the boy's tremble and how much she thought the child looked like her in that moment. And then she thought about her son grabbing the gun and placing it in her hands. How that was almost good of him. She wondered if she should hope. She thought about the rest of her children and Jessie B.'s words: *You gone be they only thing from here on out.* She nodded her head, like he was still whispering in her ear. *You can do this. You can keep them safe.* And she knew the only way to protect the others from what Bacon had done to Wayne — from what Wayne was — was to protect them from him. She could never be sure of what Bacon had planned for the shed, but she knew why she needed it — why they all did. It would right the wrong rooted in the boy. The shed would hold the evil. The shed would be Wayne's home.

169

She told him to sit down and made room for him on the step.

"We gone finish this shed, kay?" she said, taking a drag of cigarette.

"Yes, ma'am," he said, and she could see a smile tugging at his lips.

She put her hand on the middle of his back and she thought about the outhouse and about giving birth to him and about the shed to come. And she wondered why he didn't tremble under her touch.

7
JULIE B.

Tricia open the door before I even have a chance to ball my knuckles and knock on it. Me and her went to junior high and high school together. Let her tell it, she was into me back then. Let her tell it, when she come back here, I was the only person that wasn't kin that she just had to see. Real surprise for me come when she come back here two years ago to bury her momma and ain't never leave after it was done.

And then Kenzy started sniffing around, right after he become a widower, right after lonely wrap around his throat and try to kill him. Only reason Tricia invited him to dinner that first night was on count of me. I felt sorry for him. Done got old with that woman and she turn to dust and leave him alone.

Kenzy been in love with Tricia since eighth grade and she wouldn't never give him the time of day. He was a good boy back then

171

— handsome. Ball player. Went off to school in Houston and come back a lawyer what talk way over my head. Back in the day, I had a silent crush on him, but he ain't nothing like he used to be to look at. Dark circles around his eyes, like he a zombie haunting something — somebody — and he put on weight that don't compliment him none. You can tell he smoked cigarettes for a long time fore he quit, cause he dangling on the edge of losing his teeth, and he don't do a good job about keeping his hair cut on the side. Don't do a good job of hiding that that's all he got left.

Turn out, back then, when we was kids, I was crushing on him, he was crushing on Tricia, and she was crushing on me. These days, we all get together and they get what they want. He get Tricia but he got to take me; she get me but she got to take him. I can't figure out what the hell I'm getting out the deal or what it is I really want. We all get in the center of Tricia poster bed and we become one thing with no past and no future.

When I walk up to the porch of her little blue and gray house, it remind me that I ain't on the east side no more. That I might as well be on another planet. This area she live in ain't always been this nice. It used to be mainly college kids, wannabe college kids, and the not-so-well-to-do whites what lived over here. Now it's only bleach-blond college whites, black whites, and professors and stuff. It's a few folks what done come from big cities for jobs and such. They usually young white families what be pushing they babies around in them red wagons and jogging strollers. All of the folks over here now look like they used to having nice things.

Tricia standing there clutching her silk robe closed with one hand and trying to open the other one to catch me in a embrace. She so pretty about the way she carry herself that a lot times when I'm around her, I feel like I ain't really no woman. Not like her. She move and sway like seduction. She ain't no tiny woman up under that robe. She got perfect wide hips — the kind that's good for pushing babies out — even though she ain't never choose to do that. Her silver-gray hair is cropped close to her head and her teeth so perfect and white, I know they cost her a lot of money. They implants. She can't take them out. They the kind I want but can't get right now cause even with the money I found, it ain't enough for nothing like that. Went to a fancy dentist place when I found it, but what that man was trying to charge me for some teeth was way more than all that money.

When I'm on the porch, I don't step into her arm. I just kind of stand there in front of her until she drop it.

"I could tell you were upset on the phone," she say. "Is your mother okay?"

I nod my head without saying nothing, cause Tricia gone always think I love my momma perfect. She know I take care of Momma and Homer. Know Momma in the hospital now, but them surface things. Easy things. Everything else belong to only me.

"Come in," she say, and grab me by my elbow, but I don't let her pull me inside.

I shake my head and say, "Naw, I'm just here for the car."

She crane her neck around me to see what I'm driving, like she ain't see me drive up in Momma's old Buick.

"You know what I'm talking about, Tricia," I say, like I'm irritated. She make me wish she wasn't the one I come to when I needed a place to store the first new thing — the first real thing I ever bought myself.

She look at me and I turn my eyes from her. I cried the whole way from Alex apartment off the loop to her place on 21st Street. Dried my tears before I got out the car, but some folk can tell when you been crying. Tricia see I been crying, she gone call me out on it and try to make it right. Gone want to know what cause my tears, so she can try to fix it.

We ain't gone never be in a place where I can tell her about my kids. About what I held on to and what I didn't. I think she know that. Sometimes I can see it in the way she look at me, squinting her eyes, like she trying to put together the pieces — trying to make sense of what's in me. But she ain't gone never know how I'm like my momma in that don't neither one of us know nothing about saving our children. We both did the wrong damn things, and I got to live with that. I want to make amends with mine, but I don't even know where to start. Tricia think she want all these parts of me. She don't know the half of it.

"Go around," she say, pointing her finger a bit, and I smile.

I make my way around to her detached garage and she disappear into her house. I'm still smiling when she walk out the back door and sashay her body to where I'm standing in front of the garage door.

She stand next to me and extend her hand with the remote in it and the garage start to rattle open.

I smell the mango lotion coming off her

body and turn toward her a little bit. She mad with me. Seem like her lips stuck out a little bit, so I get close enough to her that my nose almost touching her neck. Close enough to where the back of her body is almost curving into the front of mine.

"Thank you, Tricia," I whisper, and she close her eyes and her head droop back a little, like she high or something. "You the best kind of friend," I say, trying to make my voice low and sexy. "The best kind."

My new car ain't nothing big, but I like to drive it when I go to the bank or the mall or a place where folks don't know me. Ain't nothing big, but it got a sunroof and leather seats and I was the first to ever put my ass on them. Momma always had nice cars and things. Updated her Buick every five years, but I ain't never had nothing like this in my own name. Title say *Julie B. Walker* in bold print. I ain't never had nothing this serious before.

When we was coming up, we didn't never know we was poor. We was the first blacks in Parkley, always had the best clothes, and ain't never go to bed hungry. Momma provided for us in the way she was posed to. Most folks thought we was well off and them thoughts kind of scraped off on us.

Now I know better. Momma was better with money than most folks was, but we wasn't nowhere near well-off. Momma ain't never have to go to the welfare, like I did. Never worked a day in her life, but she could always lend twenty or thirty dollars to folk when they came knocking. They ain't see the corners she cut for us, though. They ain't see the deals she got from the shoplifters and the men she let blow in her ear. They ain't pay attention to how often the insurance man come by our house — to how Momma took out life insurance policies on everybody she knew. That's why people thought we had. Cause they wasn't looking hard. My momma did things what made men want to take care of her. That's what we had. We had that kind of momma.

After what happened, Ruby Nell had problems with her mind — with her emotions — but they ain't stop her from being whole. Ain't never stop her from opening her mouth and getting what she wanted too. She ended up with a man what took care of her best he could. Man what loved her too much to put his hands on her. Sometimes, when I think about her, how she lost herself like that, I feel guilty cause I know her big break — her final break — trace back to me and Dale. Me being with him when she was being broke down in that way. Other times, I'm just glad I ain't sitting nowhere with my mind gone, too.

And I used to think Dale put his hands on me out of love. I'm too old a woman not to know better now. Dale lost me some of my teeth. Got a bridge when I found that money, though.

When I pull up to the bank, it's still early in the morning but the sun got a burn to it. I sit in the car a while and let the air conditioner blow in my face. Since Momma ain't been well, ain't been no updated Buicks or trades. The a/c in Momma's Buick been done gone out. Car ain't worth more than five hundred dollars and it damn sure ain't worth no fifteen-hundred-dollar compressor.

I make sure I scope the parking lot out good, even though my windows tinted dark as the law allow. I don't need nobody seeing me and getting it back to Punkin or Homer or nobody else that they seen me in a new car. Seen me with my new teeth in. Seen me looking like somebody that come from somewhere else.

I stop by here every other morning. I just go in and do a balance inquiry and make sure that the last four thousand dollars all right. Make sure it's still there and I'm all right. When I see ain't nothing but white folk sitting in the parking lot and walking in and out of Monarch West Bank doors, I grab my handbag and get out.

I found the money when Momma first started losing herself. I figured she had been saving and collecting it over the year. SSI from our father's death, before we was grown and before she married Homer, the money from the different men what thought I was they child, and the little bit left by her daddy and brother after they was gone, and all the life insurance policies she bought on random folks that had died over the years. That always seemed like a good thing — a nice thing to me, the way she buy them policies and be there to help folks bury they people. Folks who ain't got the same foresight as her. Now I understand that she always got something after them folks was gone. Always got what was left from they lives — from they deaths. I ain't even know about the envelopes Alex was sending every month until I was the one doing all the cleaning. Until after she got sick. Everything what got to do with keeping up the house was on me. I found all the monies in different places at different times. Some pushed deep inside Momma's old shoes, tucked away in the back of her closet. I found money frozen in Ziploc bags at the bottom of the deep freezer, underneath meat older than my kids, and I even found money, rolled tight and thick, stuffed in through the leg of a hollow ceramic leopard our daddy bought her a long time ago. After my daddy died, before Wayne become somebody ain't nobody know, Momma and him put up an old rickety shed in the backyard. They got out there every day and worked on it together, quick and in sync in a way that made the rest of us think they finally had something special between them. It turned out to be horrible thing. A thing that made Wayne hate. A thing that lasted too long in our lives.

After Alex was gone, we left that shed be and grass eventually grew so high around it that we just kind of silently agreed to give it over to the snakes. When Momma got sick, I hired a few crackheads to get in there and clean it out. They had to fight the snakes off with shovels and hoes, but for fifty dollars crackheads'll do anything. I was surprised they was honest when they called me out to show me the corner of liquor bottles and three Sparkling Water jugs full of change. I can't know if they snuck bottles off quiet before they called me, but I counted out almost two thousand dollars from the shed when I sat down with what was left.

And all the moneys I found was twenty-one thousand two hundred and thirty-two dollars and fifty-eight cent. I left it be for a long while fore I touched it. I wanted to see if she was gone come back to herself. And she ain't come back and she ain't coming back and I got four thousand left to spend.

I'm glad to see the nice Asian girl at the teller window. They done replaced a lot of the tellers with these old kiosks right in the middle of the bank, but I like to have somebody write my balance on a slip and hand it to me and smile at me so I can smile back and be proud of my teeth. These days they usually only have one teller and then a banker that try to meet you at the door and direct you to the kiosk.

I like real cashiers and bank tellers, real people to handle my money. The man teller, Matt, be here sometimes. He huff and puff about giving me my balance. Roll his eyes in a way that make me know he don't want to do it. Last time he say, *You know the kiosk can give you the same information?* And then he pinched his lips and say, *Right, Ms. Walker?* The girl, she smile from her tight eyes and say *Welcome, Ms. Walker* every time she see me. And that's what she doing when she set her eyes on me. She even throw up her little hand and give me a excited wave.

When I make it up to the window, she don't say hi or nothing like that. She hold out her hand and say, "He proposed to me. He did it." And I smile cause I know she been waiting on the boy she talking about for months.

"Well, look at there," I say to her, and smile at the little silver band she show me. "Congratulations, baby," I say, and try to be happy for her.

As I make my way to take the car back to Tricia's, I think about my children. How they have a hard time loving and being loved. How all that might be my fault. And I feel like something that's fertile and unfertile at the same time. And I try to believe that they won't be like me, a old woman who ain't never had nobody slip a ring on her finger and ask her to walk with them till one of us die.

8
LYDIA

When I walk through the automatic hospital doors, I think about my babies. I remember how panicked and afraid we were with the last one. We had just come in from the airport. I'd flown to Houston with Walter. It was just an overnight trip. We'd gone to celebrate the birthday of the wife of one of Walter's friends. I'd felt slight cramping off and on for most of the day, but it was so slight that I hadn't said anything to Walter. I hadn't wanted to ruin such a wonderful trip.

We had just made it past the first trimester and the doctor had told us that everything was looking good. At the party, I'd watched him share the news with his friends and I blushed when they made us sit in chairs in the center of the room and sprayed us with money. Walter blamed himself the whole ride over to the hospital. Kept apologizing and saying, *This is my fault. I put too much on you. The whole Houston thing was just too much.* And I let him blame himself, but I knew the truth. I knew that all of it was my fault. That I'd let my love for him, my desire to please him, allow me hope. That I'd tricked myself into believing that I could be a mother, and that was wrong. I was wrong. I wasn't meant to have that.

I stand just inside the automatic doors and tell myself that I'll be okay. I remind myself that I'm not here to give birth or leave something I've carried behind. *You can do this,* I tell myself.

When I make it to Grandmoan's room, I stand over the hospital bed and look down at her. She isn't awake, like I thought she'd be. There are no flowers in this room and the curtains are pulled shut. I can't pinpoint the smell that floats around us, but it was the same in the hallway and the elevator, too. Like medicine and candy and steel.

I remember her as powerful. Someone who could change things — change people with one word. I don't remember her this way. Her sleeping form is tiny in the huge bed, and the IV and tube in her mouth and other connections to the machines remind me of a cyborg. Her eyes are closed and her skin is almost gray. Her lips are around the tube and the corners of her mouth look like

184

they are cut and infected. Half her hair is braided neatly in finger-sized cornrows and the other half is wild against the pillow.

I reach my hand out and shake hers. It's cold, like she's already dead, so I twist my thumb around until I find the place where her pulse should be. I gently shake her wrist and whisper, "Grandmoan, it's Lydia. Do you remember me?"

And then I go silent and think back to all of those times I was dropped off at her house. We — Aunt Julie B.'s kids, me, and some of the second cousins Grandmoan babysat for — were always confined to the driveway in the summer. We'd play patty cake, red rover, and red-light green-light, then think. We'd drink stale water from a pitcher that she'd tossed out with us, then think. We'd listen to her vulgar curse words at Aunt Marie, Grandmoan's youngest daughter, or the characters on her soap operas and tremble with fear, hoping we weren't next. After her voice trailed off into bitter mumbling, we'd go back to what we were doing and even do some cursing ourselves.

"That Jerusalem heat was brutal in the summertime," I say. I watch her face and it remains still. I've heard that comatose people can hear you, even though it appears they can't. I laugh a short laugh and say, "Sometimes me and Jan thought we would fry under that big orange sun, with all the slippery Blue Magic pomade our mothers used to sculpt our hair into the perfect ponytails."

I don't say anything else for a while. I place my elbow on the arm of the chair and rest my cheek on it, as if I have grown bored. After a while, I stand up and lean over her face. I let my lips get so close to her ear that if someone were to walk in, it might look like I'm about to kiss her. I open my mouth and whisper, "What did we ever do to you? What did we do to make you put us out like that every day?"

My parents hardly ever argued, but my father would pout and fuss about me going to Grandmoan's. *Your momma. Your sister's boy. They got mean ways,* he'd tell my mother. *Lydia shouldn't be there without one of us.*

Mother would bring her face close to his and say, *She more them than us, honey. You got to learn to take it all in and let it go. Family gone be what they is.* Then she'd kiss him and promise that I'd be okay.

Grandmoan wasn't the type of grandmother who was waiting for me anxiously when we got there, but she always seemed happy when Mother handed her the twenty dollars a day she charged to care for me.

If it wasn't too cold out, as soon as Mother was gone, she made us go outside. When she first put us out each day, we were all shiny and soap-scented, but by the time my father arrived to get me, I was way past dusty and sweaty.

The stink of hog pens is what did it. The dull blue paint peeled off the house, and the iron bars that protected its windows were rusted to tired orange. Back then, I thought that the paint peeled and the bars rusted because they were old. But after I escaped the thick stink of the small-town air, I considered that maybe the horrible odors of cow shit and slaughtered hogs outside of town caused the wearing of the house.

Liquor was sold outside of the Jerusalem city limits. My grandparents had a small hog pen out there. They lived so close to the edge of town — most blacks lived so close to the edge of town — they caught all the shit that blew in from the business of livestock keeping and slaughtering and drinking.

I don't know how Granddaddy got all those rusty barrels, but when Grandmoan put us out of the house, we'd turn the oil-stained barrels and buckets that lined the front of the house upside down and use them for seats.

The yard had a dip that looped right around the center, and barely greening grass sprouted from it like the dip was its own plant pot. It looked like someone had dug it to place a fountain once and never quite finished. We dreamt of duck-duck-goose in the sacred, wonderful dip each day, but it was off-limits.

Grandmoan had an old window unit for air conditioning, and, to her, even with all its loud huffing and spitting, it was worth something. Our only goal of every summer day was to break into her fortress and sit quietly in the coolness of her sweet air. She always made a fuss about us letting flies in and air out, so as soon as eleven a.m. rolled around we were sentenced to the driveway with her rattling on about how we were terrible children and ruining her stories was the last thing she'd let us do. She would always end her sentence — a death sentence in our juvenile minds — with *And you bet not get on my grass or leave out that gate. Play in that driveway. If you don't, I'll whoop you niggers' asses.*

Every now and then one of us would

venture off to the side door, which was the common entrance to the house. She'd had the garage converted into a den long before any of us were born. I don't ever remember entering from the front of the house. Ever. That entrance was sacred in her eyes and unless you were white or visiting from out of town, you could not enter that way. The den was where everything happened. Where she took company and watched her soaps. That's where we wanted to be.

You could see the front room from the kitchen, but only through a small window-like cut in the wall. Back then, it was frightening. I had no desire to enter the bronze jungle. A huge bronze cagelike fixture hung from the ceiling in the center of the room. Inside the fixture was a fake bird trapped inside of a spotlight by plastic bars that dripped oil onto the bottom of the fixture. Large leopard statues, one of them with a broken paw, were displayed and plastic flowers were scattered throughout the room. The dark furniture was protected by an untouchable plastic, at least untouchable to us.

Every now and then, we tapped on the side door with requests for water or food, to relieve our bladders, or to feign sickness. Jan liked to be the one to tell her that Mr.

Chavez, the elderly insurance man, was approaching. He never missed his weekly visits, which were consistent, even though most Wednesdays he could hear her yell from the window above us, "Tell that nigger I ain't home!"

We'd stumble over each other trying to be the one to make it to the door to tell her he was there, but I always let Jan beat me to it. We thought maybe when she opened the screen the lucky one standing there would be blessed with the air that we imagined wanted to escape from inside the palace as much as we wanted in.

I remember the day I didn't let Jan win and I was the one to announce Mr. Chavez. She flung the huge orange door open but stood behind the screen door. She didn't say a word, just looked at me with expecting eyes. She wasn't an ugly woman at all. In fact, if you could get past the floral housecoat, the plastic cup with the brown liquid that made her mean in one hand, the bags under her eyes, and how she never smiled at us, she was pretty. She had strong features, high cheekbones, and a pronounced nose, and the greasy curl she wore was almost nice.

I shifted my eyes past her to the small television that sat on top of a larger, older floor model. There were picture frames of her children and of us, a small porcelain black mailman, and a half-empty whiskey bottle sitting on top of the old floor-model TV that had been pictureless since before I was born. A familiar Mr. Clean commercial sang out and I knew *The Young and the Restless* would be back soon on the small thirteen-inch TV resting on top of the broken one.

When her eyebrows rose to indicate her impatience, I opened my mouth and told her that the insurance man was coming.

She took a drag from her cigarette and blew a wide puff of smoke through the upper part of the screen with her head tilted toward the sky. A hopeful feeling from the kindness she exhibited by blowing in the direction opposite my tiny face tickled me.

She slurred her words out to me, telling me she kept her window open. That she could hear everything outside of it. Her eyes became tiny slits when she told me to get away from her door or I could go take a nap. Her voice rose with every word. The ones that always stayed with me were *Don't come to this goddamn door no more today.*

I stepped back just as Mr. Chavez walked up to the door, and her face changed instantly. She offered him her most spurious smile and allowed her open-faced gold tooth to sparkle at him.

She unlocked the flimsy lock on the screen door and allowed Mr. Chavez to pass through. It was the first and the last time she'd ever hurt me with her tongue. I stayed out of her way after that.

"I wrote you letters," I say to her. "They were SOS calls or something like that."

In the part of Dallas we lived in, South Dallas, a lot of children were being raised by their grandparents or at least had grandparents in their lives. The girl who sat next to me in fifth grade lived with her grandmother and her grandmother's boyfriend. Her name was Camesha Wallace and she was very well cared for. Her hair was always in perfect ponytails and her clothes were always new. She had the best packed lunches and sometimes her grandmother baked cookies. I didn't know where her mother and father were, but that whole year, I wanted Camesha's life. I wanted someone — a grandmother — to step up for me and bake me cookies and buy me nice things.

"I asked you to bake me cookies. Told you that Mother needed help," I say. I close my mouth because I can hear trembling in my throat and my hands are shaking.

I take a deep breath and let it out. I keep

doing that until I don't feel like I'll cry.

"I hated you for not writing me back. For pretending you thought I was okay with Mother when I was visiting those summers. Until I found the letters in her drawer when I was a grown woman," I say. My tone is even. "You never gave me a reason to want you, but still, I wanted you."

I found all twenty-six unsent letters in Mother's underwear drawer the day I packed her life into two boxes and moved her into Quail Oaks. She sat silently on the edge of the bare twin bed that had once been part of a bunk set and watched as I packed. I held the letters out toward her, like a gift. There must've been so many tears and so many questions in my eyes.

She looked at me as if she was confused. She was more herself that day than she had been in a while. She knew that I was putting her away, but she didn't judge me. She had spent the day telling me stories about my father. About how much he loved us. About how much we'd loved him. She reminded me of his innocence and of the death he didn't deserve.

What? she asked, focusing her gaze on the envelopes in my hand. *What, baby?*

She leaned in to get a better look at the stack of envelopes in my hand, and recognition and tears clouded her eyes at the same time.

She shook her head and apologized. She kept repeating, *I didn't know, baby. I didn't know what to do with them.*

"If Mother had mailed those letters, would you have come for me? Would you have kept me that first summer when I came back?" I ask my grandmother.

"All I needed was someone," I say.

And we're both silent.

9

JAN

For almost a year, I sat next to her every weekday morning. We ain't say nothing to one another, but I'd go to her after I dropped my kids off at school. She look out at the yard that was hers. That had been hers for more than forty years. Be done just got up out the bed. I ain't even sure if she was in a condition to brush her own teeth, but she be done put on them big brogan tennis shoes and throwed a thin housecoat on to cover up her gown and made her way outside. Out to this porch. Most days, Granddaddy be in there getting her coffee, making her colored pancakes. Singing. She sit on that porch and just watch Colgate Street in silence, like it was hers and she was some kind of guardian.

First time I come by and end up sitting with her, I didn't mean to be quiet. Had something to say. I had just talked to my housing counselor about porting my voucher to Dallas. About going to school in a foreign land, where ain't nobody — no history to distract me. Counselor told me I been in the system long enough to request a port out at my next recertification, in about a year's time.

I wanted to come right out and ask her about the money. Wanted to see if I had it in my memory the right way. Wanted to see if what my momma had in hers was right. I wanted to stick my hand out and finally get something worth having from somebody in my family. Even a couple thousand dollars was enough to get me going. Momma talked about Grandmoan having a way with money. Knowing how to save. If all that was real, if she was saving like Momma always said, she could spare it and I was gone get it.

That first day, I walked up to where she was sitting in that drive and stood in front of her for a while. Her white hair stood wild all over her head. When I saw how her eyes darted all over the place, how that oxygen tank was at her feet and that tube in her nose, how she looked up at me like something that came from faraway stead of deep inside her, I thought it wasn't no use. I just sat down in that chair next to her and listened to her rattled breathing. And listened to mine. And we lived that way for one hour each weekday morning for a year, until earlier this week when her system went down. When her body attacked her.

Before her body attacked her, I had watched a movie what had a vulture stalking over a starving child, waiting for it to die. It was one of them movies about war in Africa. Can't remember what had done happened to the child, but it was dying and when it did, that big hollowed-out-looking bird perched itself up on that baby and looked out to where the sky touched the earth, like it was waiting on whatever vultures wait on to tell it to eat. That was a real small part of the movie, but I couldn't stop thinking about it. Made me go to the library and check out all the books they had on vultures. I probably shouldn't have did that. Found out that they used to have sharp talons and real strong feet. Used to be able to hunt, kill, and carry they own food away. Now they just got to eat where the roadkill lay. Don't know why that made how I was feeling worse. Something about the way I went to Grandmoan every day made me feel like that bird, like I was waiting on the worst part of her life to happen, like wasn't nothing else I could do but be there with her, cause my own survival was wrapped up in

that. Then sometime after that, I was helping Javon with a school book report about
birds in Central America. Book said some
of the traditional folks, ones what practice
more ritual stuff, believe if you bury a
person in the open and let the vultures get
them, it free the spirit. I don't know why,
but that made my sitting with her feel worth
something. Feel like I was doing good.

Now I sit out here by myself and listen to
Granddaddy bang pots and sing inside the
house. He don't sound nothing like somebody who wife dying. Don't sound sad and
I can't really blame him. He probably been
walked over his whole life. He ain't smart.
Can't read or understand nothing really.
Momma read him his mail and sometimes
his conversation get so far off track, I
wonder if he the one with dementia stead of
his wife. I feel sorry for him most times, but
I ain't really in no place to feel sorry for
nobody.

I lost three jobs last year on count of my
thyroid messing up. McDonald's, Target,
and Walmart, jobs like that don't take kind
to folks calling out weeks at a time, no matter what they medical history of problems
look like. My boss at McDonald's was cool
enough to let me sit on a stool and work
the drive-thru, but when I passed out one

morning, he made me go home. Seem like after that, I just couldn't get back. Eventually had enough problems to wind up in the hospital, which gave the government cause to give me Medicaid. Got my thyroid took care of, but I ain't interested in working none of these low-paying jobs no more. I just want to go to school. I want to study animals and they behavior. I don't know what I can do with that. What kind of money I can make, but it seem like all the answers in them. In the animals. I just want to do something different.

"Jan, Jan, Jan. My little darling, Jan," Granddaddy say, coming out the front door, balancing a food tray in his hands. "Granddaddy got something for you. You used to love my rainbow pancakes," he say, smiling.

He ain't got his teeth in, but he smiling like he do. Even without his teeth, though, I think Granddaddy look happy and kind. Even with one dead eye, I think my granddaddy a nice-looking man. His smile been the one constant thing in my life. When I was little, I always thought it was disrespectful of my momma and her sister and brother to call him by his first name. They call him Homer right before us, and I wondered why Grandmoan didn't cuss them. I was a grown woman before I realized he wasn't none of they daddy. He was always good to them like he was, though. Like them and us was all he had.

"Hey, Granddaddy," I say, sitting up from my slouch in the chair.

The weather nice right now. Too early in the day to be hot and too late in the season to be cold. Me and Grandmoan sit out here no matter what the weather, though. Get too cold, Granddaddy bring big bedspreads out for us to keep warm with. Rain don't matter either since we was shielded by the carport.

"You ain't had to do this for me, Granddaddy," I say when he place the tray on the little table that sit in front of the chairs.

When I see the plate, I know he done put forth his best effort. It's a blue pancake, a green one, and a pinkish-reddish one. They all seem to be crumbling and a little soggy, and that make me remember how he never could get the food color to bind in them when we was little. He still at it after all this time, and that make me smile on the inside. Still, the bacon undercooked and the coffee black, just like Grandmoan like it.

"Hush up, gal," he say all playful with a half smile on his face. He stand up straight and put his hands on his sides, kind of gripping his back. He stretch out a bit and look

200

out at the street. "Your granddaddy like cooking. Always have." He make a loud groan, like stretching his back feel real good, and he look down at the chair Grandmoan usually sit in. He point to it, and I nod.

"Have some," I say, pushing the plate toward him.

"That's for you. Your granddaddy get up with the chickens and eat with them, too. Go on. Enjoy," he say. I see thick spit crawling down his lip. He sit back in the seat and clasp his hands together over his stomach and watch me. Wait for me to take a bite.

I ain't really that hungry. Don't never really do more than coffee in the morning, but Granddaddy been insulted his whole life. I don't want to add to that. I break off a piece of the blue pancake with my fork and put it in my mouth. I nod my head and close my eyes cause I know he watching. It got a good taste. Like something from scratch, not out the box, but I'm not hungry so it's hard for me to get it chewed and swallowed down.

"Good, ain't it?" he ask, wiping the spit off his lip with the back of his hand. His voice still smiling.

"Mmm-hmm," I say. And he break into a chuckle. I use the paper towel he got on the tray to wipe my mouth and swallow the rest of the piece of pancake. My mouth feel dry now and I know I can't eat another bite, so I talk.

"You miss her, Granddaddy?" I ask before he can stop laughing all the way. And I watch him slide his big, rough hand down his mouth, like he wiping away his smiles and laughter altogether.

"Your Grandmoan always been something else," he say, fixing his eyes on the Scotts' old house across the street. "She was a strong woman when I come long. Raising them kids. Had done lost a husband and all her close kin." He sigh.

"Granddaddy didn't have nobody. Not really. My sister lived on that corner yonder," he say, pointing his finger past a diagonal to us, across the road, where the street pause and turn into another street.

"I member her. Aunt Annie Maul?" I ask. "You used to let us walk around there with you after work."

He smile and nod his head. "You got you a good memory, girl. Granddaddy sure did let you and your brother and your cousins come with him. Y'all was little then. How you member that?" he say, pushing his perched lips out into a pout and batting his eyes all exaggerated like.

"I member everything, Granddaddy," I

say, and I can tell by how his eyes change, I done shifted the mood.

He sigh again. "Granddaddy ain't have nobody. Annie Maul give me one hour a week. Said I talked too much for anything more than that. I figure if I take y'all, she let me stay longer. See my sister, Annie Maul, she the only one move up here with me. Her and my momma." He cough and I hear the rattling in his chest.

I make like I don't hear nothing. Just wait for him to stop. When he finally stop, he smack his lips together, like he trying to get his mouth wet or something, and I'm close to asking if I should get him some water cause I need some for myself. Before my words slide out, his do.

"They was hard and soft together. They probably would've made it if they had been one person, but they wasn't. They was too much of one thing, you know? You member my momma, Jan? We call her TuMomma?" he ask.

I shake my head and he continue on.

"She probably dead fore you was born, but Marie knew her. Marie was here, she member. TuMomma loved her some Marie. She was a baby when I come to your grandmomma. I'm the only daddy Marie knowed." He sit up and wipe his lip with the back of his hand again. He put both hands on his lap and just look down at them.

I think we both take a moment and think on Marie. What she was to each of us. Hate how she ain't nothing to nobody no more. How it don't seem right that we forgot to remember she was here when she was and how it seem like she wasn't never here now that she gone.

"Seem like y'all was getting close before all this," he say, and I look at him, wondering what he mean.

He read my mind and say, "You and Grandmoan. She loved you when you was a little baby, but you wouldn't have nothing to do with her. Never would have nothing to do with her. Then out of nowhere you start coming around. Granddaddy was happy to see you, Jan. Happy things was working out," he say, and then he put his eyes on me. The glass one ain't really looking at me, but the good one, the deep brown one, seem like it's digging inside me. "She might not have been all there, but your grandmomma was happy with y'all mornings. Weekdays was her best ones. I think cause of you."

I shake my head. "I wasn't here to be no comfort," I kind of spit out. "I wasn't here to make her days good." I got a mind to ask *him* about the money, but I'm sure he don't know. I'm sure of that. Momma always complaining about how his retirement don't stretch enough. How the cable off or the auto insurance done lapsed. How she filling in the gaps for food with the home health aide money she get for taking care of Grandmoan. If Granddaddy or Momma knew about the money, wouldn't none of that be happening.

Granddaddy good eye get wide, like I done cussed him or scared him or something, and then it just go back to normal and he sit back in the chair and let his hands rest on his stomach.

"You member old pissy Vera? Your grandmoan friend?" he ask, but he don't turn to look at me. Don't see me nod my head.

"Your grandmoan always hung out with older peoples. Vera was about ten years older than her. That's why she was peeing her pants. Why your grandmomma was always cleaning her up like she was some type of child. She was old. And, boy," he say, dragging the word *boy* out like it's a song. "She was a shit-starter, too. Me and your grandmoan used to party," he say, and a smile break across his lips.

"I hear tell it," I say. And I had. My whole

life I'd heard whispers about who she was. Never straight stories. My momma didn't talk about anything, but our town is small so other people talk. Didn't take long for me to find out where I come from.

"One night, we was out past the line at a little juke joint with a pool table in it. Your grandmoan was jealous. She wasn't gone have nobody looking at her man," he say, sliding his hand across the top of his head. I can see the spit on his lip again. I look down at my hands.

"Vera got it in Grandmoan head I had looked at some other woman and Grandmoan pulled out her gun and shot at me right in that juke joint." He chuckled and slapped his knee. "Boy, I tell you, I left that place running. I run all the way back to the east side sloppy drunk. At one point, I was thinking I was surely dead when I saw the headlights of a car rolling real slow up the highway. I was close to a underpass, so I just hid under there, and sure enough, it was her and Vera, driving slow, looking for me." He stop talking and throw his hand in the air.

"Morning, Johnny Ray," he say when his next-door neighbor come out his front door. The neighbor don't say nothing, just nod and move toward his car, and that make me so mad I say something.

"You hear my granddaddy speaking to you. He your elder. Folks act like they don't know how to show respect," I say loud as I can. Johnny Ray stop in his tracks and look over at where we sitting. Momma told me about Grandmoan cussing him out on count of his dog messing in her yard. Momma say he been mad ever since. That was years ago, fore Grandmoan even slipped away from herself.

"O-oh," Johnny Ray stutter. "Morning, Mr. Homer. I didn't see y'all sitting there. Morning," he say again, and then he hurry to his car.

Granddaddy sit quiet for a while after that. So long, I wonder if I should've shut up with the neighbor or about Grandmoan or if I should just leave. And right when I'm ready to get up and leave, he speak.

"She ain't come home that night. Reckon she stayed with Vera and sobered up. She come home the next morning, looking like the day before, and I ain't know what was gone happen. I was standing in the kitchen, washing the dishes I had done messed up making breakfast. She walked up behind me, and I was still as a possum under a axe handle. Didn't move or look back or know if she had her gun or what." He stop talking and get this faraway look in his eyes. The sides of his mouth twitching like he want to smile but he don't.

He shake his head and say, "She walked up behind me and kissed me on my neck, like the night before wasn't nothing. And I knowed after that. That's when I learned her the most. She drank to forget," he say, laughing. "And it really worked, ain't it? Made her forget to whoop Granddaddy butt." And he nudge me with his elbow, so I can laugh, too. And I do. I laugh a little before all the laughing trail off and we sit there quiet.

When me and Granddaddy say bye, it's still early. He watch me get in my car before he wave and go in the house. And I just sit there for a while, thinking about my next move. I open the glove box and pull out the envelope with the housing voucher — the one my housing counselor gave me to port out to Dallas with. After yesterday's moving briefing at the housing authority, I feel like I got more of a plan, but I'm scared. I don't have everything I need to do this, and I'm scared. More scared of not having nobody than I ever been. So scared of failing and having to come back here.

Grandmoan picked me up from school when I was in pre-K. When my brother was in pre-K, she let him walk after he did his half days. But she told Momma, *She a girl. She ain't walking that block by herself.* She could've easily handed over her keys to my momma and let her get me, but for that whole school year she got me herself.

She was something beautiful them days. I could smell rosewater on her, and she was always dressed nice. Creased jeans and floral blouses. After she got me, she take me to Bill's Drive-In and buy me a milkshake, or sometimes we drive to the west side and visit with Vera, who lived in the servant's quarters of some rich white folks house what she used to work for. That's where I heard her first talk like she loved me. Talk like she wanted something good for me. She said, *Yes,* kind of dragging the word out, like song. *Vera, I ain't done a lot I'm proud of. But this . . .* She sighed and lowered her voice. *Maybe this turn everything. Maybe this'll do it.* And then she looked over at me and smiled soft, like a grandmother. *Yes, ma'am,* she sang out. *I'm gone make something good of this. You just watch and see.* And I done held on to that year after all this time. Granddaddy wrong about me never taking to her. He wrong about that one thing. I took to her once. That whole year I took to her. That's the year she became Grandmoan to me.

HELEN JEAN
1976

The night she found out what Wayne did was the same night Bacon died. That was the night she thought she'd break the covenant and do what she first meant to. Before that night, she had almost forgotten what it was like to be held down by the actions of men. She had learned to be free after Jessie B. After Bacon. Occasionally, a man would come along and make her remember what it was like to be a subject under someone else's rule, and she'd throw him back to the world. She liked being king herself. But that night, she felt hollow in a way that reminded her exactly where she came from.

When Helen Jean walked through the door that night, after leaving her brother's lifeless body in the hospital morgue, she expected her grandson, Alex, to be waiting for her in the den. Some nights, his momma left him there, sleeping in his old infant seat.

Even though he was more toddler than infant and his whole body didn't really fit in the small seat, he liked that better than being with his mother. He didn't sleep well with her. He slept better with his grandmother.

Sometimes Helen Jean felt guilty for loving the boy more than the girl she'd given birth to just over a year before. Her and Julie B.'s pregnancies had overlapped shortly, which was more than a little embarrassing for her. And she hadn't wanted that child. Not for the same reasons that led her to the outhouse all those years ago, but because she'd learned that children complicated life. But because there was the covenant from all those years earlier, she kept her.

And then the girl, who she'd named Marie, was born slow. It wasn't a recognizable slow. Strangers couldn't tell it by looking at the child, but from the moment she was placed in her mother's arms, Helen Jean noticed the same empty gaze in her eyes that she had seen in her brother's. In Herbert Lee's.

And that scared her. The night she was born, Helen Jean worried about what the world would hold for the girl. She imagined the most horrible things. She'd seen first-hand how people dismissed and took advantage of the vulnerable. The weak. What she feared the most was what would happen when people began to know. She imagined her being taken, strapped into one of those jackets. She imagined white men in white suits, telling her they'd take care of her daughter just fine. She thought about her youngest brother. He wore his slowness on his face. His teeth hung out of his mouth and his eyes sat crooked in his head. He never learned to speak. Never learned to do the most basic things.

After her mother died, her father let them take him. Herbert Lee died in a place that was even worse than the only home he'd ever known. A place with pea green walls that smelled of feces. A place where they strapped him down when he was having a sad day or when he was probably just missing his momma. A place where they opened his skull and played in his brain. Helen Jean didn't want that for her daughter, so Helen Jean didn't want her daughter.

Marie's father was one of those men Helen Jean wanted to throw back out into the world, but for as long as he could, he wouldn't allow it. He was kind of man that lived life like a weasel. Sunk his teeth into the soft part of her flesh and never planned to let her go. He was the type of man that beat and threatened her to keep her his. Type of man that bound himself to her so tight that he forced her out on secret drives to far east Texas to meet with conjure women. The kind of man that made her want to believe the remedies of those women so badly that she did everything from put drops in his food to buried bone-dolls in his likeness formed with some of his real hair a few counties away. She never knew which thing it was that worked, but one day he just left. Never even knew his child was growing inside of Helen Jean.

When Vera called her to come down to identify her brother's body, reminded her that they hadn't married and Helen Jean was his only true next of kin, she hadn't wanted to go. It had been years since she'd seen Bacon. He'd tried reaching out to her — tried to make amends for what he'd done to them — but she'd never told him he was forgiven. Their cousin Ernestine had tried to bridge the gap between Helen Jean and her brother, thinking it petty that Helen Jean would let the relationship die over something as small as money, which was the reason Helen Jean had given her. Truth of the matter was that Helen Jean had never wanted her cousin to pity or judge her or her brothers because of what their father had done to them. Ernestine and nobody else would ever know the true extent of Bacon's sin.

Ernestine left Jerusalem for Dallas in '72, but before she left, she made an elaborate meal of oxtails, white beans, and cornbread and invited Helen Jean over for a beer. Something in their relationship broke for good when Helen Jean arrived to find her brother at her cousin's table waiting to be served.

All the times before when she had snapped at Ernestine, she hadn't meant it. But when she'd shouted at her, *Stupid bitch! Got no idea about this evil motherfucker!* she'd meant every word and she never took them back.

Even still, when Bacon rose up from his seat that day, she'd wanted to tell him that he'd been forgiven before they'd ever left their father's house. That he'd been forgiven the night she woke up to him whimpering into his pillow as their father's body hovered over him. The night, from her side of the tiny room she shared with her brothers, she realized that her father took turns moving through each of his children. The night she kept quiet because it wasn't her turn. But it hadn't felt right to say those things to him.

Saying those things would've been cheating the child she gave birth to. When she looked at the boy, she was ashamed for still loving her brother and she wondered what it meant that, after what he'd done, she could still love Bacon and struggle to look at a thing that came from her.

So she never told Bacon that he was forgiven. Always let him believe he was hated. And on the night of his death, with eyes swollen from crying, she scanned the dark room hoping to set her eyes on Alex's seat tucked away in a corner. In the midst of all her grief, it was his face she needed to see.

She'd had the garage converted before the last pregnancy, before the final child. Open concept was how the remodeler explained the opening the size of a doorway that stepped up into the kitchen. Through the doorway, she could see the dim light over the kitchen sink that was always left on at night, but aside from that the whole house felt still and dark. Alex was not in the room.

She stood there in that dark, wearing her coat, clutching her purse for a long time before she moved over to the couch and sat down. The plastic crunched underneath her body and she thought about Vera's words at the hospital.

*He been strange since . . . You know. Y'all
ain't speak no more. I don't know what Bacon
had got hisself into.*

They'd found Bacon's body beaten and
tossed into a ravine outside of town. When
Vera first called to tell her about it, Helen
Jean didn't get upset. She hadn't wanted to.
Not in front of Julie B. and Ruby Nell.
She'd excused herself from the kitchen,
where they had been sitting at the table eating dinner, and she had gone into her room
and held her hand over her mouth and let
the tears roll down her face. Though they
never talked about things of old. The shed.
The segregation of Wayne. She knew to hate
Bacon on the surface as a service to her
children.

She wanted to cry and miss her brother
and regret how things had ended right there
at the dinner table, as soon as Vera told her,
but she simply said, *I'll be there when I can
get there.* She wished that all she felt was
relief, but there was something about him
being her brother, about their shared pain,
that made it impossible to shake her love
for him free. And that made her feel guilty.

She shook her head to rid herself of
thoughts of her brother and that's when the
footsteps on the kitchen floor stilled her.

She knew it wasn't Alex. These feet was

older and more intentional. She listened quietly in the darkness of the den, until she heard the scraping of chairs on the kitchen floor, until she heard the whispering and what sounded like weeping.

"I don't like it, Julie B. Dale ain't never been right for you, but if that's what you want to do . . ." Ruby Nell exhaled and then sniffed.

"It ain't about wanting or not wanting, Ruby Nell," she heard Julie B. say, cutting her little sister off, and Helen Jean could hear the tears in her voice. "It's about you leaving after you graduate, it's about you moving in with Aunt Ernestine out in Dallas. I heard her when she called. She invited you to come stay with her. That's why I'm thinking about leaving with Dale. Cause I need people all the time. And you not gone be here no more . . ." She smacked her lips. "You gone leave when you graduate. I know you is," she said, like she was asking a question.

And then they were quiet.

Julie B. was always the pretty one. Helen Jean gave her a hard time for years because she was so shapely and perfect. She always reminded Helen Jean of her own mother. Pretty and weak in ways that would destroy her.

She kept her head down and stayed out of her mother's way, but as she grew older and more beautiful that didn't seem to be enough. She wasn't as tough as Ruby Nell. Never had been, so most of the time Ruby Nell stood up for her. Ruby Nell liked to remind her mother that Julie B. was her daughter, too. When Julie B. was sixteen, Helen Jean's anger faded out and turned to pity for her. That was after Dale Lusk came into the picture. He was eight years older than Julie B. A lot of the girls and women called him Pretty Dale. But Helen Jean could see nothing pretty about the way he liked to hit Julie B. and how he couldn't stay away from drugs. When he came along, she could only see her mother in the girl.

"You don't need him," Ruby Nell said, raising her voice.

"Don't wake them up," Julie B. whispered. And Helen Jean guessed that the children were sleeping in the back room.

Helen Jean had given birth to Marie six months after Julie B. had Alex. When Marie was born, Helen Jean's sloppy parenting showed more. She was still a heavy drinker — had drank straight through the pregnancy, and it took a lot out of her to try to keep up with the new man, Homer. The man who owned a small farm, more so a hog pen, outside of town. It was a tiny operation. About a dozen chickens, two goats, fifteen hogs, and a horse. And Helen Jean loved it. She took to farming like it was her true nature. She was better at it than anything. Mothering, loving, and even drinking.

And Marie was so little and helpless. To Helen Jean, it seemed that the child just got in the way, so Julie B. and Ruby Nell became her parents. They stood in the gap as far as she was concerned.

"I can't live with *her* anymore, Ruby Nell. Not without you, I can't," Julie B. said, and Helen Jean knew exactly who *her* was. "Somebody named Snopes came to the door yesterday. Said he my daddy. He the second man to do that. All she did was laugh, Ruby Nell."

"Julie B.," Ruby Nell said softly. "Jessie B. was both our daddy. We know that for sure. We look just alike." She sighed. "Sides, Momma named you after him."

Helen Jean cringed at those words. She knew her children had heard the conversations over the years. Conversations about her and other men. Though he never spoke them out loud, after the girl was born, Helen Jean knew Jessie B. must've had questions about Julie B. in the same way she knew he never had to question where Ruby Nell came from. That one entered the world wearing his face.

"We thought so. We did, but if they keep coming . . . If all these different men keep coming and saying . . ." She started crying again.

"The possibility of it and her laughing and saying, 'Let that nigger think what he want. Let him buy for you like he your daddy. Don't get mad.' If she can — if I can let him think that . . . She was with him. She was with that other one, too. It's possible and that mean I'm not me."

Helen Jean had told the girl to milk it because what was done could not be changed. She had learned to milk men. To show them — to give them the part of herself they wanted and make them pay. And she had learned to be good with that money. To put most of it away. In her heart, she had no idea who Julie B.'s father was. It was one of three and Jessie B. was still a possibility.

The girls were quiet again and Helen Jean sat there trying to ignore the sweat the plastic from the couch was creating. She could feel the dampness under her arms and between her thighs, but if she moved they would hear her. They would know she was listening. There was something in the intimacy between them that she wanted to hold on to.

"I'm gone leave," Ruby Nell finally said. "But it ain't cause of Momma. It's cause of . . ."

Helen Jean could hear a tremble in her voice and it scared her. Ruby Nell was the tough one. Had been since she was in the womb. When Helen Jean carried Wayne, he moved inside her sly and sneaky, almost like he wanted her to believe that he wasn't really there at all. Julie B.'s movements had been fidgety and nervous-like. There were times that Helen Jean swore she could hear her crying inside of her. Ruby Nell had surprised her mother with bold, hard kicks, and she never seemed to sleep or let Helen Jean get any. She was an annoyance that meant to let Helen Jean know that she was alive inside her and she would have her every need met. So that tremble in her voice frightened her mother and made her remember that she was the daughter too strong for trembles.

Julie B. sighed. "What? Cause of what, Ruby Nell?" Julie B. asked, and Helen Jean knew that she had heard the tremble too.

Ruby Nell's sigh felt like a brewing storm.

"The year before I started high school,

before Wayne moved away . . ." Helen Jean wanted to move in the direction of her voice. But she sat still. Frozen. The mention of her son's name unnerved her, made her feel uncomfortable.

"You was with Dale — and that was fine cause most days Momma be in her room lying down, still sleeping off the night, you know?" she said, rushing her words in a way that made the question more statement than anything. "That day she wasn't here at all. It was just Wayne and some of his friends from school. And they was in the house, not in his shed, like he was posed to be."

Helen Jean's hand moved instinctively to her chest, to her heart.

"What happened, Ruby Nell?" Julie B. asked again. "Just tell me."

"He watched . . ." Helen Jean held her breath.

"He — he watched his friend do things to me," she said, and then she started sniffing, like she couldn't control it.

Helen Jean clasped her hand over her mouth and her eyes felt warm all over again. She struggled to match the silence in the kitchen. She wanted to storm out of the house. She wanted to scream. She wanted to tilt her head toward the night sky and let her voice rip it wide open with all the sound she had in her. She wanted to get into her car and drive to Wayne's house and blow his brains right out of his head. She wanted to do what she had failed to do that night in the outhouse, but the thing that always stopped her came back and reminded her. *Bear it or perish yourself.*

"Wayne told him I wanted him to do filthy things to me. He stood there while his friend hurt me," Ruby Nell finally said.

Helen Jean closed her eyes. She could feel tears catching in her throat, like bile. She hadn't wanted that for them, for her daughters. Surely hadn't wanted it in her own house.

"He said she wouldn't believe me. She wouldn't care," she heard her daughter say, her words coming out clearer than they had been before. Her words coming out like strength.

"That's not true, Ruby Nell. He wasn't even supposed be in the house. She would've killed him — she would kill him —"

"That's the problem, Julie B. That's always been the problem. Wayne what he is . . . That's on her." Ruby Nell sighed.

Helen Jean held her breath. She wanted to break in and correct her daughter. Tell her that Wayne was what he was because of what he was. She wanted to explain that she tried to save them. But telling them that would've been telling them too much. So she just listened.

"I'm telling you, Julie B. But don't nobody else need to know. Please," she said. "I'm telling you, so you can be ready. Cause I ain't felt right in my head since it happened . . ."

Helen Jean wondered if she would continue. She wanted her to. She wanted to listen to all the things she wasn't supposed to hear.

"I don't want this to be my thing," Ruby Nell finally said. "To be the thing that break me." She sighed like an old woman. "Long as he my brother. Long as I know about all the things done to him by. . . . He gone always be our brother."

Helen Jean sat listening to the quiet between them, and her mind went back to her own brother. Family was family. To her knowledge, nobody had ever found a way around that. She'd grown up with Bacon — with all of her brothers. Had known them in ways that nobody else ever would. Loved them like brothers. She never learned to see monsters in any of them. It didn't matter who he was out there in the world. It was hard not to love Bacon in her heart.

She hadn't imagined that her girls would feel that for Wayne, but she understood as she listened to them that just as Bacon was always her brother, Wayne would always be theirs.

She closed her eyes and imagined Julie B. rubbing her sister's shoulders, shaking her head, like their lives had been some pitiful things. And she would've sat there and listened for much longer had the phone not rang. Had Julie B. not hissed at Ruby Nell and said, "Get it, Ruby. Hurry before it wake the babies."

She heard the chair scrape against the linoleum in the kitchen and she imagined her daughter making her way to the other side of the room and grabbing the phone from where it was mounted on the wall.

Helen Jean tried reaching back and recalling a day when her son could've hurt her daughter. Tried reaching back and making sense of how she missed it. If something in the girl's spirit broke and she missed it. And then she thought about how Ruby Nell's sad and quiet spells reminded her of her mother's. How Julie B. was her mother outside, but, at some point, she'd known that Ruby Nell was her mother inside and she ignored that part of her. Ignored the broken parts of her because she didn't want to see them, and that's how she missed what Wayne had done.

And she believed Ruby Nell because she'd always known what lived inside Wayne, and she knew that even with the world she built for him, she should have been waiting for her daughters to come to her. And she was disappointed in herself for missing it all.

"Hello," she heard Ruby Nell say, and she imagined her daughter resting an elbow on the washing machine, and because she heard it squeak, opening the door to the hot water heater closet next to the wall, and holding it open with her hip. They all used the inside of the door to jot down telephone numbers. There was a number on each slat. Most slats had three or four numbers. Ruby Nell had started it in junior high and it never bothered Helen Jean too much. She wanted the children to carve out a place for themselves. As they grew older, she wanted them to feel at home, even, to some extent, Wayne. After all, he had come from her, too.

When Wayne started elementary at Parkley, she never imagined they'd have numbers on that door. It had been so white and pristine, like most of the people at the school. But the people at school, the kids and teachers, had been so hateful to Ruby Nell and Julie B. and Wayne. Ruby Nell's first-grade teacher, Mrs. Goode, called her dumb when she couldn't see the blackboard from the back of the room, but she still refused to let the girl sit closer to the front. Ruby Nell was the only black girl in the whole class — in the whole first grade — and even though she wasn't one to come home crying about it, her mother was sure that all of her classmates treated her like she had the plague.

But all the whites were gone from Parkley by the time Ruby Nell was in middle school. The tornado of '67, the one that destroyed Little Guadalupe, where all the Hispanics lived, made the houses cheap enough to bring more blacks in. When that tornado destroyed the Hispanic neighborhood, the city took a look at all the vacant houses the white folks left in Parkley and bought them cheap. They lowered the prices of those homes even more than what they'd bought them for to keep those Hispanics from moving to the west side — the white side. But not even the Hispanics wanted to live with the blacks. Some of them came, but more stayed and rebuilt Little Guadalupe. With the depreciated value of the neighborhood, the costs were more affordable for black folks. A lot of them wanted to live in nice homes that had been built to a certain standard because they were built for whites. Black families thought they had arrived because they could afford to live in Parkley. So they settled the neighborhood by the droves. And Helen Jean didn't mind that her kids celebrated by tallying up their friends on her door. She let them have it just like the white folks let the blacks have Parkley.

Now the door held hundreds of numbers. Bob's Burger Stand. Wayne. Ernestine. Sam's Hair Palace.

"Speak up, Aunt Vera. I can't hear you," Ruby Nell said, and she knew what was being said over the phone.

Though she had tried to hide it, she knew Vera had seen the disturbed look in her eyes when she gently grabbed her shoulder, pulled Helen Jean's body into hers, and whispered, *It's okay to cry for him, Helen Jean. Y'all wasn't talking, but that was your brother.*

When Vera finally let her go and Helen Jean prepared to leave the hospital, Vera said, *You be sure to call me and let me know you made it home.*

"What?" Ruby Nell said in a voice loud enough that it caused the babies' crying to erupt from the back of the house. "She ain't made it back yet. Is that where she was going when she left here after dinner? I'm not sure I . . ." The girl cleared her throat and said, "I'll be sure to tell her to call you when she get in, Aunt Vera."

Helen Jean heard another chair scrape against the floor and the quick steps of what she knew was Julie B.'s feet.

"Okay," Ruby Nell said softly. "We'll be here when she get in. We'll be here for *her* — if she need us. And we'll get a hog burnt if that's what she want."

And then Ruby Nell was quiet.

After a while Helen Jean heard the rotary dialer spinning. She waited for her daughter's voice and told herself everything would be all right. Dale would get himself together and give Julie B. a good life. Buy her and that baby the home she wanted. Ruby Nell would stop being sad in the way her own mother had been prone to being. She would be as strong in her mind as she as was in her spirit and she would be okay. And she promised herself she would love her little girl as much as she loved her daughter's little boy. She'd stop drinking and be a good mother. Everything would be all right.

But when she heard Ruby Nell call out Wayne's name into the phone in the next room, she felt tears well up in her eyes. She put her hand over her mouth and whispered into it, "Everything will. It will. Everything will be all right."

10
LYDIA

Jan isn't happy to see me when she arrives and finds me in the hospital room.

When she walks in, I say her name with so much excitement that I surprise myself. When I wrap my arms around her to embrace her as family should, she doesn't raise her arms to hold me back. She lets them hang limp at her sides.

Her eyes are dark beads surrounded by dark circles. Her hair is pulled back in a bun, but I can tell it's thinning. When I embrace her, she feels so frail, so thin, that I think I'll break her. She can't weigh more than a hundred pounds. She looks like an old woman and she's not even forty yet.

When I let her go, I return to my seat in the chair closest to Grandmoan's bed and she sits in the chair across the room, right beneath the television. We don't say anything for a while, but I can tell she's having a hard time keeping quiet because she keeps

232

taking deep breaths and smacking her lips.

"You still walking around not believing in God or nothing?" she finally asks with her face all screwed up.

I shake my head and say, "It's not that I don't believe, Jan. I'm just not sure." I make sure my voice is calm and try changing the subject. "You think she'll come back from this?" I ask, nodding in our grandmother's direction.

The last time I was here, Jan was huge with child. She was beautiful, but she judged me about what I was doing with my mother. I'd come as a courtesy to the family. I wanted to let them know where Mother would be. Thought maybe they'd finally want to see her. That they'd finally care.

But Jan sucked her teeth and rolled her eyes when I told them that I was putting Mother away. When she spoke, her words were short and snippy. *God don't want you driving your momma away. Black folk don't do that. We take care of our own.*

When she said that, I looked at my hands and told her I didn't know what God wanted. That I'd never heard his voice. That I wasn't sure I believed in him.

My aunt, her mother, didn't say a word. Just sat there in silence. Grandmoan cleared her throat and told Jan to hush her mouth.

233

You don't know nothing about nothing you saying, she said. And for a minute, I thought she cared for me.

"If God want her to be all right, she be all right," she says. "That old woman got a whole lot to pay for, though," Jan says now.

"We all have things to pay for, though, right?" I say.

She smacks her lips. "Grandmoan was mean and ain't no cause to be how she was," she say. "This all she got right here." She sighs. "This all she got left right here," she says again, and her voice cracks a bit and I think she might cry.

Jan clears her throat and says, "I don't understand why you trying to sound so positive and understanding about her, like you really knowed her or something. You ain't even got the Lord in your life. Ain't nothing positive about you."

I want to tell her there is no reason for her to be hostile with me. But when I look at her all I can see is the high cut of her cheekbones — all I can remember is seeing her face pressed against the pillow on the bed she shared with her mother, and I decide to allow her the punch.

"You think she ever smiled at Granddaddy?" she asks. Her voice is less judgmental and calmer.

And I consider the question. After work, Granddaddy would step out of his beat-up once-yellow Ford pickup that we all called the hog pen truck. The bed was full of oil barrels that were full of corn and other slop from businesses that Granddaddy had made arrangements with to keep his hogs fed. He'd step out of that truck and slip into serving his wife, into making her happy in whatever way he could.

He was no more than fifty-something then, but he looked more like ninety. Life had been rough on him and it showed, but much of that had been before he met our grandmother. He was the oldest of eleven children. After his father died, when Granddaddy was still just a kid, he quit school and helped his mother raise their family.

They say Grandmoan took his right eye when he walked in on her with another man. Supposedly, that happened before Jan and I were born. The glass one that wiggled around loose in the socket was all we ever knew. When we were kids, some people on the east side would laugh at the way he tried to comb his kinky, processed hair from one side of his head to the other in a pitiful attempt to hide the bald top, but we thought he was beautiful.

When he stepped off the truck after work

each day, he'd step on the barely green grass, taking slow and tired steps across the yard to get the hose. He'd use his finger to half cover the opening, spraying the old window unit that cooled the room where Grandmoan watched her stories. Granddaddy would do this sweating and smiling, even before changing from his work clothes.

Before I can respond to her first question, she asks another one.

"Member when she used to let Alex go to the hog pen?" she says. "She didn't never want us to come, like we was some kind of burden or something."

I remember the hog pen and how Alex hated going when he got older. He would hide in the big dumpster right behind Grandmoan's red dirt backyard. Jan and I always begged to go, but he would actually hide to stay away from the place.

I sigh. "We were girls, Jan." I shrug. "I'm sure she had her reasons. We *were* probably just in the way. Do you remember how you and I would beg to fill up those old nasty water barrels? Granddaddy rarely let us, but when he did, we had so much fun with that water. Climbing onto the back of that truck. Seeing the whole street. That was fun for us, right —"

"She loved him better," she says, cutting

me off. "Wanted him to have everything and didn't care if we didn't have nothing. What kind of grandmomma can see . . ." She sighed. "How many times she come down there to check on you, Lil?" she says, and I know she knows the answer.

I flinch a little when she calls me Lil. She knows that I go by my given name now. I don't correct her, though. I won't. She wants a fight and she's the last person I want to fight with.

"Yeah, some people deserve to make it through they sickness," she say. "But not her. Not our Grandmoan." And her words sound final, like the law.

We're both quiet and the steady beeping from the heart and cardio monitors that have been gauging our grandmother's vital signs for the past few days scream melodies that neither of us understand. The hum of the machine that has been breathing for her makes us nervous.

Jan's almond eyes have been shifting from my grandmother to the machine since she walked in. The lights in the room were too bright, so Jan has shut them off, but there is no off switch for the sick, dying smell that has situated itself around my grandmother since my arrival.

"How are your children, Jan?" I ask, attempting to break the silence between us.

She keeps her eyes on the television screen, which is dark because it isn't even on. "They blessed and highly favored," she says. "Couldn't ask for nothing better."

I nod my head and force a smile. "I know the circumstances are horrible, but I hope I can meet them while I'm here. I'll bet they're gorgeous, just like their mother." And I mean it. Her long, narrow face and high cheekbones against her reddish-cinnamon skin make her look Ethiopian. Regal. She could be a nice-looking woman. If she were able to take care of herself, get her teeth fixed, she'd be gorgeous. When we were children, people said we looked like twins. If she could keep herself up, maybe someone would say it now.

She smacks her lips and waves her hand without looking at me. "Come to town more. Check on everybody more. You won't have to ask them kind of questions. You'll already know."

I don't say anything.

I stopped coming in the summer after that third year. I don't know if I'd expected Jan and me to pick up anew each summer after that first one, but I thought we'd at least talk and play and be close again.

That third time my cousin Joy met Aunt Julie B. at the halfway point, Jan wasn't in the car. It was just us. Aunt Julie B. and me. We rode the one-hundred-plus miles in an uncomfortable silence. I responded to the occasional question about school and friends, and I waited for her to ask about Mother. She never did. Eventually, I asked my aunt where Jan was.

She smacked her lips and said, *Ain't want to come.* She shook her head. *That one ain't gone never smile. Ain't gone never be kind.* She went on to explain that her daughter loved me. She whined and asked me to be patient with her. *She just need to remember that y'all was always close. Don't listen to her mean words. She want you here too.*

That's when I realized she didn't. That's the moment it became real. No one had ever said it. Had ever made Jan's dislike for me real with words. I made my decision not to return right at that moment, so it didn't bother me when Jan rolled her eyes when I walked into the house behind her mother or when two weeks rolled by and she still hadn't said anything to me.

"Anyway, when you gone have some kids? We ain't getting no younger, girl. You gone let your little eggs shrivel up on you," she says, laughing and clapping her hands.

She fixes her eyes on me and waits for my response.

I don't say anything. I just imagine my eggs shrinking to raisins and my heart starts beating fast. That's something doctors have been concerned about. With each passing year, the risk of danger is higher because of my age. The older I get, the less likely my chances are. I know Walter is worried about that. I stand up and fix my suit jacket. "Excuse me," I say, grabbing my purse from the small table next to my grandmother's bed.

When I make it out to the hallway, my chest is rising and falling rapidly and I'm completely out of breath. I steady myself by placing one hand on the wall and I make my way to a small waiting room. I'm glad to find it unoccupied. Jan's words swirl around in my brain and I think about my babies, struggling to stay alive inside me. I take a seat in one of the chairs, open my legs as wide as my skirt will allow me to, and let my upper body fold over until my fingers touch the tips of my high heels. I feel the blood rushing to my head as I kind of dangle there almost upside down, but my breathing begins to slow and I feel my breath catching.

I think of Walter and his arms around me

and I promise myself that as soon as this passes, I'll sit up and call him. When I think of this, of calling my husband, my heart begins to pound again. "Be still," I whisper to myself. "Be still," I repeat. My husband is my life and I'm losing it. He is important to me, but I have never been a fighter. I'm not sure that I even know how to fight for this. But I don't want to be alone again. All those years with just Mother. All those years with just me. I'm so afraid of that.

When I'm me again, I dig through my purse and retrieve my phone. I dial my husband's number and feel my nerves falling away from me. When I hear his voicemail, I'm both relieved and disappointed. If we were on good terms, I'd hang up and call him until he answers. But we are not us right now, so I wait for the beep. I'm conscious of the nervousness in my voice when I begin to speak. "Walter, honey," I say. "I'm with my grandmother. She . . ." I exhale. "She's dying. I — I miss you."

I hang up quickly and sit in the waiting room until I can go back to Jan with a smile on my face.

Jan has moved to my seat when I get back to the room. I make my way to the seat she occupied earlier.

We don't speak, at first. Me, because I'm

not sure what to say or how it'll be taken. I'm not sure why she is quiet. And then she smiles at the dark television screen mounted on the wall above my head. I can see the gaps in her mouth where teeth should be.

"Maybe you can just make your peace with them," she says, nodding toward the inside of the room. "Your momma, your daddy, her. Maybe that'll bring you to the Lord and he'll set you free." She sighs. "You remember your daddy?" she asks, fixing her eyes on me.

Her concern almost feels real with her eyes peering into me, expecting a stutter. Still, I can tell she likes reminding me of the things that hurt. "Yeah, I do," I reply as a lump fills my throat.

And I do remember him and what a good father he was. When I was old enough to understand what he'd done, I was disappointed in my father, but I always loved what he was to me.

He tucked me in every night of my young life. Before our world was torn apart, my father had a weekly schedule that included activities, meal plans, and all kinds of other stuff. School year or not, I was at Grandmoan's until five on weekdays, after which he would pick me up. Mondays, we ate at McDonald's. Not the drive-thru either. We went inside, where he made me decipher the overhead menu and order both our meals. We'd sit down and eat together, during which he'd ask for every detail of every part of my day. And finally, he'd give me twenty glorious minutes in the play area, during which he'd pull out a book, a cookbook or something on Africa or some other faraway place, which he'd mostly just hold between his hands while watching me from our table. Tuesdays we went to the park, where he let me skate or we fed ducks. After that, we'd go home and he'd make oven-smothered barbecue chicken with baked beans and potato salad. Wednesdays were library and homemade burger days, and Thursdays and Fridays, Mother's off days, she picked me up from school or from Grandmoan's in the summer, as she used her off days for errands and business, despite my father's protests. She made dinner those days, so the menu wasn't as consistent or set in stone as it was when my father was in charge. But I loved Thursdays. That was *The Cosby Show* day. We'd sit down on that couch together and find joy in that TV family. I'd sit between Mother and my father, both their arms draped across the couch behind me so that their fingers intertwined.

I want to tell Jan that I'll never forget him, but all I can think about is what my mother told me less than twenty-four hours ago. That my father is not my father. And I want to let her words go. To treat them like they should be treated. Like the words of a mad woman. They were wrong words. Hurtful, breaking words. If ever I should let anything she has ever said go, this should be it. But I can't. There is something in that wrongness that I fear feels right. If I open my mouth and say anything about my father, I'll probably come undone.

Instead I let my mind shift to Jan. To her problems and what her life must have been like across all of these years. Aunt Julie B. fell in love with my cousins' father, Dale, when she was still in high school. He was a yellow man with green eyes and big fists. I think he ran off and left, so she and her children ended up in Grandmoan's back room. Aunt Julie B. had two kids by Dale. Alex and Jan. But to me, when we were young, they both seemed so alone in the world. Not at all what I imagined having a sibling to be.

And there is something that has haunted me for years. Something I saw as a girl. I never told anyone what I saw, but Jan hates me anyway. I close my eyes tight and shake my head to rid myself of it. When I open them, I still see it. I used to feel guilty about it, but now I'm convinced it's why Jan can be a mother and I cannot.

"Where is he now?" I ask her, without looking up. She looks over at me through her lazy eyelids, and I can see the question in her eyes.

"Who? Soweo?"

She doesn't know who I mean. She still doesn't know that I know.

I sigh, "Alex, Jan. Where is he now?"

She shrinks in the seat, making herself tiny, and shrugs. "I don't know. Why you ask me? How I'm posed to know?"

All those years ago. Seems like there was one great explosion between him and Grandmoan that everybody else seemed to miss. He was always her favorite. We all knew that. She never made an effort to hide it, but then he was just gone. I've always wondered if she found out what I knew. What Jan knew.

11
JAN

Lil done pissed me off asking me about Alex, bringing him up out of nowhere. But I can't show her that. She won't never know nothing about growing up here. About having a brother that ain't really no brother. Me and Alex was close until I was six. Then we turned into something else. And she won't never understand how that was. How, at first, I thought it was normal, until I knowed it wasn't.

We was a real family before my brother ever touched me. He felt like a real big brother and my momma felt like safety. Didn't matter that we lived in Grandmoan back room. My momma started a tradition that I still keep with my kids. Friday night movies. She said she couldn't never remember a time when Grandmoan gathered them up like a family after her daddy was dead. He was the family one for them. He was the drive-in movie type of daddy.

Well, on Fridays, Momma used to have movie night with us. It would be me, her, Marie, and Alex. It was really the only time Marie come out of the front room — the one that was Uncle Wayne's before he left home — outside of her cleaning. She was always excited about movie night. Sometime Momma let her go to the video store with her and pick the movie. She'd smile wide if all of us liked the movie she picked. She'd get all sad in the face if we didn't. Sometimes, I looked over at her sad face and it felt like my fault. I can't rightly explain how come, but it felt like something I was or wasn't doing made her sad. When I looked over at her face drooping down like it was about to slide right on off, I liked to pretend the movie she picked was the best thing, even if Momma and Alex said different. I'd clap my hands and say *That was good, Marie.* Her sad eyes was so constant that it made her look alive when she spread her lips all over her face like she did when I supported her like that. Made her look proud, like she had made some kind of difference.

Momma would make us popcorn and pour us sodas and we felt like we was really at a movie. Most nights it was kid-friendly stuff. *Space Camp, The Goonies, Pee-wee's Big Adventure, Care Bears,* stuff like that. I think Momma got bored with all them baby movies after a while, though. She took to renting two movies, a baby one and something for her. I usually fell asleep after the kid movie, but Alex and Marie stay up for the adult one. I was about five or six and Alex and Marie was around nine or ten the night she rented *Cat's Eye*. That night, Momma played *Back to the Future* first, which I liked so much I was still up when the credits rolled.

After the first movie ended, I snuggled close to Momma on the couch. I was planning to stay awake as long as I could cause I'd heard my brother say he heard Chucky was scary. When I snuggled into her, I remember my momma saying, *Damn, girl. Give me some space. What's wrong with you?*

I couldn't tell her I didn't want to fall asleep. I didn't want her to throw me over her shoulder or tell my brother to throw me over his and take me into the bedroom we shared. To put me in the dark by myself like. Not after all the scary Chucky talk.

And just when my feelings was about to be hurt cause my momma didn't want me laying on her, Alex, who was sitting on the other side of the sofa, opened his arms and let me lean on him. *You can sleep on me, Jan,* he said. *You don't have to go to bed. I know you scared.* When he wrapped his arm around me, I knew I was safe from Chucky. And that's the last time I remember feeling that way with him.

Lil don't know what it's like to have that. To have that safety and then it become torment. She don't know nothing about that kind of love or that kind of torture and what it do to your brain. She don't know about losing a brother what ain't lost to this world. And it ain't my place to tell her.

"You . . . You still talk to your momma?" I ask Lil.

She don't say nothing. Just sigh and look at me like she don't know what I'm talking about.

"I don't blame my momma for nothing got to do with me." I pat my chest. "What I didn't agree with. I just got to do better for mine."

She nod her head, like she already know, like I'm telling her something she done heard before. And I want to ask her why she always got to have everything. To know everything.

"We aren't the same, Jan," she say. Her head is still down, kind of like she looking at her hands, but her eyes on me. "My mother isn't like yours. Our journeys," she say, waving her finger between me and her,

249

"just aren't the same thing."

"Humph" is all I got for her.

After her daddy went to jail, after Marie was gone, my auntie took Lil and moved away. I ain't see her for a long time. She ain't never call. Ain't never write. Just left me, like I wasn't nothing, and it took me a long time to get over that. She had been my every day for as long as I could remember. And then she was just gone.

And then one day, Momma say she coming to spend the summer. I was so nervous for that. Didn't know what she was gone be like after so many years away. When she got there, it seemed like we was gone be all right, but she wound up hurting me again when she wanted to choose Alex — when she wanted to see him. Eventually, she did what she was good at and stopped coming altogether. Didn't even try to fight for us. Just left. Me and Lil ain't been close in a long time, but I know what I know. We both had mommas and they did they best. She come a mother, she'll know that's all we can do.

My momma didn't never really have no authority in Grandmoan house. Even the simple things she couldn't choose, like whether a clean house should smell like pine or bleach. But I could see her trying to be a

250

mother to me and Alex, even when Grandmoan was Alex favorite.

Alex used to have nightmares. Real bad
ones. One night, I was about four or five
and he was about eight or nine, Alex
screamed out from a nightmare, and I felt
the raggedy springs of me and her bed
move. And then I heard her sit down on his
bed and her voice was so soft and smooth.
*It's all right, son. It's all right. Momma here.
Momma right here,* she whispered.

She gasped when he said in a real sleepy
voice, *I want Grandmoan, Julie B.*

Shh, shh and soft patting on his back was
all I heard until she climbed back in the
bed with me. It took a while for me to really pay attention, to understand what I was
hearing after that, but Momma laid in that
bed and sniffed and cried until the sounds
of her sadness put me to sleep.

And these is things Lil will never know
nothing about. She ain't got siblings to live
through tough things with, and she give up
on her momma. Just give her up to strangers. My momma ain't do nothing to save us
from Grandmoan and each other, but she
was there and she still here and I still got
her.

"I thank God for my momma," I say. "She
raised us and did the best she could by us.

251

I'm sure my auntie did her best by you too. Don't matter how different our journeys been. Our mommas did the best they could."

She nod again, like she know. Like this old news to her. "Aunt Julie B. is a strong woman. A very strong woman," she say, like she know her.

"Your momma strong, too," I say. "Been through all she been through and you give up on her. That summer broke her, too. You ever thought about that?"

And she don't say nothing. She just turn her eyes toward Grandmoan.

Laverne was Marie best friend. And though it wasn't all the time, sometimes Grandmoan let Marie out the house to play on the sidewalk or across the street at Laverne's, which was much better than the driveway in our young eyes. For Marie, the sidewalk was still too close to home. She always wanted to be at Laverne's, but Grandmoan had to be feeling real good to let her go. To let Marie out her sight. I can probably count the number of times on my hands I saw her go inside Laverne's house. Of course, Laverne wasn't allowed at our house. Nobody in they right mind let their kids play at our house. Grandmoan's reputation wasn't good in a way people wanted to set up playdates with her children or their children. But at least Marie and Laverne had the telephone and the driveway. They connected in them places as much as they could.

We called Laverne "Bald-Headed Laverne" behind her back on count of her hair being like a desert trying to grow grass and flowers. It always looked thirsty and never had more than a few tight auburn patches randomly stretched across her scalp. We laughed at how her teeth bucked from where she still sucked her thumb like she was closer to our age, instead of Marie's. We giggled at the stink of her armpits and other private parts that we was still too innocent to understand. Too young to understand that something was wrong — slow about both them, Marie and Laverne. That that's probably the tie that bound them together. But Marie and Laverne didn't care nothing about what we understood or didn't. They raced down the sidewalk happy and free. Alex taught us to taunt, though — made us do it. When he was around, we was brutal. We wanted to please him — we needed to.

Even back then, being a boy made you freer. Grandmoan started letting Alex leave out the driveway when he was about twelve years old. He'd leave, but he came back throughout the day on count of the plate of sandwiches and the pitcher of water she set out when she put us out in the morning being there.

And when he came back, we was mean for him, so he wouldn't be mean to us. His punches hurt. His insults did, too, and he had a talent for making up the meanest and catchiest chants.

Bald head, bald head
Where have you been
Playing with Marie
Cause she your best friend

Laverne's face always seemed to shine when she was with Marie, and Marie's would do the same. Looking back on it, after everything what happened, I know they was the brightest spots in each other's lives. On regular days, when Grandmoan had plenty of work inside for Marie, Laverne would stand at the edge of her own driveway, lean against the edge of their flimsy wire gate, and call for our attention with a hopeful look on her face.

One of us would always yell back something rude or hurtful. Laverne would ignore the insult and ask if Marie was coming out that day. We'd throw over a real rude "No" and some more insults to top it off. And Laverne's smile crack right before our eyes. She'd turn around and walk real slow back up to her front porch and sit by herself on one of the three orange plastic chairs that matched the color of her house. She didn't never seem to want to go inside, even though she didn't get put out like us. So she'd watch us play in Grandmoan driveway, like wasn't nothing better than being where we was.

"Seem like a long time ago," I say out loud. "And it seem like yesterday."

Lil looking at me like she confused, like she don't know what I mean, and it make me feel some kind of way, like I'm dumb enough to believe she don't remember.

I smack my lips and say, "That summer. Remember?"

Her eyes get wide and she gasp, like I done slapped her right across her face. Her face flushing out a little bit, turning red. She put her hand on her forehead and let it run down the back of her head.

She sigh, like I'm getting on her nerves. "Yeah, Jan, I remember."

And her tone almost make me reach across the room and snatch her up by the throat. She ain't got no right to have no attitude with me. She the one left and forgot about everybody. Forgot about me.

I take a deep breath and ask God to help me hold my peace. And then I say, "Ain't no need in getting mad. I was just making a comment about that summer. You the one acting like you don't know what I'm talking about. Making me dwell on it."

She don't say nothing. Just look down toward the floor.

"Just saying it's hard to think about is all." And I mean them words for real. That summer might be the worst thing for some folks, but it's when all the bad stuff stopped happening to me. It's hard for me to know how to feel about it.

"I miss Marie the most," I hear myself say out loud, and I can't really believe I'm saying it. Don't nobody talk about her. About what she did. Everybody walk around like her whole life never happened.

Lil nod and her face kind of soften. It almost look like she smiling without smiling.

"Before we left Jerusalem, I used to love it when you guys would sleep over," she say. "Remember that time you and me wanted to run away?"

I do. I know exactly what she talking

256

about, but I don't tell her that.

On Friday nights, before everything fell apart, Grandmoan have everybody come over and drink Coors and Budweiser and brown liquor. The blues be playing loud enough for the whole block to hear, and all the grown folks we know be laughing and dancing at Grandmoan's. Cept Soweo. I want to remind her that, but I don't.

Ms. Sane lived next door. Grandmoan said she was a voodoo queen, but she sold popcorn balls and cakes to the whole neighborhood. They was good. Buttery and sugary and bound together perfect. Them balls was about the size of baseballs. And she sold them for only twenty-five cents. Momma used to buy them for me when she could, but Lil loved the popcorn cakes. They was fancier. Dipped in food coloring. Lil loved them. I only got the cakes when Aunt Ruby Nell was around on the count of them being fifty cents more than the balls.

"Mother wouldn't buy us popcorn cakes that night and we got mad and planned a whole getaway," she say, slapping her hand on her thigh and laughing. "I had that Big Wheel and bicycle at home. We were going to hitchhike to the west side of town. To our duplex, sneak past my father, and pack all my things."

I can't help but smile a little thinking about it. "You was gone use your jump rope to hitch the Big Wheel to the bicycle." I say. "We thought we could take the freeway back and live in the old empty Wilson house down the block."

Both of us laugh until we don't. When all our laughter trail off, I watch her eyes roam the room slowly, until they set on me, and then I shift my own to the floor.

"I didn't have much, but I wanted to share everything I had with you," she say, and pause, until I look back at her. Then she smile. "Because you were my best friend, Jan."

I look back down at the floor. Of all people, Lil ain't gone be who make me cry. She don't want me to be mad with her for playing dumb. She just trying to be nice. She don't mean that.

"But Aunt Marie, I felt so sorry for her. It was like she was invisible. No one ever paid attention to her," she say.

And that make me feel guilty cause I can't help but think about all the times I wanted to play with Lil over Marie. Myself over Marie. Marie wasn't never my first choice. I didn't hate my aunt or nothing like that. She was just so quiet, so slow, and, to me, she didn't know how to play like everybody else did. If we was playing beauty shop with my Barbie dolls, I'd have to tell her that two of the clients was having a fight at the shampoo bowls — that we had to make them fight. If we was playing school, she wasn't a good student or a stern principal. Looking back, though, Marie ain't have a lot of playing time anyway. She was always cleaning and helping around the house. Always being like the maid.

I don't say nothing cause I'm thinking about being brought up with Marie and not calling her "aunt" like Lil do. Nobody ever tried to make me and my brother see her like that. I used to think it was cause we grew up so close, like siblings more than anything, but now I think it was all a issue of respect or disrespect for her mind. The shame from that wash over me suddenly and I don't want to sit in it no more.

I shift my bottom in the chair and look at my watch.

"I'm glad she had Laverne in her life," Lil say, and nod her head, like she said the best thing. "She was suffering — lonely — and no one around her knew, but I'm glad she shared what she must've shared with her friend."

I want to ask her what she know about suffering. What she know about sharing, but all this talk of Marie is making me feel guilty for something that's way past where I can do something about it.

I close my eyes and pray to myself. Ask God to have mercy on Marie soul. And then I open my eyes, look down at my watch again, and feel myself let out a big breath and say, "It's almost three. I got to get my kids. I wonder when my momma coming up here," I say out loud but to myself.

Lil shrug. "Maybe she wanted to stay with Granddaddy awhile. I'm sure this is torture on his blood sugar," she say, and her face look like she pity him or something, like she feel sorry for him, like he weak and need that kind of look from her.

"Humph." I let out a grunt and I hate that I did it as soon as I hear myself. It remind me of how the hogs used to sound at the hog pen, but I end up doing it a lot when folks say dumb stuff, like Lil just did. Don't she know how strong he is? Ain't nothing wrong with him. When they told him he had the sugar diabetes, he rebuked that diagnosis in the name of Jesus. Granddaddy changed his diet and started walking three miles a day and God healed him from whatever them white folks tried to put on him.

"Granddaddy fine. He ain't got no diabetes. He gone outlive us all. He be up walk-

260

ing Parkley fore you even think about opening your eyes in the morning," I say, standing up, pulling my purse strap over my shoulder.

"If she *do* wake up, she ain't gone do nothing but fuss at you anyway," I say, nodding in Grandmoan direction. "Wearing your hair short like some type of man." I look at her hard. Lil would be real pretty if she had hair on her head. Got real pretty features. Nose ain't too big and she got just the right grade of hair to call "good." When folks used to say we looked like sisters, I'd smile inside. These days, I'm shame of that.

"Me and you always had the lightest skin and the best hair out of everybody. Sometimes I really used to wonder if that African man was really your daddy. I mean if he was, wouldn't you be black like him and your momma?" I pause. Her face look like I ain't said nothing about her daddy. About her crazy momma. About her.

I smack my tongue against the roof of my mouth. "What make you go and cut all that wavy hair off your head? Black folks spend big money on hair and you had your own." I run my hand through my own shoulder-length, thinning, wavy hair. "Money," I answer after she don't say nothing. "Rich folks is the fools of the world and they look

261

at us like we ain't got good sense."

"I am *not* rich," she say through clenched teeth, like she mad.

I can tell she hate it when I say she rich. It piss me off that she *is* rich and think I'm too dumb to know she lying about it.

I hold up my hand to stop Lil. I don't care if she see me sticking my lips out and smacking them. I ain't even trying to breathe and control my temper no more.

"You married a man — a lawyer that come from money, Lil. You gone sit up here and lie about having money? Child, please. Who you think I am?" I slide my hand up my hip and purposely buck my eyes at her.

She drop her head, like a coward. She won't argue with me. She think she too good for that, but that don't stop me. I don't ask nobody for nothing. This thing with Grandmoan, this thing with *that* money, is the closest I done ever come to it.

"Ain't nobody gone ask you for nothing. You ain't got to lie to me." I want to stop, but I can't help it. I keep going. My momma say it don't take much to get me started. She say I'm like a toy doll at the store that say "Push me" through a little hole in the box. I laughed when she said, *You stick your finger through that hole one little old time and you'll never be able to get that doll to hush.*

"Humph," I grunt again. "Like I said, I got to get my kids from school cause I ain't got no rich husband. It's just me. No nannies, no sitters, no nothing — just me. Shoot, I can't even hold down no job cause I got these kids, so don't treat me like some beggar you got to lie to. I don't want your money." And I mean that. I don't need nobody lying to me cause they think I want a handout. I make my own way in this world. My own way with the Lord.

"I'll see you later, Jan," she say softly, and it make me feel bad for going off on her.

"Um-hmm," I say, and turn on my heels in a hurry to get out that room. I don't offer no good-bye, *See you later, Lil,* or nothing. I just go.

12
ALEX

Even though I know about Grandmoan being in the hospital, I'm not allowed to go see her. I've sent money each month across all these years because our family, Julie B., Jan, and I, always had a home in her. I've sent money because I've learned that family takes care of family. No matter what. Sometimes, I ride by the house when I patrol Parkley. The house is different these days. Looks like some type of stone fortress. It doesn't fit well in Parkley, Jerusalem even. I don't know what type of updates they've made inside, but the outside makes me nervous for them. Predators will think they have something to take. I like to keep an eye out. My partner complains about us rolling by, but he took the day off to deal with the knot he got last night, so I plan to stop in on Granddaddy. I haven't talked to him in years. Julie B. fills me in on what's going on with everyone, but she's not enough. Never has been. She decided to be in my life sometime around that very first time she showed up at the ranch, though. That's when she told me that she'd always be there. *No matter what,* she said. She's managed to stay true to that, however late she might've been. I can't take that away from her.

"Anything else, Officer Walker?" James wipes the tiled counter with a rag that was probably white when it was new. He eyes me, and I know hearing no from me is all he really needs. His shift is almost over. Hearing the answer to my question will be his last task of the day. I eat lunch, usually the first meal of my day, right before my shift, at Holly's most of the time. Food here ain't as good as it is at some of the barely standing burger stands on the east side, but I'm comfortable here.

I shake my head and slide off the stool. "No thank you, James. I'm done for today."

His face lights up and freckles smear all over it when he smiles.

"Well, I'll see you tomorrow. Got to get out here on the beat," I say, nodding at him across the counter.

I shake my leg to make sure the hems of my dark blue uniform pants slide down and touch my shoes. The door to the small diner chimes and I hear cackling children and a mother trying to quiet them.

"Y'all better stop. Look, the police here to get you," she says in a loud whisper.

When I turn around, I see the young mother struggling to carry an oversized toddler on her hip, while trying to wave two preschool-age boys back toward her.

"Momma, no," one of the little boys whines, hurrying back to her. "I don't want go to jail. I'll be good."

And that makes me remember the police on the east side when I was young. How afraid I was of them. How all of us were. How Grandmoan told us about what they did to black children. What they did to black folks. Looking at these frightened, wild-eyed little white boys makes me wonder what their mother tells them to make them so afraid of me.

I smile at the woman, who's actually more girl than woman, before sliding two dollars under my empty plate. As I pass the tiny family, I notice how tight the boys are gripping their mother's legs. Her eyes are glassy and blue and holding as much fear as theirs. She lowers her small face when our eyes meet and I know her fear has nothing to do with my uniform. She reminds me of Julie B., so I pat the top of the tallest boy's head. He's about four or five and the stringy greasiness of his hair makes me think about lice.

"Be good for your mother. Okay, boys?" I say.

Even though neither of the kids peel their faces from their mother's legs, I know they hear me and I know she does, too. She lifts her oily face, offering a slight smile, and I nod at her before heading out the door.

I like helping, but I also like the power my police uniform takes away from me. Some people don't understand the power that comes with lawlessness. They look at police brutality and think cops got all the power. Cops that get all out of order with power like that are the ones with no real power without their badges. Cops like that think they're free to be lawless in their lawfulness. Whole idea is an oxymoron. Lawless people got more power than anybody in the world. Some people just don't understand the power that comes with lawlessness. I do. I think Grandmoan always kept me away from the house because she recognized my power — maybe saw herself in it.

"Hey, Alex," a soft, sultry voice says. I know who it belongs to. It's Veola. She seems to catch me sliding into my squad car, leaving this place every day. I was supposed to call her this morning — meet her for breakfast — but this morning was rough. Plus, I don't know. She wants something from me that I don't think I can give. The whole thing with Samra's got me questioning everything.

"How you doing today, Veola?" I ask, looking up at her from my seat in the car. I can't really see her face because she's positioned to block the sun. I know it by heart, though. She's pretty. Her momma is a white lady and serves food at an elementary over here on the west side of town, and I ain't never seen her daddy, but I can tell she got the best features of both of them. She's smart too. Didn't go to college or nothing like that, but she got a real good job at the light company.

It's usually hard for the black girls in town to get hired on and keep a job there. Veola's been there for five years. She makes no excuses about life. I should probably be drawn to that. We've been seeing each other for a few months. We usually meet for dinner or a movie. Went bowling once and on a couples' date with Chavis and his wife. I've never taken her back to my place and never taken her up on an offer to go to hers.

She says she needs more from me. Says she wants me to meet her kids — two little girls. For a while, I was thinking maybe it was time. That I can have a normal life. Maybe start a family of my own and let go of the one I've been holding on to longer than it was willing to hold on to me. Thought maybe Veola and her daughters were a good place to start. Was beginning to think that I could be a good man in their lives. A partner for Veola. A father for her daughters. But what happened with Samra. How I saw her as my sister and then as something else. How I wanted her without wanting to. That scared me.

Before that, I liked to tell myself that the things I did when I was young, I did *because I was young,* but now I don't know. I'm afraid of who I am — of who I can be.

"I'm good, Alex," Veola says. I still can't see her face. She tilts her head to the side in a way that lets the sun beam down directly on me and I have to squint just to look up at her.

"You were supposed to call me. We had a date, mister," she says, and I can hear the smile in her voice.

"Yeah, I know. I'm sorry. My mom came by this morning. Said my grandmother's sick," I tell her, realizing myself that this is all a real thing.

She squats down beside the car and makes

herself small beside me. "Alex, I'm sorry. I hope she'll be okay."

I don't say anything and we're both quiet for a while.

And then she says, "Well, let me know if there's anything I can do to help."

Her head is tilted and she's looking up at me and I know Chavis is right. She's a beautiful woman. A good woman, and she doesn't deserve what she thinks she does.

I nod and wish it was easier to be better for the people around me.

After Grandmoan said I couldn't sleep in the house anymore, made me sleep outside in the shed, I thought I could show her I was better. Thought I could do better by her and by everybody and prove my way back inside. And then Marie was gone and Grandmoan wouldn't even look at me. Wouldn't let me come through the house after that. So I left. I just up and left. I was fourteen and on my own. Most nights, I slept in abandoned houses with junkies. Other nights — cold nights — I stayed with Uncle Wayne, wherever he was, and let him do whatever he wanted to me for heat and a meal.

The look Grandmoan gave me when I walked in the night she put me in the shed is something I'll never forget. I walked into that den through the side door that night to her and Julie B. and Granddaddy sitting there watching TV. Her with a plate of sliced tomatoes sprinkled with salt and pepper sitting on her lap, which had probably been there for an hour because she always ate real slow.

I'd never come home looking the way I did that night, so it might've been the welts and scratches still left on my face. It might've been that she was remembering in that moment that she hadn't seen me in a few days. It was likely the long tear beginning at the collar of my T-shirt and ending at my navel that let her know that I had struggled with someone. I've imagined her putting it together in her head and all her love turning over before she could finish chewing her tomato slice. Whatever it was that gave me away, I knew as soon as her eyes widened like I was a ghost that she knew what I'd done.

Julie B. stood up like I hadn't even walked in, like she wanted to cry, like she wanted to hide. She tilted her head to the side, swallowed real hard, and left the room without a word. Grandmoan moved the plate to the coffee table and walked over to the spot where I stood frozen. Granddaddy just sat there, like he was holding his breath.

She grabbed my face between her index finger and thumb and turned my head to get a better look at the scratch on my eye. "Mmm-hmm" was all she managed to say before she pulled her hand back and let her palm slam down across my cheek.

When I gained my composure and met her eyes again, her lips were clamped tight and I could hear her teeth chattering. She shook her head and closed her eyes.

"You don't know what you done made me do," she finally whispered in a cold, hard tone.

She kept her eyes shut tight and pointed toward the back door and told me to go out back because I was no longer welcome inside. Told me Julie B. would gather my things. I could no longer sleep inside. When I left on my own, I was still just a boy, but nobody came to look for me for months. It was almost like it took a while for them to know I'd left at all. Then one day, about three months after I left, Grandmoan came and did the best thing she could have done for me. Her eyes were almost tender that day, and I swear she was crying when she came back out of Uncle Wayne's. She took me to Spur Ranch for Boys and told me I was ruined and she didn't ever want to see me near Parkley again. Momma wrote and told me Uncle Wayne was dead, and I could smell her salty tears like dry dust on the paper.

Veola thinks I'm a gentleman. Says she's never been with someone like me. She can't believe that I don't make a fool of myself just to sleep with her. She doesn't know that I've sliced away at the soft parts of my flesh for a long time now. For a long time, I thought as long as I kept cutting, nobody had to worry about seeing that part of me ever again. But that night with Samra, that kiss, she got close and I got hard and I almost forgot how the skin on my cuts heals thick and ugly, like leather. I don't feel like I can trust myself anymore.

"Thank you, Veola," I say.

She stands up again and nods. I can see her long curly hair bouncing like a lion's mane around her invisible face. She turns to walk away, and I reach to pull in the handle of the door.

"You're a good man, Alex," she says, without turning back around. I shift my eyes from the door handle to the gravel on the ground.

"Don't ever let nobody tell you you ain't." She adds, "You're a good man, Alex Walker."

And she doesn't have a clue.

HELEN JEAN
1982

Helen Jean learned to hear her daughters when they whispered. There was always telling and intimacy between the hushed words, in that almost silence. She'd been sitting in the darkness of the front room, the room she no longer allowed anyone to enter, waiting. She'd been resting quietly in her recliner, waiting for Homer to return.

Her daughters likely thought she was out. Probably didn't imagine her sitting there, holding her breath to their words. Ruby Nell, who'd been back and forth between Jerusalem and Dallas since after high school, had recently returned from an eight-month stay in Dallas with her little girl a few weeks earlier, explaining to her mother, *I ain't here to stay. Just looking for a place for me and my family.*

Helen Jean had shrugged at the girl. Had told her, *Y'all know I don't care about y'all being here. This much y'all house as it is mine.*

274

But she really wanted to tell her that she was glad to see her. That she'd turned out to be a pretty girl. That her hips had spread nicely, and she'd grown into her teeth, and her Jheri curl was perfect in the way that it touched right at her shoulders, and the open-face gold on her front tooth was becoming. That she looked good on the outside and she hoped she was good on the inside — in the mind.

But she didn't say any of those things to her. They passed each other in the house, but Ruby Nell's face only lit up for her little girl, her sisters, and her nephew. That light made it clear that she wasn't there for her mother. And Helen Jean learned to be okay with that. She'd also learned to pretend to be okay with the man Ruby Nell had chosen. There were things about him that seemed dangerous to her. At first she'd thought he was African. She had only met a few Africans and found them to have strange ways — wicked ways — like the one Ernestine had messed with before she left for Dallas. He knew roots in ways that East Texas folks could only dream about. Twisted, wicked roots. Then Julie B. explained that Soweo wasn't African — that he was raised by, fostered by an African. That he made the name up to honor the man. But something else concerned her, even more than that. Soweo promoted the same isolation of her daughter that her father had forced on her mother. Leading her to Dallas and then to the west side of Jerusalem. Only wicked men cut their feeble-minded wives off in that way. Helen Jean was afraid for the baby girl that Ruby Nell carried around on her hip. She was afraid for Ruby Nell too — that she would leave the child with the monster as her father had done her.

She sat there and listened to Ruby Nell beg from the other room. She couldn't hear tears in her voice. There was conviction — a certainty that what she was saying was real. That it was right.

"Julie B., I need you to take her while we get settled in. I know she's little, but we'll send money. It's just for a while; me and Soweo — we ain't — I ain't doing good. I need to get myself together. We found a place where I can get help," she said, and Helen Jean noticed the panic in her daughter's voice, how her words spilled out and crashed into each other.

She waited for Julie B. to say something, waited for her to tell her sister that she could barely take care of the one she gave birth to, but what she said was different from that.

Julie B. said, "I'm sorry, Ruby Nell, but I can't. You promised that y'all . . ." Helen Jean could hear the snot from tears in her sniffles. "I did *that* for you. I did it for you. You said it would make you better. Besides . . ." Her words disappeared again.

Ruby Nell sighed. "I know, big sister. I thought it would. I just don't know what else to do. I didn't know I was still gone struggle, not like —"

"I done messed around and got — I'm pregnant again," Julie B. said, her words charging out like a rushing wind.

Helen Jean shook her head and closed her eyes. She thought about her oldest daughter bringing another mouth to feed into her house. She pitied how she was stuck on Dale and knew he would never be stuck on her. Helen Jean thought about her daughter being the same type of mother she'd been — that she was. There but not present. And she thought about the danger in that.

She shook her head and thought about saying something. About being present for them this time. About telling them what she knew about destroying things. She wanted to tell Julie B. that she didn't need another child. No matter what, she didn't need another one. But then she remembered the covenant from the outhouse — for her life — and she knew couldn't tell Julie B. to kill what was growing inside her.

"Awww, Julie B.," she heard Ruby Nell say. "I'm sorry. I didn't know."

She listened to her daughter tell her big sister that it would be okay. That they would all be okay. And Helen Jean smiled because she wanted to believe it.

The conversation she'd overheard was on her mind when she stood in the chicken coop with Alex that next day. She was thankful that Julie B. had gotten that right. That she had kept him. He was his grandmother's brightest spot those years following the death she refused to mourn out loud. He wasn't even two years old when Bacon died, but it was as if he'd known how to handle her grief. He'd stand in the entrance of the front room, making sure not to step over the invisible line she'd made for him and Marie. By then, the front room belonged to her alone, and everyone knew it. Alex would stand there and sing nursery rhymes that she couldn't understand. After a while, he'd take a seat, Indian style, right there in the doorway and chant *I luh loo, Momma* over and over until he couldn't sit up without leaning on the wall behind him, until he'd chanted himself to sleep.

"Grandmoan, how come we eat eggs when they come straight from a chicken ass?" he asked her in the chicken coop, keeping his gaze on her and his face straight, even when she threw her head back in laughter.

The way he said *Grandmoan* tickled her more than anything. It made her laugh and bend over him and kiss him on the head. She missed the days when he easily called her *Momma.* Julie B. had taken to correcting him, making him aware of who his mother was. That seemed to hurt the boy. Take something from him. But then he'd taken to calling her Grandmoan instead of Grandma and that felt like something new. Something beautiful and between just them. She came to realize that grandmothering was different from mothering. It was a deeper and richer love and there was opportunity to express her growth there. It was so pure that, at times, she felt bad about it. That she could be a better grandmother to Alex than mother to Marie.

She wasn't mean to the girl. She provided for the child in all the ways that one would provide for a child they loved, but she was such a worrisome thing. Such a burden. She spent most of her time in the bedroom that Helen Jean had fixed up just for her. Pink walls and curtains and ruffles and a canopy.

She was the only one in the house who had her own space, but Helen Jean knew deep down it was the only way she could protect her. She wasn't like Herbert Lee, but she was like Herbert Lee. Helen Jean had never thought to put the girl away. She wouldn't do that. But she'd keep her safe as best she could. And Julie B. pulled the slack wherever it needed to be pulled, and Helen Jean knew that what Julie B. was capable of would never be enough.

She could feel Wayne's eyes on her from across the field, where he stood next to the aluminum tank. She thought about putting some space between herself and Alex. Wayne was jealous of their relationship. Her and the boy's. She knew without him speaking a word about it. She also knew he had every reason to be jealous of the boy. Not just Wayne, though. Everyone did. She loved little Alex the most and for reasons that she couldn't really explain. There was no burden in what they shared. It was as if they'd reached across generations and chose each other. She was careful with Wayne because of that and so many other things.

Helen Jean had wanted to kill him or to lock him back up in the shed since the night she'd found out what he had done to Ruby Nell. But the night before, Homer had decided he wanted him to learn about the hog pen.

He the only male child you got, Helen Jean, he said when he arrived home the night before. *Is it a reason you don't want nothing to do with him, honey?* he'd asked with real concern spread across his face.

Helen Jean had shook her head and looked down at her feet. She could never tell him that. She felt shackled by the same thing that kept her from telling him about her father. About Bacon. Except this time there was a shame because the monster came from her. Her father had been placed upon her by a mother who closed her eyes. Her brother's sins didn't fall on her, but Wayne's . . . He was hers. There was a time when she was still pregnant with Wayne that she thought about giving him up when he was born. When she mentioned it to Jessie B., he wouldn't hear of it. *There are worse places this baby could end up than with its mother,* he said. As she stood there looking at her feet, that moment came back to her. She wondered where Wayne would be, what he could be, if he wasn't tied to her — to the memory of what made him. He was hers only because she let him be, but if he had been someone else's, maybe things would different. She wondered if the monster in him could have been suffocated by love. A love she always knew she was incapable of.

The night before, Homer had said, *Well, good,* nodding. *We got to prepare him to inherit this thing. We got to get him ready.*

Flies landed on Wayne, near him, all around him. It was hard to keep them away from the tank, which was filled with a mixture of corn, green vegetables, canned meat, bread, and other things that had gone bad at Brooks Grocery Store. Homer had a contract with Brooks. Homer was good at begging, so he'd begged Brooks for his scraps. Promised him he'd haul them away each day. Every evening he'd fill his own drums with Brooks's scraps and then go out to their land and dump it into the twenty-five-hundred-pound water tank. Over time, all those scraps would begin to spoil and liquesce, and before it got to the hogs and other animals willing to eat it, it all looked and smelled like vomity slop.

She watched Wayne take a sip of his Coors. Homer had bought him a six-pack for coming today, but he hadn't come for a six-pack. He needed money and his mother, and that worried her. Homer had searched for him deep into the night after Wayne's young wife called and told Helen Jean he hadn't been home in two days. *It's not like him,* the girl said. *Wayne always take care of home.*

Homer had found him in the corner house on Lorraine Street, the house that sane and solid people kept away from. The house that saved folks threw oil and water at without even stopping to see where their offerings landed. The house that sons and daughters walked into for a good time or to follow friends and walked out as shells of themselves or ghosts.

When they showed up at her door, Homer holding Wayne up, like something worth saving, Helen Jean had pointed her finger toward the backyard and said, *Nuh-uh. He ain't coming in here. The shed. I'll get the key.*

And she'd known as she rummaged through her dresser drawer that Homer must have thought she said that because Wayne was high. The next day, she protested his joining them at the hog pen, but Homer insisted.

You — we got a duty to that boy, Helen Jean, he said. *I can't watch you watch him die. He your only son.*

The whole ride to the hog pen, Helen Jean had tried hard not to touch her son. When Homer pulled into the liquor store, she'd

283

volunteered to go inside but her husband gently patted her knee and told her he'd be right back. She had been sandwiched between her husband and Wayne in the single-cab pickup, holding Alex on her lap. When he left them in the truck, Helen Jean had thought she would suffocate. The quiet air had become thin and her chest rose and fell, until she reached over and pulled the handle of the driver's-side door and released herself and the child into the parking lot.

Standing by the chicken coop, Helen Jean watched Wayne push himself away from the tank and call out to Homer.

"Over here, son." She heard Homer's voice on the other side of the land, where the pens were sloppily set up to house the hogs.

She watched Wayne move to the sound of Homer's voice.

"Grandmoan," Alex said, tugging at her sweatshirt. "Grandmoan, can I get the eggs out the henhouse?"

She looked down at him and his wide eyes looked up at her. For a moment, she was lost in them. The wideness of them spread all across his face, leaving just a little room for his mouth and nose. And there was light and innocence and hope in them that made her almost believe in the direction her life had taken after that night in the outhouse.

"You all eyes, boy," she said with a chuckle. "Yeah, gone and get the eggs."

He smiled and turned toward the little dwelling inside the coop and she gently slapped his back. "You be careful with that old mean hen, you hear?"

She turned her attention back to Homer and Wayne. Her son stood watching her husband, who she couldn't see from inside the coop. She knew he was inside the pen with the hogs. She could hear him calling to them, "Here, sooiee, sooiee."

And then she heard his voice say, "Hey there, son. I hear you —"

"Ain't your damn son," Wayne snapped at him.

Helen Jean could hear the violence in his voice. She could hear her father.

She stepped out of the coop, making sure to fasten the door behind her. Jessie B. had always been patient with Wayne. Loved him even though Helen Jean couldn't figure out how to. Years after he was gone, she reached far back into her memory and tried her best to do right by all of her children. Even Wayne.

Once, after Jessie B.'s death, before she found out about what Bacon had done, before she banished Wayne to that shed, she felt something tender toward him. Bacon had belted him badly for an accidental spill. Helen Jean hadn't stopped or corrected her brother, but the beating had unnerved her enough that she felt she needed a drink. When she passed her son's room, heading to hers, where she kept her good liquor, she saw him sitting on the edge of the bed, legs dangling and head hung. He looked so sad, so broken, that he reminded her of her, and something in her shifted. She took a step back and entered his room, a thing she had never done.

The boy sat up straight and wiped at his eyes — eyes that were confused and trained on her.

She let her eyes roam the room. It was neat and tidy. It was easy for her to determine which side of the room had become her brother's. Bacon's side held one of the twin beds, which was unmade with clothes thrown about it.

On the side that belonged to Wayne, the bed was made with military precision and she wondered where he'd learned to do that. His shoes were neatly lined up at the foot of his bed. There were sheets of notebook paper taped to the wall about the head of his bed, spaced in a calculated, almost perfect manner. She allowed herself to move in closer, to lift a knee and lean over the bed, to get a better look, and she found herself surprised by the pencil sketches. There were several automobile drawings so detailed that it was like looking at photos. There were dog sketches, food sketches, and even a sketching of Jessie B.

"You did these?" she asked, peering at the sketch of Jessie B. His face appeared stern at first glance, but as she continued to gaze at it, she could see a smile curling at the corners of his lips.

"Yes, ma'am," Wayne said, standing up. "Mr. Pratt says I'm good enough to maybe go to art school one day."

Helen Jean moved her knee from the bed, stood up straight, and looked at him. He was fidgeting with his fingers and she knew he was nervous. That her presence made him nervous, and in that moment, it made her feel ashamed.

He was such a long and lean boy, but he didn't stand up straight before her. His shoulders turned in and his back hunched a bit. She'd always known that his stance was a matter of confidence. But as she stood there staring at him in that awkward way, she realized that she saw more of her than her father in his face. The jawline, the nose. She realized that he might've been handsome to her if she didn't know what made him.

And she stood there and watched him shift his weight from leg to leg before turning back to the sketchings and finally saying, "You don't say. Where'd you learn to draw like this?"

Wayne shrugged and smiled. "I don't know. When I was little, I'd color at the shop with Daddy and he would tell me I was good. I kept coloring and drawing cause of that." He shrugged again and blushed a bit. "I guess Daddy taught me."

She let her eyes find him again and nodded. She looked toward the bedroom door and Wayne's eyes took in the cue, as he shuffled his feet to make room for her to leave.

When she made it to the doorway, she called his name without turning back to face him.

"You real good at drawing. You keep that up and you might be all right," she said, and she wanted to believe it.

"Yes, ma'am," she heard him say before she disappeared down the hallway.

Homer wasn't like Jessie B. He wasn't like any man she'd known. But he worked hard and brought her everything he earned. He was a good man, even if he needed detailed instructions on how to do things. He wasn't brave and that was all right with her. Matter of fact, it was one of the things that attracted her to him the most. Helen Jean had come to realize that she'd always lived in the kingdoms of men. Always thought she needed the protection of one, but no more. She could do the protecting. Exact the justice.

She inched her way in their direction.

Homer came out and headed toward the coop. Like a gangly, goofy hound, Wayne followed close behind him.

"Hey, Homer," Wayne began. His words were slow and low. Almost a whisper. "I need to get paid for today."

Homer seemed to speed up when he heard Wayne's words, and Helen knew they could both see her, less than fifty feet in front of them.

"You hear me?" Wayne tried whispering, through gritted teeth. "I ain't come out here for no goddamn beer. I need money."

Homer stopped at the water tank and stuck his gloved hand in, searching for the bucket they used to scoop out the slop.

"Boy, I can't put no money in your hand. I can't help you kill yourself," Homer said. He didn't holler, but his voice was loud enough for her to hear. She thought it was a cry for help.

She moved in their direction, and, as if she hadn't been paying attention at all, she asked, "What's going on over here?"

"You old scared-ass, snitching-ass nigger," Wayne said, not bothering to whisper anymore.

Homer blinked his eyes and flinched, lifting his hands toward his face, like some form of protection, like he was afraid that Wayne would hit him.

"You owe me that money anyway," Wayne said, turning to face his mother. "It's the least you could do after everything. You can at least give me that."

"I don't owe you shit," Helen Jean said, pushing Homer out of the way. "I done everything I could to save you. Everything I could to make you something better than what you was gone always be." And she thought about all the things she done in service to Wayne. Marrying Jessie B., allowing Bacon in and then putting him out of their lives, and building the shed. She thought about what she knew he'd always wanted. To be loved by his mother. And she knew that maybe she did owe him that.

She looked at him. He had her pronounced jawline. Her father's. His eyes turned down like sad half moons and that almost made her pity him.

"Don't raise your voice at my husband. He the one come and get you. Trying to save you. You gone respect Homer," she said, nodding her head and looking in his eyes. Her voice was even. She didn't yell at him. She moved close to him. He towered over her, but she wasn't afraid of him.

"This here my husband," she said in a low voice. "You disrespect him, you disrespect me, and you don't want to disrespect me," she said, moving her face even closer to his. She put her finger under his chin. "Stop smoking that shit fore you get lost in it, son," she said softly, and she meant her words.

His eyes moved from her face to Homer, who stood behind her. He gently shook his head away from her fingers and looked down at the ground. His lips quivered.

"You don't get to be my momma now," he said, raising his voice a bit. "You was locked in your room when I needed you to do that," he said, slamming a fist into his chest.

Helen Jean stood still. She could feel Homer's eyes on the back of her head. Her hands began to shake.

Wayne shook his head. "And you didn't have to lock me in that shed at night. I wasn't gone hurt nobody. I wasn't. It was me. I was the one hurt. All I needed was you," he said, and then he turned his back and began to walk away.

Helen Jean looked down at the dirt. It was red and dry and dusted her shoes, causing them to look orange instead of the white they had once been. When she lifted her eyes, they were on Wayne's back and he had become small with the distance his steps made between them. She thought about calling out to him. Asking him where he was going, but she wasn't sure that she really cared. She watched as he walked past the barbed-wire fence and out onto the county road. She stood in that spot and thought about what he said. *You didn't have to lock me in that shed at night.* And she knew he was wrong because she knew she was right. Even after Homer returned to the pen with his bucket full of slop and Alex called out from the chicken coop, she stood there watching where Wayne had disappeared.

13
LYDIA

I don't know why I stand up when Jan storms out of the room. I guess I want to chase her. If I had the nerve, I would and I'd grab her by the shoulders, turn her around to face me, and tell her that we don't have to carry the tension between us. I'd tell her I miss her. Share all the happiness and hurt that has spanned across the years we missed together. I'd share with her the things I've held inside — even from Walter. And I'd tell her that as much as I want the end of my marriage to be about all the dead babies, I know it's more than that.

I don't chase her, though. I stand there and think about that summer. The summer Laverne Scott went missing. That's the summer everything fell apart.

I remember not wanting to leave my grandmother's house during the time Laverne was gone. My mother, my father, and I lived on the west side, the white side of town, not too far from the university. The rest of our family lived in the Parkley neighborhood on the east side — the black side. We were far from rich. We lived in a tiny two-bedroom duplex that was cramped but cozy and tidy. Simply living on the west side made us rich to our family, though. My father was from Dallas, but my parents moved to Jerusalem when I was a toddler and we only ever lived on the west side of town after that arrival. All I can ever remember is feeling like an outsider when it came to Parkley. But I can't remember that bothering me except for during those few days Laverne was missing.

I will never forget all the fuss and how life on my grandmother's block stopped the two days Laverne was gone. Before then, white folks might've stayed away from Parkley because of their views or beliefs regarding black life, but the neighborhood was actually pretty safe. Most people slept with their front doors unlocked and kids were safe to play without fearing strangers. Some people locked up due to the troublesome tendency junkie relatives had of breaking in and stealing treasures they'd grown up with. But even junkies only stole from relatives — never from neighbors.

I remember the search parties those two

days and how my mother was part of that. I remember the sad faces of the adults as they came in without Laverne at dusk the second night. There was a buzz in the neighborhood, a busyness that we had never seen before. What I recall most is that Aunt Marie came home with us, even after Grandmoan protested and told my mother she couldn't, and I left Jan there.

Even though our mothers told us not to do it, Jan and I would often plot to ask if she could spend the night at my house after each visit. Outside of our aunt, we were the only girls, so we were pretty close. Jan loved spending time at my house, and I loved having her there. So we had plotted and I was supposed to ask my mother if she could come home with us that night. But before I could ask, an argument started up inside the house. We heard my mother and Grandmoan shouting at each other through the window. Mother looked so strong when she emerged, pulling Aunt Marie by the arm. She turned and yelled back at the house, "You gone keep my husband name out your mouth and I'll take my little sister if I want! You don't pay her no mind no way!"

And I meant to tug at her shirt and ask her if Jan could come, too. But Mother continued to fuss and mumble about

Grandmoan, even when she grabbed my hand and pulled me to the car along with her and Aunt Marie. I was still waiting for her mouth to stop moving when we drove away. I had no idea that it would be the last time Jan and I plotted anything together.

By the time December rolled around that year, my father was gone and my mother was losing herself. A few months after my father was put away and transferred to a unit in New Boston, Mother packed us up and hit the highway in the burgundy Riviera she'd bought a year earlier and headed back for the safety of Aunt Ernestine in Dallas. Said we should be close to my father. Said he'd been wanting to get back down that way. She reasoned that upon his release, we'd make a life there.

Still standing in Grandmoan's hospital room, I think how if Walter leaves for good, I'll keep bathing and taking care of my body. I'll still brush my teeth and, if I could have them, play with my children. After my father left, my mother stopped breathing. She changed. She'd leave me with her aunt for days at a time, only to return to eat and bathe, placing shitty kisses on my forehead before disappearing again.

She just grieving, baby, Aunt Ernestine would say. *God got your momma in the cup of his hand. Just keep praying for her.*

During those years I often had panic attacks. The world around me would shake right before my watery eyes, and my heart would beat so fast and hard in my chest that I'd think I was at the end of everything. I didn't know they were panic attacks then. I didn't know what they were until I was in college, but I carried them on my back long before I had a name for them.

After a while at Aunt Ernestine's, the housing authority sent a letter saying they had an apartment available for us. We got our own place and moved to a public housing property. It wasn't long before I longed for Aunt Ernestine's full refrigerator, constant electricity, and running water. We were always lacking. That's when I began to notice my mother's struggle to keep it together mentally. She moved from job to job because she was so inconsistent with who she was. Some days she sat soaked in her own piss and stared into space with drool dribbling out of the side of her mouth. Other days, she was my mother or someone from one of the stories she'd tell. Sometimes she could function and we could be real, like a family. But sometimes just wasn't enough.

I took care of Mother until I was grown,

but I learned early in life to take care of myself.

As I ride the elevator down to the ground floor of the hospital, I try to clear my mind. I close my eyes and breathe in deeply and then I feel my phone vibrate in my purse. I dig for it clumsily and smile when I see Walter's name on the screen. The elevator dings and the doors open. I step off and bring the phone to my ear.

"I got your message," he says before I can even say hello. My heart begins to thump wildly in my chest.

"I — I don't know why I called. I wanted you to know," I say, and I hear the shakiness in my voice.

"I'm sorry, Lydia. I really am," he says. "I'd like to be there for you. I'd like for you to want that."

My eyes dart around the lobby as I consider his words. For a second, it is as if he's watching me, and then I remember what he wants from me. I know if I tell him where I am, he'll be here within a matter of hours and we'll have the same mountain of mess between us. I don't say anything.

He calls my name several times before I answer. "W — Walter, honey," I stutter. "I don't want to . . . I just wanted you to know —"

"Okay," he says, and then I hear him sigh. "I see. Is there anything else?"

There is silence on my end. I don't know what to say, and I can tell by the loud exhale he releases that he's irritated with me. I don't know why I let us get to this point. I guess it all just got away from me. But now, I don't know how to turn back and make it right without ruining everything.

"I have to go, Lydia. I can't — I won't do this anymore."

"I — I miss us," I say.

There is silence on the other end of the phone. I look at the screen and find that Walter is gone.

I am greeted by the smell of cattle and baked cookies when I pass from the entrance to the hospital parking lot, and I can see all of downtown from where I'm standing in the center. I've always hated how the whole town is leveled. It's impossible to feel above anything here.

Walter's last words ring in my ear. *I won't do this anymore.* His words were so final. Everything with him is that way these days. Deep inside, I know he's gone.

I lean against the rental car for support. I'm reminded that my tweed skirt and pumps are a bit much for the weather. For the whole town. My armpits are sweaty and

I can smell the faint scent of my own musk. The heat reminds me of endless summer days in Grandmoan's driveway. Those days before Mother and I moved away. After I was no longer a Jerusalem resident, when I became a visitor those three summers, Grandmoan would let us inside, but before that, there was no in, only out. This heat, the sweat beads forming on my forehead and above my upper lip, they bring it all back to me.

I remember sweat beads forming above my lips the day Jan peed herself and Grandmoan belted her and made her go inside. I remember the salty taste of it as I tucked my lip underneath my teeth, as I watched my cousin, prayed in my head that she could turn the water off, that she could hold it, from the edge of the driveway.

We weren't allowed on the lawn. It was forbidden, but the water faucet was there. We'd often wait for Granddaddy to get home instead of creeping across the lawn ourselves after the pitcher of water Grandmoan put out was empty or spilled or polluted with flies, gnats, or bees, to avoid knocking on the door, to avoid being cursed at or sent to take a nap.

I still blame myself for that day. We had been playing hopscotch in the driveway. It was one of those rare days that we were alone out there. No second cousins to play with. Just me and Jan. We liked those days. We played hand-clapping games and church and were finally playing something that I loved to play, but it was me who'd bumped the pitcher when I tripped over the hopscotch rock during my last turn.

And I hadn't become thirsty right away, but after a few rounds of our game, I said, *Let's take a break. It's hot and I'm thirsty. I think I might throw up.*

Jan's eyes widened. She began to press the palm of one of her hands into the knuckles of the other. I knew she was nervous.

The last time I'd thrown up at Grandmoan's, gotten sick, my father had taken off work for three days and kept me home. Jan shook her head and whispered, *Don't throw up. Your daddy won't bring you back. I'll get it, Lil. I'll get you some water.*

I should've stopped her, but I didn't. I knew the rules — I was the oldest. But I let her break them.

I watched Jan slink across the lawn, like a sneaky cat, looking back at me every now and then for encouragement or warning. I was supposed to keep watch. I was supposed to let her know if Grandmoan came

301

to the window or to the door. I don't know what we'd have done after that, but I was supposed to let her know. After all, I was the one who'd turned over the pitcher. I was the reason the mission had been taken in the first place.

When she slinked through the small forest of tall banana plants that guarded the faucet, I was relieved. She'd made it. Hadn't been caught. We were okay. Her tiny body disappeared for a moment into the green brush and I smiled. I was still smiling when my grandmother's voice ripped through the air. When she said, *Gal, I'm gone beat your little ass if you don't get out my yard.*

And I turned to find her standing behind me, wearing her housedress and a frown and furrowed eyebrows.

I looked back toward the lawn and saw Jan's face peep through the plants, her eyes wide with fear. She disappeared quickly and the plants swayed from her touch, which caused me to grimace because I knew that the plants were the only beautiful thing in the yard. Grandmoan was proud of them.

Grandmoan took a few slow steps forward, until the tips of her slippers were right at the place where the concrete ended and the lawn began and she was standing right next to me.

Did you hear me, gal? Get your ass out my yard! she shouted.

I — I got to turn the water off, Grandmoan. I got to —

Turn it off now! she shouted. *If I have to come get you — you don't want me to have to come get you,* she said.

It won't — it won't turn, Jan called through the plants, and I could hear the tears in her voice.

You better turn it off and you better do it now, my grandmother said. *I mean do it now.*

I got to pee, Jan called out. *I can't hold it, Grandmoan,* she whined.

You better turn my water off since you want to be grown and do what you want and you bet not piss yourself, my grandmother responded.

Jan started to cry and my grandmother crossed her arms. I watched the plants. I prayed that my little cousin's face would emerge and that we would be okay.

Now, my grandmother called out to her. *Shut it off now.*

It felt like minutes passed, and I stood there holding my breath. Eventually Jan emerged slow from the plants. Her eyes were on her feet as she took slow calculated steps, holding the empty water pitcher against her chest.

Did you shut my water off, gal? Grandmoan asked.

Yes, ma'am. It's off, Jan responded in a quiet voice.

And I exhaled. Wanted to jump up and down. Wanted to shout out in triumph, until she moved closer and I could see the wet that covered the front of her shorts. The wet that crawled down her leg.

I wanted to speak up for her. To say, *Grandmoan, it's just the water. She didn't pee. It's the water.*

But I stood there in silence. Grandmoan shook her head and followed Jan into the house. It seemed the world went silent, until I heard her screams erupt through the open window and Grandmoan's harsh words with each slap of the belt. When it was over, Grandmoan said, *I bet you won't step on my grass no more. And I bet not never catch you pissing your britches either.*

And we were careful after that. We never got caught stepping on her lawn again.

My rental is one of the only two cars I see on 44th Street — downtown 44th Street. A young woman with bright red braids is driving the other car, a little Honda that I can hear rattle, as if it wants to stop. We pull up to a stop light at same time. Her music is loud, but I hear a child screaming over it.

304

The windows are not tinted, so I shift my gaze to the back seat. I can see a baby sitting in a car seat in the back. The baby's face is wet with snot and tears, but the mother never turns to look at the child. She is bouncing to loud music and jerking her head so hard she looks like a bobble-head. She catches my gaze and smiles, revealing a full set of gold teeth.

I turn my head back to the street and think about how long my mother has been mourning my father. I think about how she's given her mind over to that. I can't help but pity her. If Walter doesn't come back home, I tell myself I'll be okay. That I can survive this. That I can come out whole. That I am nothing like my mother.

When I make it to my grandmother's neighborhood, the first thing I notice is that the fences of the houses that used to greet guests and visitors are barely standing. The planks of most have been painted colors like off-white or powder blue, none of them replaced and some completely missing. The chain-link fences have bends through the center or are missing the cover poles, so they are half fences as well.

The houses I pass all look abandoned. Some are boarded up and some look as if they should be. Aluminum siding has been placed sloppily in random places on roofs, and some people have used Sheetrock and long wooden beams to make carports over their driveways. In the Pepto Bismol–pink house on the corner of my grandmother's street, a lady who looks to be in her forties stands in the doorway with a blue flyswatter in her hand. She is wearing a bra, a half slip, and a black satin bonnet on her head. She makes no effort to cover the extra roll of fat that separates the bra and the slip. I can't see behind her, even though she's holding the door wide open. There is a blue tag stuck on the pane of the door, so even though it's daylight, I know darkness waits inside for her.

I park the rental at the curb in front of my grandmother's house and look at it from where I'm sitting. The driveway I grew up in looks huge, which is strange. Most people say the devices of their torture are actually smaller than their memories draw them. There is a police car there and I know who it belongs to. I let my eyes take it in, wonder how he ended up doing what he does. I should be proud of him. It should mean that he's a better person.

The house is one of the only two on the whole block that have been updated. The white stone makes it look like it should be in another neighborhood, another country even, and a huge stone carport now covers the newly extended driveway. I can't tell if the house is set completely in stone or if it's just facing. It's beautiful, whatever it is, and it doesn't fit here. Not even the yard, with its stone fountain in the center, which is not as large as I remember it being.

"They must have torn it down and rebuilt," I say to myself.

I turn my head to the house across the street, Laverne's old house. It's boarded up now. The once-bright-orange paint that made it so wonderful to look at from our spot in the driveway has dulled and almost completely peeled away, and the chain-link fence is gone on one side.

I open the door and step out of the car and lean against it for a moment. I need strength to go inside. I wish I could pray, like Jan, but unlike her I know prayer is useless. I finally gather the strength from somewhere within to push myself away from the car. For a while, I just stand on the sidewalk and look at the house and then a Buick pulls up behind my rental.

14
JULIE B.

Alex police car parked in Momma's space in the drive and I'm so focused on that, I almost don't know her when I pull up in front of the house. Almost forgot I begged her to come because of how busy this morning been. The closer I get to her, the more I know I'm looking at the girl my little sister tried to raise. I used to feel guilty about her. Used to wonder if I should've done more by that child, even more so than what I tried to do for the ones I raised. Ruby Nell made it clear from the start that she wanted to raise that baby without intercession. And I just wanted to give my sister something so she could maybe be happy, so she could stay my sister and stop falling to pieces. Then she came back begging and I couldn't help her and I always felt guilty about that. Well, that and that I wasn't there that day to save her — to look after her in the same way she was always there for me.

Me and Ruby Nell should've been happy we was pregnant at the same time, but Alex was still too young and I had just got rid of another one. I couldn't be happy with that. I already had one hanging off my tits. I knew when I realized I was pregnant again that I didn't need no nother one. And then Ruby Nell lost hers.

The way my sister cried scared me and moved me at the same time. Strings of snot running from her nose and saliva running from her lips. But wasn't no sounds coming out her mouth while we sat on the floor of the only bedroom I done ever had. Me cradling her in my arms.

This make two, she said into my shirt. Her voice was muffled and afraid. *Ain't gone never have none. Something always wrong with me.* And all I could think about was all the nights she held me on that floor when I couldn't stop crying about not knowing who my daddy was, when I couldn't stop crying about Dale. All the silent cries she coached me through.

Lydia walk up to the front of her car and meet me halfway, and when she open up her arms we hug and then I hold her away from my body and say, "Let me look at you, niece. You so pretty." But I really think she look just like Punkin. Just like Dale. They all got the same light skin and wavy hair, but when Lydia was a girl, back when she had all that beautiful hair, it grow long and thick while Punkin's grow in real thin.

"Girl, you just like Ruby Nell for the world," I say, and I watch her face to see if she believe me. Watch her to see if she see that I don't even believe myself. Her long and narrow face ain't nothing like them round faces Ruby Nell and Soweo had, but her bowed legs always been just like Ruby Nell's. Folk always said Lydia was bow-legged, just like my sister and just like Jessie B. Them same bowed legs gave me a secret hope, though. Helped me believe that despite the other two men that claimed me after Jessie B. was gone, he somehow really was my father. Me or none of the ones I raised had legs like that, so her legs meant something special to me, just like they was something to gel her to Ruby Nell.

Lydia smile her perfect teeth smile and that make me remember I forgot to take mine out. "You look good, Auntie," she say, and I know she probably talking about my teeth. But maybe it's the money she seeing, too. Money look good on everybody.

"How you doing down there?" I ask her. Then I sigh and say, "How y'all been doing down there?" And I hope she know I mean my sister too. That I done always meant my sister, too. Even though I ain't asked about her in all these years, I love my sister — done always loved my sister. I can't tell Lil that, though. Can't tell her that it ain't cause I ain't cared that I ain't asked. But I know. I know that not asking is the only way I been — I'll be able to keep holding the only thing my sister ever needed me to hold to myself.

And when I say that, Lydia drop herself from our hug and set her eyes on the ground. She smack her tongue against the roof of her mouth and shake her head but she don't say nothing.

I stand there waiting on her for what seem like forever, before I start to get nervous and think maybe she know. Think maybe after all this time my sister done cracked enough to tell the truth. If she ask me, if she just come out and say it, I ain't gone deny it cause ain't no benefits to that. To keeping up the lie.

"Did you know?" she ask me without looking up. And then she start raising her head all slow and letting her eyes crawl up my body, like so many roaches. "Did you know Soweo wasn't my father?"

I exhale and put my hand on my chest and kind of stagger, more surprised than I expect to be. And I don't know if I'm

311

surprised that she don't know the rest or if I'm surprised that she know anything at all.

"What?" I say, dragging the word out slow. "Who . . . who told you that, baby?" I ask, wondering why Ruby Nell just didn't tell the whole damn story.

"After you called, I visited Mother. She told me," she say, and her chestnut eyes seem to be asking me for something.

She sigh and look down at the ground and then back at me. "Is it true, Auntie? Was my father not my father?"

First time I come up pregnant, I didn't tell nobody but Ruby Nell at first. She was still in school and I thought I was gone leave her behind and I wanted her to be ready for it. That was before Dale found heroin. That was before he got too mean. He'd slapped me around a few times, but only cause he was jealous of me with other boys. I should've wrote that down as a sign, but he was gone get me out my momma house and that's really all that mattered to me.

He borrowed LaCarl Minor car the day after I told him I was pregnant and we rode out to the west side, past the west side really. Wolfforth. Pulled up on a patch of land that had a *For Sale* sign posted on it. The high yellow grass waved all around that tall commercial sign, and I thought it was beautiful, like *Little House on the Prairie.* The land was so flat, all I could see off in the distance was where the grass met the sky, and I imagined the moon and stars out there would've been something to make me believe that God lived there.

This it, he said, smiling wide and kind of true. *I'm gone enlist and serve and get out and set us up right here. And you ain't gone never have to be afraid no more.* I walked that fifteen acres with him and built our home out loud. It was right next to a stream and a old oak tree. He put his hand on my stomach and said, *We gone have six in all. Boys. Got to be all boys. First they gone help with land and then we gone make us a band.* And I laughed, but I was so happy, and he knew that so he laughed with me. And we kept laughing until we made our way to that ground and made love right there on our future.

By that second pregnancy, I was broke by Dale. He was whooping my ass all the time and was strung out by then. I wasn't ready to carry all that and another baby too. I wasn't having nothing else with him until he was clean. I got rid of it and wound up pregnant again just a few short months after.

I drop my eyes to the ground and think about maybe telling Lydia that. Think about

313

being real with myself. Speaking my truth to somebody. Maybe some type of healing can happen for all of us. I'm about to open my mouth and tell her, *Yeah I knowed, and I knowed more than that, too,* till Ruby Nell face pop up in my mind. Her face when she was protecting me all them years. Her face when I missed protecting her that one day I should've been there.

I see her watery eyes the day she lost that last baby, the day I told her not to worry cause mine was disappearing too. I remember her saying, *Julie B., don't kill it. I can take it. Raise it — me and Soweo — like our own. Don't nobody have to know.*

It was my idea for her not to tell nobody she lost her baby. To carry *something* with me during the pregnancy. That was before Soweo was her husband. When they was just courting and she was still running back and forth from us to him. We figured it wasn't gone be nothing for him to have her gone for four or five months since she had been stretching herself across two places in that way anyhow.

We drove to Hobbs when the time came for me to deliver. Let a Native woman in a barn pull the child out into the world and when we made it back home, we was equals. Sometimes I wonder what Soweo must of thought when she come back to Dallas cradling that baby that ain't look nothing like her and nothing like him. But he loved Ruby Nell and he saw how much she wanted him to love that baby and I like to think he tried to hold on to that. And then Momma had her way on his life and he broke.

I lift my head and look back at Lydia and I know what I got to say. Even though my sister can't be who she was, I can't take this from her.

"Yeah, honey. I knowed," I say. "But it ain't a thing nobody was ever trying to hide from you. All that life shit — all that what happened. It just kind of got in the way," I say.

She nod and look down at her shoes. "Maybe if I'd have been real to him. Something to lose — something he loved . . . He never would've did what he did and wound up in prison in the first place."

I shake my head and keep shaking it, like I ain't buying what she selling, like how I do Jehovah's Witnesses when they approach me outside the bank or the mall. "Nawh, Lydia. Don't think of it like that. It's more than blood what make somebody your daddy. Soweo," I say, and point my finger at her, like I'm telling her the truest thing.

"Don't matter what happened. That man loved you best he could. Both them. Him and your momma did the best they could. It don't matter that it ain't his blood in your veins. He chose to love you long as he could."

And we stand there in the quiet of everything until Punkin and my grandbabies drive up.

15

JAN

When I was carrying Javon, I'd ride outside of town to where the plains turned to hills, just past Synder and Post, pull over to the side of the road, and scoop up big Tupperware bowls full of red clay dirt to eat. It was something so real about sitting on side the road tasting them first few scoops. Made me feel like I come from the earth and having it in me was natural and connected to something bigger. Keesha told me about Argo cornstarch halfway through my pregnancy. By the time I came up pregnant with Jazera, I wasn't driving outside of town for dirt no more. I'd stick a straw right through the box and get my dirt fix that way. After the pregnancies, I just got a permanent taste for the soft earth-like powder on my tongue. Now, it's a habit.

I wonder what Lil would've thought if she'd have walked in on me stuffing big spoons of dirt in my mouth. It's such a country thing. Lil wouldn't know nothing about it, but that craving come to all of us when we carry. My momma say craving the dirt was always how she knowed she was pregnant. I wonder what Lil would've thought if she knew that the whole time I was in Grandmoan's hospital room earlier, my box of Argo with the straw sticking out sat in my purse waiting for my next suck. That even after I wasn't carrying nothing inside me no more, the craving for dirt stayed with me.

I hate the way I stormed out of the hospital room and let Lil win again.

When I got in the car, I was so mad I balled up my fists so tight my fingernails was cutting the palms of my hand. I slammed them against the steering wheel of my truck so hard I had to shake my hands to stop the ringing in them afterward. I turned the key, but the truck only coughed and went dead. I turned it again and it did the same thing. "Lord, you know I got to get my babies," I said, and thought about how the car ain't gone make it through Dallas, ain't gone make it to Dallas. And I felt like I was gone break down cause I ain't got no other way.

But when I turned the key again, it stuck, so I put it in drive and pulled away from the hospital. My eyes was blurry from tears that wanted to slide down my face. I wiped them away before they had the chance.

And I turned my mind to Laverne Scott. Anything to make me stop thinking about myself. I can still see Laverne body draped over the pole that connected to the chain links on their fence that day. Her patchy, nappy head and her crooked neck cocked to the side. Seemed cruel for any kid to be born with a condition that weakened the muscles on the left side of the neck so bad that it looked like she was walking around cradling a phone between her head and her shoulder. But Laverne was born that way. She was always smiling her big buck-teethed smile, though.

The day she went missing, she called out across the wide street to us, *Hey, y'all.*

I can't even remember what we answered no more, but I do remember that her smile was hopeful, even though half her face drooped into a frown, like some kind of stroke victim. *Think y'all grandma'll let Marie walk to Ms. Loodney's with me?*

Even though I was the youngest, just seven years old, I was the one to answer that day. The one to say *Nope, I bet she won't, so you bet not even ask.* Then I twisted my middle and index fingers together and shot them

319

up at Laverne while sticking my tongue out at her. She dropped her head to the side as much as her neck would allow. I think she knew I wasn't giving her the real middle finger, even though I didn't.

Okay. My momma gave me a dollar for penny candy, she said, without raising her head. She looked up and smiled her normal warm smile. *Tell Marie I'm gone bring her some back . . . Yeah,* she said like she was answering her own question. *Tell her I'll bring her some Tootsie Rolls back.*

We shrugged at each other and didn't intend on telling nobody nothing. Laverne loosened her grip on the pole and skipped away from her yard toward Bates Street. She didn't look like her normal self. Like a thirteen-year-old girl in a seventeen-year-old's body as she headed toward Ms. Loodney's. She looked like a happy little girl skipping away in a dull yellow sundress that tied at the shoulders, eager to get candy for my aunt. We continued about our business of swatting flies and trying to get inside, and as the day grew old and the heat died out just a bit, we forgot to remember to watch for Laverne to come back.

One thing I'll never understand is how Grandmoan got it fixed in her mind that Lil daddy was the one that took her. I know she didn't like him. Used to talk ugly about him around the house. Called him a crazy African. Possessive, but that ain't enough of a reason to accuse him. I guess after Laverne described who took and kept her in that old abandoned house on Bates Street, Grandmoan thought she knew for sure.

A few days after her disappearance, Laverne came back all on her own. After all the searching and scavenging the neighborhood, she just appeared on her parents' doorstep on her own. When she heard Laverne was back, Grandmoan put her liquor-filled plastic cup down on the coffee table and headed to her bedroom. She came back out twenty minutes later, wearing a shoulder-length black wig, slightly twisted to one side. She had on a pair of deep-creased, dull pink slacks and a purple blouse with pink flowers all over it. She shifted her weight from leg to leg slow, steady like a cowboy. She looked like she was a hundred carrying about three hundred pounds instead of someone in her midfifties carrying just over a hundred. It was the kind of walk that made me want to hold out my hands and catch her cause I was sure she was gone fall. *Gone check on this gal,* she said, making her way across the street.

She was the type of person people talked

to, looked up to, and expected stuff from. Some people called her the "Godfather of Parkley," cause a lot of times what she said went. She was part of the first black family to buy a house in that neighborhood, and, for the people that followed, it was as if she was the one that settled the land. Wives came to tell her about cheating husbands, and she gave them remedies like *Pour lye water on him when he sleep* or *Shoot him in the toe this time, but next time aim for the head. He won't try you no more. Mark my words. He won't try you no more.* She whooped folks' kids for them when they was too soft to do it theyselfs, and she showed men how to cheat on their home insurance policies so they could have extra money for they kids at Christmastime. But for all the wrong she did, she did some right too. She gave out meat to needy families when Granddaddy killed chickens or hogs. She took Chester, the neighborhood imbecile, to the hog pen with them to earn extra cash, and she opened up the den she'd had the garage converted into every night and let the neighborhood come in, no further than the den, to drink and dance like it was Friday. Like it was payday.

That goddamned African, Soweo, she cursed when she got back from the Scotts' that night. *Them folks got nasty ways, I ain't never liked his black ass.*

My momma tried to talk her down. *Momma, she didn't say it was Soweo. She said the person what took her had red eyes and big hands. That could be anybody. Sides, Soweo ain't no African. He was just raised by one.*

You shut your fool mouth, gal! she yelled at my momma. She wasn't slurring. She wasn't drunk — she was mad. *She was talking bout Soweo. That black-ass nigger been gone since she went missing. Catering in Dallas, my ass. This shit stops now. Men can't continue to do this to these girls and go unpunished. This shit stops now. You mark my words.*

When I pull up to the car pool of my kids' elementary school, I don't turn off my car. It's a draw between preserving gas and not being able to start it after they get in. I can always get a few dollars for gas from Omar. It'll be a shame to not be able to start the car in front of they school. I don't want to embarrass them like that.

Ain't no other parents here. Most kids walk home. A lot of parents ain't got cars or think the school too close to come get they babies. Others just don't care. It's the same elementary school I went to — my momma went to this school, too. When we was little, Aunt Ruby Nell told me, Lil, and Marie what it was like before it was a black school — before it was a all-black neighborhood. The glass windows was all there. None of them was boarded up like they is now. The yard in the front of the school used to be covered in grass. Now, it's covered with scattered patches of yellowing grass that remind me of Laverne hair.

A dry wind sweep through the window of my truck and head over to the basketball court. Ain't no cement on the court, just dry red dirt. The wind cause the loose dirt to twirl around in circles. I hope it stop before the bell ring. Jazera a dust storm chaser. I hate the way the bathtub looks after she done caught one.

I wonder what schools like in Dallas. I wonder if the basketball courts made of hard dirt. Maybe they ain't. Maybe everything cemented and modern-looking. I don't know what I think about that, but it make me hope something nice about leaving this place. It make me feel like I really can.

Lil and her momma loved Soweo and then he was gone. Maybe that's why it was so easy for them to leave and restart. Some nights, before it all fell apart, Aunt Ruby

Nell would take me and Marie home with them. We'd go to they house on the west side. That was like being in some kind of paradise. Lil had her own room, something I didn't get to have until the housing authority give me one. She had a huge white wicker bed that filled up most of the room. The headboard was its own attachment, with a mirror and cabinets and all kind of shelving. Bed was so big me and my momma and brother could've slept in it together. All of us. She had Cabbage Patch Kids, stuffed Glo Worms and monkeys, and Rainbow Brite all sitting atop her pink and white flower spread. Even had stickers on the wall to match the spread. She had everything.

When we go over there, Soweo cook for us. Sometimes he cook African food. Doughy stuff him and Lil eat with they fingers. Sometimes he bake chicken or make pizza, and me and Marie follow Lil into the kitchen to help him. He have music playing and be dancing round, dusting our faces with flour and telling us where to pour what. When we get to putting the food on the table and Aunt Ruby Nell come in talking about how good everything look, Soweo give us all the credit.

Don't look at me, woman. These girls gone

make some real fine wives some day. He be rubbing her shoulders and smiling proud at us in they west side duplex. And I be sitting there coveting all of it. All Lil had. Her daddy, her momma, and her room. Anybody see how Soweo was with us, they know he ain't do what Grandmoan say he did to Laverne. I knowed it wasn't him from the start. I also knowed who it was always.

I didn't understand the love they shared, Lil and her daddy. Mine left before I was born. I didn't know what a daddy was meant to do till I got pregnant with Javon. I was twenty-something by then.

Omar used to talk to Javon while he was still in my stomach. He was a good father then, and he still a good father. I can't take him in for me, but he love Javon and Jazera. I guess I love him for them. He pick them up and keep them at his place one weekend every month. Come to field day at school and even come to see them recite they Easter speeches at church when it's time. Put on a dress shirt and slacks and everything. Omar give me four hundred dollars a month to help with they upkeep and he try to be there whenever I call him. Whenever he can. He better than what I had, as a man, a father.

The only memory I got of Dale, the man

half responsible for me being here, is from behind a bullet-plated glass. I was seven years old. Had just turned seven that very week, and I think visiting him was part of my birthday present. I didn't think nothing about Momma staying up all Friday night doing hair. She cut Alex's first, which was something she taught herself to do when he was young cause she couldn't afford to take him to the barber. Said she wanted her boy to look like something, so she practiced on his head till she got it. And after she was done with him, she straightened mine, and then she rolled it up with torn paper sack like it was Easter or something.

When she woke us and up and dressed that Saturday morning, I didn't know what was going on. Maybe I thought it was Easter. Can't remember too well what was going through my head, but I knew it was gone be a different day when she pressed our Sunday clothes, dressed us, and told us to sit down in the den with Grandmoan, and dared us to get up before she was dressed and ready to leave.

She came out wearing all red. Red dress, red pantyhose, and red pumps. And she was bright like Christmas lights. Devil bright. Her lips was as bright as her outfit, and I'd never seen the gold costume jewelry she was wearing. I thought she looked beautiful. More beautiful than the tired Momma I was used to seeing. But Grandmoan, who sat in a recliner in the corner of the room, smacked her lips and said, *All that for a nigger behind bars. Nigger can't father no kids from there. All that for shit.* And she chuckled and looked back at the TV.

Still, she let Momma load us up in her car and drive us to Lamesa to see Dale in prison. Momma had to go in the bathroom and take off her bra cause it had wiring in it. She carried it in her hand and some of them men what wasn't on solitary visiting restrictions whistled at her when she walked by with it dangling in her hand. I can still remember how mad Alex looked in his eyes at them men. He was only twelve, but he had so much fire in his eyes, I know he could've killed one of them convicts.

I had never seen Dale outside of photographs till that day. After my brother sat in front of that glass, it was my turn, and I was nervous. Unsure of what the person on the other side of that glass was supposed to mean to me. I hoped the ribbons in my hair meant something to him.

When I sat down and Momma handed me the receiver, I moved my face close to the filthy, scratched-up glass and tried to get a good look inside. Looking at that man was like looking at me. His skin was yellow, the kind with a red tint. His eyes was green and his smile was crooked just like mine.

Baby girl, he said, smiling through the glass. *Man, she done grew up,* he said, looking up at Momma, who was standing over me. She couldn't hear him, though. She didn't have the phone.

"Hey, Momma," Jazera say when she open the back door of the truck and steal me from my thoughts about the past. She look almost like me with the two braided ponytails my friend Angie weaved in last week. Unlike mine, her skin is the color of pecans. She seem to get excited about us missing teeth at the same time, her the front teeth and me the side ones — the ones that rooted out. I wonder how she'll feel when she ain't in elementary school no more. When she got all her teeth back and her momma teeth still gone.

"Javon in Principal Brown office," Jazera say.

"What he do?" I ask.

"Fighting." She slide her arms through her backpack to release it from her body and throw it into the back seat of the truck right fore she swing her leg in and hoist herself up to the seat. "Again," she add before slamming the door and sitting back in her seat.

"Ugh," I exhale. My son got anger issues. His doctor, Lynda Fan, tried to label him with some ADHD or ADD type of mess, but I think what he really needs is a good old-fashioned whooping. Now I have to sit in the car pool another fifteen minutes. I personally know Willard Brown, the principal. He used to like me in school, but now he look at me like he feel sorry for me. I know what his punishment for my son gone be. He give it all the time. Not because he don't like Javon, but because Javon always doing something to deserve it.

I reach over to the passenger side of my front seat and fish around inside my oversized purse, which used to be Jazera baby bag. Feel like I'm fishing through junk forever. I can feel my fingers shifting through Medicaid IDs, my SNAP benefits card, and the last three dollars and sixty-eight cents I got to my name. I smile when I finally find the stiff cardboard box. Leaning my head back on the headrest of my seat, I close my eyes and listen to Jazera hum a tune from some cartoon show.

I put the straw to my lips and suck in what taste like earth. It's a art to eating dirt or cornstarch. Take training and skill. Real smarts. I don't swallow as soon as the grainy tenderness bust from the straw and hit my tongue. I wait. And hold it. I savor the taste of myself and everybody else I know. If I don't, I might choke, so I just hold it. I think about how wide I love Jesus and how much I hate sex. And then I swallow, and I keep on sucking and swallowing until my son get in and slam the car door.

"I know you ain't slamming my door, boy," I say after Javon slide into the back seat next to his sister. I see creases in his forehead, and I can tell he about to talk back.

"Satan, I rebuke you in the name of Jesus!" I shout. "And don't think you ain't getting holy oil drops in your bathwater tonight. What you doing fighting, boy?"

He turn his head to look out the window. He want to talk back, but last week when he did I took him right to Omar, and he whooped his butt real good. Since he getting older, body turning to a man's, I got to take him to Omar. I want him to feel his whoopings. He don't feel them good with me.

He don't want that again. To go to Omar's. To feel that belt. Omar don't care that he be in middle school next year. He make him lay cross that bed and tear his butt up. I ain't never made him drop his pants. I don't let Omar do it neither. That's crossing the line. I don't believe in that. But I do believe in a good whooping.

I turn back and look at Javon again. I think about cutting the Mohawk I let him get for good grades as a punishment. I can't see his eyes cause he still looking out the window. I'm glad. I melt underneath those eyes — eyes like mine.

I put the car in drive and finally leave the elementary school car pool.

The kids' school is only two streets away from Grandmoan's. I decide to drive around the corner instead of heading to my house on the other side of town. I need to check on my granddaddy, and my momma still live there. I'm embarrassed that I grew up in the neighborhood as we ride the two streets over. All the grass in the yards we pass is gone, and I can't figure out why. Grass should be green and beautiful in May, but not in Parkley. It's plenty patches of golden straw, but no grass. Dogs tied to trees in front yards with rope, and something off about how they just lay there and gaze out at the dusty air with their tongues hanging out of the sides of their mouths. Broke-down cars that been jacked up for years sit in every other driveway. When I stop at the sign that mark the turn onto my old street, a junkie named Sukey smile, revealing a bald mouth. She wearing a bright pink sweater so thick I can see sweat beads forming on her forehead from my car. Her denim shorts so short and tight the hug they have on her cooch look like it hurt.

"Hey, Jan," she say. "You got a few dollars?"

"Nawh," I say. "But I got this." I hold up the Bible I keep on my dashboard and Sukey smile fade.

"Fine then, bitch." She spit at me. She try to make a graceful turn on her fire-engine-red six-inch heels but stumble. She find her balance and look back to make sure that I didn't see her. She see I did. She throw up her hand like she gone wave me away, and then drop all fingers except the middle one.

"I'll pray for you!" I shout out the open window.

"Pray for your own goddamn self!" she shout back. "You the one look like you got the AIDS!"

I shake my head. "I got to get out of this town," I say out loud without meaning to.

"Momma, where we going?" Jazera asks.

"Baby, don't mind me. I'm just talking. We ain't got nowhere to go. God put us where he wanted us to be," I say. I ain't told my kids about Dallas. I don't want them to know till I'm sure.

In the past, I done slipped up and found myself making foolish dreams in front of my kids. I don't want to lie to them no more. Give them hope where ain't none. I got to be sure I can stand outside of this place. I got to be sure in my heart.

As I get close to Grandmoan house, I notice other cars is there, but the only one that make me want to slam harder on the gas and speed right on by is the black-and-white police cruiser. What he doing here? What he doing here?

He the police now, but that don't change who he really is. Matter of fact, that probably make him worse. I can feel my heartbeat speed up. I can't speed by cause my momma and Lil standing next to a fancy car. They done spotted me and Momma waving. I roll up the windows on my truck and pull close to the curb across the street, in front of Laverne old house.

"Granny, Granny," Javon and Jazera start chanting as soon as they spot my momma arms swimming through the air.

I hear the door behind me click and I can't even turn around and tell them to look both ways before they cross the street. My heart pounding and my eyeballs dancing around in my head. I can't breathe. The street zooming in and out. I rub my hands together and try to concentrate on praying. I take short breaths, blowing them out harder with each one.

"Lord, please," I manage to gasp between the heaviness of my lips. Somebody tapping on the driver's-side window, but I can't look. If it's Alex I'll scream and my heart'll stop beating.

"Jan." I hear the tapping again. I know the woman voice ain't Alex, so I look up. Lil is drawing circles in the air with her finger, asking me to roll down the window. I crack it. My momma loading the kids into the old Buick that used to be Grandmoan's. Lil see my eyes on them.

"She said she wanted to take them to the supermarket with her. She needs to pick up a few things for dinner. I told her it — I told her it was okay," she say, looking at me like she waiting for me to throw tomatoes at her or something. I don't get mean with her, though. I'm trying to catch my breath.

"Can I get in?" she ask. I nod and she walks around to the passenger side. I want to tell her it's hot in here. I ain't got no air in here. I want to tell her she don't want to get in here, but I can't. Maybe she'll see my sweat and get it. She get herself situated in my passenger seat, and we sit quiet until the deep rising and falling of my chest softens.

"You okay?" she finally ask. I still can't talk, so I nod.

"Look," she say. "I'm sorry about what happened at the hospital earlier."

I want to say something back, but I ain't got my breath back. I see her fidgeting with her fingers from the corner of my eye.

"The problem with our people is . . ." I turn my eyes to her. I want to see why her voice is trailing off. I want to say something, but I still can't find my words. She turn her head and look out the window. "Secrets," she say. "I have panic attacks sometimes. Take medications to control them, but some things you can't escape by swallowing pills."

I don't know what no panic attack is, but I want to ask her about it. Find out what she mean. I smack my lips because my words won't push through, and she sigh and look back at me. Her eyes look like she about cry, but ain't no tears fell down yet.

"I have a secret, too, Jan," she say, and her lips quiver a little bit.

"What?" My voice hoarse.

She put her hand on mine and I think about us being little girls. She was there, too. Just like me. She was there with him. And for the first time in a long while I feel like I understand my cousin, what she trying to tell me.

I almost respect her more than I respect myself cause I know the words to say what she trying to say don't come easy. I always thought I was the only one. I look at her. She seem perfect sitting beside me. Her flawless makeup, expensive jewelry, and designer suit look perfect, but she sitting here telling me she messed up, too. That she ain't coming out and saying the words, but he got her, too.

She don't say nothing. She just look down at her hands.

"We was so scared of him," I finally whisper.

"I should have told somebody," she say.

HELEN JEAN

1990

Helen Jean began to forget things when she was around fifty-one. Around the same time, she broke the covenant. She didn't say anything about the forgetting to anyone. In fact, she welcomed it. It irritated her that it was only the small, trivial things that would slip away from her, like birthdays, ages, and middle names. Nothing that she really wanted to forget.

She could still remember that Alex was lost to her, that Marie had made herself a ghost, and that Ruby Nell's mind was completely gone. So many animals she'd burned to move on. And still she thought of each of them.

There were so many things being held in her head that she wanted gone. Things that wouldn't leave her. And what she forgot was that Julie B. and her daughter were somewhere in the house that Saturday afternoon when Wayne's mother-in-law, Betty Ann, came by. She arrived as if she'd been invited, like Helen Jean's home was a familiar thing to her. The fact was that she had never been invited because Helen Jean didn't care for her at all. Although she drank and cursed just as much as, if not more than, Betty Ann, Helen Jean hated that she considered herself a woman of God. She hated that the most. Said people that play with God were the worst kind of people out there. And there was another reason she hated Betty Ann. There was all the talking she did when her daughter left Wayne. Said horrible things that Helen Jean believed but didn't want to hear.

The whole time she sat across from her in the den, Helen Jean talked about how ugly the woman was in her head. She was a short, stout woman with skin black as tar and it looked tree bark rough. And she looked like a frog in the face. Extra wide mouth and thin lips. Eyes set far apart like they were on two different faces. And no neck. She had no neck.

She sat there making small talk at first, like they were friends, and Helen Jean cut her off with a voice that let her know they were nothing. "Betty Ann." She called her name, like she wasn't sitting on the other side of the room. Called her like she had once been prone to calling Marie when she was already out back at the clothesline and had dropped a sock or pair of underwear or something on her way. She thought of that when she called Betty Ann's name. Thought of her daughter and how much of her own face she saw on the child when they found her like they did.

Helen Jean closed her eyes to rid herself of the image and went on. "I reckon you come by for something. Can you gone and get to it? I got things to do."

Betty Ann bucked her big eyes, like a deer caught in front of the bright headlights of an eighteen-wheeler, like a thing that was aware that an end was to be met, like a word needed to spoken and she didn't want to speak it. And then she sighed in a way that Helen took to mean that she was glad to say what she had come to say, that she was glad to be the one to bear this news.

"Ms. Helen, I ain't no gossip. Last thing I want to do is talk about folks. I mean, it was folks what talked about Jesus," she said, adjusting her shoulders so that they were straight, so that she looked proud.

"Well, I don't know who said what about Jesus, but you need to say what you come to say to me. Shit," Helen Jean said as she pressed the striker wheel on her cigarette lighter. There was a long pause and then the wheel stopped. When Betty Ann spoke again, though, the cigarette that rested between Helen Jean's lips slipped and burned a hole through the hem of her good pants.

She moved from the den to the front room after Betty Ann left, and she sat there thinking long after she was gone, long after she brought her business that was supposed to be just Helen Jean's. She thought about all the ways she went wrong with Wayne and about finally making the crooked paths straight.

She hadn't expected her, but Julie B. came from the hallway up to the front room after a while. Just emerged from the back, clutching her daughter's hand, like that was the last thing she had to hold on to. Helen Jean sat in the faithful recliner, which she had come to think of as her thinking seat. She jumped a bit when she saw her daughter standing in the front room doorway, quiet and breathing like she'd just come in from a run.

Helen Jean chuckled, holding her hand to her chest, and said, "Girl, I ain't even know y'all was here. Shoot, like to scared me to death." She tilted her head and looked at her. Saw something frightening in her eyes.

341

Something new. "What's going on, Julie B.? Something wrong?" she asked.

Julie B. looked back down the hall, like she wanted to turn and go back, but when Helen Jean saw her shoulders rising and falling like she would explode in some way, she knew she had heard the conversation with Betty Ann.

"Momma, what Betty Ann saying is true and you got to go get him," she said, looking down at the top of her little girl's head. "It got to be you. You the one put him away from here. Tried to shed him." She looked down at the top of her daughter's head and took a deep breath. "And you always been his one. Go get my baby. He ain't but fourteen. He ain't gone make it out there on his own. And he ain't going in no shed," she said.

Helen Jean could see her teeth gritting and she had never seen anything like that from her. "He ain't going in no shed," she repeated, and Helen Jean saw tears in her eyes and speckles of spit pushing through her lips. And it was the first time she ever felt proud of Julie B. She knew that Julie B. knew what saying that meant. She knew that her daughter was giving him up because she knew it was impossible for them to allow him in the house with what he had done.

With what was in him. And for the first time ever, she wished she had done for her own son what Julie B. was suggesting for hers. She wished that she could've put Wayne away from them all.

And a few hours later, Helen Jean found herself at Wayne's house. It was Alex who came to the door and it broke her heart when his face lit up upon seeing her, because in the same way she had never been able to do anything for herself, for Wayne, she knew that there was nothing she could do to save him.

"Grandmoan," he said, unlatching the screen door, and she heard his voice as a little boy's. All she could do was close her eyes to it.

"Go get in the car," she told him soft as she could. "Get in the car with Grand-daddy." And she watched him and saw that the child must've thought everything was all right. But she knew that he also must've thought that everything was wrong, too.

She watched Homer help him into the back seat of the Buick and swallowed hard as she entered her son's home.

It was a naked place that she couldn't help but compare to her father near the end of his life. Wayne had spent most of his adult life trying to be normal, trying to surround himself with nice things. But when she looked around his place that day, she knew the truth had found him. Wayne had taken pride in all the furnishings and decorations he brought home to his wife at the beginning of their life together, and all those things had passed away. His whole life had. He was a junkie, but she knew that was just the surface of him. Wayne's wife left him when he stopped being able to cover who he was. When he stopped even trying to be human. The whole town knew that.

The house was quiet when she walked through. So quiet she could hear the drip of a faucet somewhere. She found Wayne in the den. The room that he was most proud of when he begged her to come over and see his home for the first and only time, more than a decade before.

There was no carpet on the floor. No tile. It had been stripped to the concrete and the walls were completely bare. The light switch and the outlet covers was gone, and there were no sheets on the queen-sized mattress that lay in the middle of the floor.

She stood there and watched as he held a tiny piece of foil with one hand and let the flame from the lighter burn underneath it. He balanced a clear glass tube between his lips, lowered it on top of the foil, and closed his eyes as he inhaled. When he released his mouth from the glass, everything fell to the ground — the foil, the lighter, everything just fell to the floor. And Wayne exhaled and let himself fall back on the mattress.

His mother stood and watched him for a few moments before walking toward the mattress and kicking it. When her foot touched the mattress, Wayne's body jumped, like he was frightened and surprised that somebody was there at all. He lifted his lazy head and smiled at her. His eyes were sunken and his lips were white. He still had all his teeth, but they were yellow, almost orange, like they hadn't been brushed in a long time.

"It's you," he said, dragging the word like a song. "You finally come by to see about me."

Helen Jean shook her head, swallowed the lump in her throat, and whispered, "I come to get that boy."

And she watched Wayne on the mattress and listened to the moans that escaped his halfway conscious body before hearing words come from her throat, thick and hoarse. "You just like him," she said, kicking the mattress again. "Just like . . ." She sighed. "Just like my father. Always have been. Always," she said.

Wayne exhaled but kept his eyes closed. "Man," he said, slurring in a way that made her think he would pass out before saying another word. He sighed and then exhaled, pushing the air through his lips.

She could see spit spray and watched as some of the tiny bubbles remained on his lips. She frowned her face and cringed.

"That's why you hated me? Hmm," he asked, lazily, eyes still closed. "Yeah," he said, dragging the word out, like it was the beginning of a love ballad. "And you wrong. I wasn't nothing like him, but you let Bacon do that to me and then gave me to that shed."

She could feel the beating of her heart speed up in her chest. He'd said it. She'd always known it, but it had never been said. Confirmed with words. Truth is easy to push down, to make something else when it's an unconfirmed, unspoken thing. What Bacon had done had never been said. But there Wayne was, speaking it — confirming every suspicion she had when she set out to finish that shed with him. When she set out to protect the others from what was in him.

She looked around the room. Looked behind her before turning back to him and leaning in close enough to smell the piss and shit and whatever else reached up and

346

grabbed at her nose from the mattress.

"I never wanted you," she hissed at him. "Never. Tried to shit you out before you ever got a chance to be who you is," she said, standing up and dusting off her clothes, like she had touched a thing that could simply be wiped off.

Wayne pulled himself up on his elbows and gazed in her direction. She looked down at her feet because his eyes had always been too much for her to handle. There was something so uneven and so unreal about how his existence made her feel. She'd tried, she told herself. She'd tried.

"I done knowed who I was for a long time, Momma," he said, letting his hand dangle in front of his chest. "That your daddy was my daddy, too. Bacon give that over to me to hurt me, too." His words dragged and slurred. "I done knowed and I still loved you," he said. And then he began to weep uncontrollably.

She tilted her head to the side and could feel a tingle in her face and quivering in her lips. And then she couldn't hold her head up anymore, so she dropped it. She realized in that moment that if he knew who he was, he knew who she was, too, and locking him in that shed at night had done more to break him than to fix him. And maybe, she had gotten that part wrong.

When she lifted her head back up at him and her eyes found him weeping like that, still loving her like that, she didn't see the monster he was born as, she saw the monster she made.

And for the first time ever, he was really hers. She'd pushed him out into the world and that should have been enough, but she had never seen past all the other mess — the mess that made him. She shook her head, kneeled down beside him, and took him in her arms. For the first time in his life, she looked at him with the eyes of a mother, and she patted his back and said *There, there,* and she never asked about what he did to Ruby Nell, to Alex. She didn't need him to tell her. She knew. And she knew what had to be done.

She took the little packet of yellowing rocks that she'd bought from someone like him and corrupted in a way that could fix all the broken, and she pushed them into the palm of his hand and continued to whisper *There, there.*

After she dropped Alex off at that ranch and made it back home, Julie B. and Jan were there, waiting in the den. Waiting for her. Julie B. stood up when she walked in the door ahead of Homer. She peered into her mother's eyes, like she was looking for something, and Helen Jean wondered for a long time after what her daughter had found.

The little girl stayed sitting on the couch next to where her momma had been, but her young eyes stared at her grandmother in way that she thought unnatural for a girl so young. They talked to her, those eyes. Asked her questions. *Am I gone die cause of you, too? You gone kill me, too, Grandmoan?* Her eyes looked like judgment. So much that she had to look away from the child. So much that she couldn't bear looking at her too much after that day.

Julie B. shook her head and reached out for her daughter's hand. Helen Jean could tell she would cry, and she could tell she didn't want her to see it. So she and Homer stood there as the mother and daughter disappeared through the kitchen to the back of the house, and she wanted to call out to her, to tell her that the sons never make it.

After a while, Helen Jean turned and put her whole face in her man's chest and she thought about the son she couldn't love somewhere breathing his last breath.

16
LYDIA

As we make the short drive to the projects where Jan lives, we're silent. She's humming what sounds like a congregational hymn. I can feel sweat beads forming right above my upper lip. It's hot inside her truck, but I don't want to say anything to offend my cousin. Besides, I'm thinking about the text I just received from Walter.

I won't do this anymore. You continue to push me away. We should discuss next steps when you return.

I want to call him. To save us, but I don't know how.

"We give up easy," Jan says out of nowhere. "Something killed the fight in us."

I nod.

"I'm ugly as this whole place is," she adds.

"No you aren't, Jan," I say. "You're beautiful. You've always been beautiful."

She shakes her head and we ride in silence for a while.

"The night Laverne killed herself. You know," she finally says before sighing deeply. "Alex came back home?" She looks over at me, briefly, and then returns her gaze to the road. "Grandmoan think don't nobody know about it but my momma and Granddaddy, but I saw him, too," she says. "That's the night she sent him to that shed. You know the one that was always in the backyard? That's the night she knew what he was."

I nod. I remember the shed in my grandmother's backyard. Before everything fell apart in Jerusalem, before my father — Soweo — left and my mother lost herself, I asked Mother about the shed. I thought it would make a good playhouse for Jan and me. It was small enough. Looked dollish enough. It even had windows and a porch. Mother narrowed her eyes and seemed to leave the room without really leaving. I placed my hand on her shoulder and she jerked her body, as if I'd startled her. As if I'd just entered the room.

Y'all can't never go in that shed. Nothing good come out of there. God ain't nowhere about that mess, she said. But she never really had to worry. Grandmoan never let us play out back anyway. We were only ever allowed out front.

And I wonder what Jan is telling me. *That's the night she knew what he was.* Perhaps she's telling me that our grandmother caught him. That she had walked in and witnessed in the same way I had. Jan's little legs dangling off the bed underneath the weight of all that pain.

I sit silently as we pass the old church where we once sang in the Sunshine Band. The white paint on the building is peeling and curling up into itself. The original wooden planks are now visible. There are two white — or once-white — vans that look a lot like the ones that used to pick us up from Grandmoan's in the small parking lot. The letters are worn away, but the words *Ford Memorial* can still be made out on one of the vans.

I think about *that* night. When Laverne killed herself. It was normal — we were normal up until my father was arrested. By the time that night rolled around, it had been months since I'd witnessed what confused and shamed me for years. A shame that I had no claim to, but I carried it as if it were mine. I wasn't supposed to see it. Nobody was. They weren't even supposed to be in the house. None of us were. But

352

Jan had been sent to bed for knocking on the door to use the restroom, and, shortly after her sentence, Alex had come home to relieve himself. He had been welcomed in by Grandmoan. *Gone boy. Go use it,* she told him when he tapped on the door and told her what he needed.

And I was left outside alone, so I risked tapping on the door and being sent to be with Jan. As soon as I tapped my knuckles on Grandmoan's door I was sentenced to bed, too. When I walked through the den into the kitchen, Aunt Marie was standing at the sink doing dishes. She didn't even look up. She didn't even seem to notice me.

I walked slowly down the hall, trying to tiptoe past the bathroom. The last thing I wanted was for Alex to come out and thump me or trip me or do something mean. Those were the kinds of games he played, and I hated them all.

But when I walked into the back bedroom that Jan shared with her mother and brother, I saw her tiny legs sticking out from under his body and his pants were pulled down past his bottom. I didn't make a sound. I just stood there and listened to her muffled whimpers and watched as his bottom humped up and down on top of her.

Eventually, I began to step back slowly,

and I opened the door and ducked into the empty bathroom for what seemed like forever. When the door handle jiggled, I knew it was him. He didn't know I was there. He had left the bathroom light on as his alibi. He hadn't expected me to really occupy it. He began to tap on the door, and I took a deep breath and opened it. I squeezed by him without looking in his face, but I could feel his gaze burning through me. Seeing through me.

Jan's voice cuts through my thoughts. "I kept quiet about it. All these years, I ain't never said nothing to nobody. About what he looked like. About his eyes. I ain't never say nothing. At first, it was cause I was mad your momma took Marie and left me that night. Over there was like heaven and y'all didn't even take me." She exhales. "Then it just got so old that it was something that just belonged to me. It was ugly of me to keep it to myself. I *am* ugly. Just like this old ugly town," Jan admits.

I shake my head as she turns into the parking lot of the complex she lives in. "It doesn't make you ugly. You didn't do those things to yourself, Jan."

She shakes her head. "Nope. Nuh-uh. I should've told my auntie about Alex that night. I should've told her what I saw.

Maybe she'd be all right," she says, patting her palm against her leg.

And I realize that we're discussing two different things. I want to ask her what's so significant — so different about that night. I want to ask her what she thinks my mother should've known, but I also want to stay in this moment of us being something kind to each other. I don't want to push her away from me. I want my cousin to be better. To be less angry with me.

"Momma better bring them straight home after they leave the grocery store. I don't want them round him," she says. And I feel bad for her. I can tell that she's afraid for her kids, and in that moment, I'm not ashamed of my relief that my own haven't survived. I'm also glad that I don't live in this place. This place where the past is a constant haunting. A constant pain. Jan's stuck in this place. Living so close to him. So close to them.

She parks in front of the building where she's lived since her first child was born. It's nice for government housing. Projects. They've been rebuilt since we were children. Then, they were six-floor pea green buildings; now they're redbrick duplexes. There are potted plants — golden pothos, I think — on the porch of the unit that we are in front of. About six small pots on the ground and two larger ones hung on hooks above the walkway. The leaves of the plants are flowing from the pots to a point that they appear to be reaching out to the earth. Looks like a jungle — a small, beautiful jungle. A colorful wind chime hangs above the doorway. It reminds me of the one that Walter put up in the nursery the first time I was pregnant.

"Did you ever tell anybody about it? About . . . You know?" Jan asks as we both climb out of the car.

And I stand there and try to figure out what she means. I didn't see Alex that night — the night she's been stuck on. I wasn't at Grandmoan's. I was with Mother. We were searching for Soweo. But right before I ask her what she means, it dawns on me. She thinks that Alex *really* happened to us both. Her patience with me is so thin already. I don't want to disappoint her, so I respond, "I had to. You know, my husband. He has to know everything about me."

"Oh," she says.

When we enter her apartment, the scent of bleach invades my nostrils. I can see the whole apartment from the entryway. Straight ahead is a small, clean kitchen. There is a bucket with a mop stuck inside it leaning against the wall. To the left are bedroom doors, and to the right is a living room that reminds me of the one we could never enter at Grandmoan's. There is no television in Jan's living room, so I assume the same rule Grandmoan has about not entering her living room applies at Jan's.

Jan heads toward the last bedroom door, where I can see part of a nightstand and the headboard of a bed. "You gone just stand there?" She turns to me. "Come on in. Sit down in there." She points toward the living room. "Let me get changed."

I hesitate before walking toward the room and notice that the walls are painted a warm beige color, identical to the furniture. There are three mirrors on each of the three walls in the room, but all of them are hung far above actual eye level. An ottoman serves as the coffee table and I consider sitting on it, so that I don't mess up the arrangement of extra pillows that decorate the sofa and love seat. I lean my shoulder against the wall and gaze into the darkness that is supposed to be the window. The dark brown drapes are drawn closed. This causes darkness to swallow the whole apartment.

Walter's last text was final and I can't stop thinking about it. He always says that there is power in the tongue — in the words we speak. It's one of the reasons I've never uttered it. I've never said out loud that who I am — who I was born to be — won't let me be a mother. Walter wouldn't say something he doesn't mean because he knows that words make things real.

In the beginning, we spoke life over ourselves. We wanted four children in all. Two girls and two boys. Built-in friends all the way around. It was so important to me back then. To have children and make him happy in that way. And I still want to make him happy. I still want us to work. I want to be willing to do whatever it takes to make that happen. He's been patient with me since the beginning. I just thought . . . I don't know what I thought.

A few Christmases ago, after we lost the second child, we were walking through a parking lot of Christmas trees, trying to pick out a suitable one for the high ceiling in our foyer.

When we have children, what holiday traditions should we pass on?

I shook my head no and looped my arm around his back. *After my father — we were . . . Mother and I didn't have many,* I said, shaking my head again.

He nodded. *Yeah, I guess not,* he said. And then he smiled. *But we can create our* own. *We'll build a world no other kid has ever seen for ours. We'll . . .* The frigid air caused a cloud of cold to escape his mouth with his words.

I removed my hand from around his back and folded both arms into my chest. *It's cold out here,* I said.

He tilted his head to the side and the already slow pace of his walking stopped.

Lydia, he said. I stopped walking, too. *I know this is hard for you,* he said, making a W of himself by throwing up his hands and arms. *But who are we if we can't speak the things we desire into being?* He sighed and took a small step toward me. His voice softened and he said, *I love you, and nothing can change that. I'm here now, baby. You aren't alone anymore. I'm here and I want all of you.*

I nodded and thought about the babies we'd lost and the ones I would give him to show him what he meant to me. I promised myself that the next one would stick. And then I thought about my mother. About how she wasn't able to be a mother to me. I thought about being exactly like her, and I shivered and shook my head at the thought, before I sighed and said, *What did I ever do to deserve you?*

You better hold on to me, he said, placing his gloved hands on his chest and tilting his head to the side.

We both laughed and I wanted to keep laughing, but his laughter died away and his face became serious. *I'm here for everything, baby. Everything. Till death do us part.*

I nodded again. *Yeah,* I started, widening my eyes and lifting my brows. *We can do this,* I said, pointing my finger at the ground. *We can come out as a family and pick a real tree as a family. All six of us. This can be our tradition.* I shrugged. *It's simple, but I never did it before you.*

He nodded. *It's perfect, baby. The perfect thing to pass on.* His brown eyes were smiling, even though his thick lips trembled from the cold.

And I don't know if it was the hormones, as we didn't know yet then, but I was pregnant, or if it was my guilt, but my emotions got the best of me. I felt tears catching in my throat and then my eyes, and he must've seen them, too. He closed the small space between us and wrapped his arms around me. He rubbed the middle of my back and whispered, *I'm so glad we found each other. I'm so glad I get to do life with you.*

We must've looked so in love, standing in that parking lot, locked in such a tight embrace. I believe we were — we are. I know why he's leaving. I can't blame him for that. I know what I've done.

When he released me from our embrace that day, he stuffed his gloved hands in the pocket of his black wool coat and looked up.

I think this is it, he said as he fixed his eyes on the tree that hovered above our heads. It wasn't beautiful. In fact, it appeared narrow and skimpy. The bottom of it was wide, but it leaned to the side. A lot of the needles were browning, and even at twenty feet tall, something about it was small.

That one? I asked, scrunching up my nose.

Why not? he asked, looking back at me, then up at the tree. *Nothing is perfect. I like finding things a little rough,* he said, frowning and pointing over my shoulder toward the best tree on the lot. *If it's perfect in the beginning, we can't watch it become by our hands.*

And if ever there was a time that we were perfect, it was that day. A day when we didn't know we could lose so much and then turn around and lose each other. We planned the world out in our heads, and none of it can happen.

I reach into my bag and pull out my

phone. Wiping at the tears that I realize are on my face with my left hand, I grip the phone with my right and go into the text message that Walter sent me earlier and hit reply and type:

Our babies don't just keep dying. They are dying because of me. Because of my grandmother. My mother. Because I'm just like them. There's something wrong with me, Walter.

Then I hit send.

17
JAN

She in my living room. Wonder what she think. I know she got a fancy house in Dallas, but my place nice, too. I spend my whole tax return each year buying new stuff for it. I love income tax time. It's the only time I ever have more than the four hundred dollars I get from Omar each month. I let him carry the kids as his dependents cause I ain't never really earned enough money to get anything back for them. He give me eight hundred dollars a child. I feel rich every spring.

I kick the flip-flops off my feet, slide out the jeans I'm wearing, and toss them on the bed. I been uncomfortable ever since I first put them on. I won't try them again for a while since they done got too tight. I turn around to face myself in the mirror that sit behind my dresser.

"Want something to drink?" I yell through the open door. My lips dry and ashy, so I stick my finger in the tub of the topless Vaseline sitting on my dresser. A few hair bows and rubber bands stuck in the grease from when I do Jazera's hair. I'm careful not to fish them out as I slide my finger around the side to scrape off the extra Vaseline.

"I got Kool-Aid and Dr Pepper," I add after Lil don't answer. "I keep me some Dr Pepper."

I slide my finger across my top lip and then rub my top and bottom lip together. I look better when my lips ain't white but only if I keep my mouth closed. I rub the extra grease on my finger off on the T-shirt I'm wearing. It's old and faded anyway. The airbrushed faces of Omar and me before I got pregnant with Javon barely visible now. I comb through my hair with my fingers. I can't afford to go to the beauty shop, so most of the time I wear it pulled back in a ponytail or all over my head. I open the middle drawer and find my favorite cotton leggings folded neatly on top of everything else in the drawer. I pull them out and push the drawer back in with my knee. I back up to the bed, plop down, and start putting them on.

"Lil?" I call out again. "You hear me?" She don't respond. I hurry the tights up my thighs and stand quickly, pulling them up past my butt. I slide my feet back in the flip-flops and head toward the living room.

"It ain't *that* big in here," I say as I walk up to her. She leaning against the wall and her back is to me. "You can't hear me calling you?"

She sniff and turn around. She crying, and I see money let you be pretty even when you cry.

"What's wrong —"

"He says we can still talk about it," she say, and close her eyes and lift her head toward the ceiling.

"Huh?" I say. I make my way over to the sofa, close to where she standing. "Sit down, Lil," I offer, pointing to the love seat that sit so close the sofa that the arms almost touch. She look in the direction of my finger but cross over me and sit down on the sofa next to me.

"My husband." She sigh. "I owe him an explanation. I've kept something very important from him, like children. Why my body rejects our children," she say, and I'm trying to keep up cause all her words coming out like one, like they crashing into one another, like she throwing up something she want to keep down. She exhale and shake her head and I can hear cracking in her voice. "I just didn't want to lose him because of all of my shit, you know?" And she looking at me like she want me to say something.

But I can't speak cause my mind spinning and she cussing in my house and talking about her body and her marriage and I don't know where to put all this stuff.

When I don't say nothing, she tilt her head, almost like she looking at something pitiful. And she say, "And Jan," dragging my name out, like a soft and throaty song. "I lied to you, too," she say, almost in a whisper that she don't really want me to hear. "I — I never told about any of it because Alex . . . He never did to me what he did to you."

"Oh," I say, and it feel like she done punched me in my gut and knocked all the wind out of me. I think about how just a few minutes ago, I was feeling free with her, like I didn't have to hide nothing about myself. I was feeling a way with her that I don't feel with nobody else, and I think about getting mad with her. She done tricked me into telling her something and then she back out. I feel myself getting mad — ready to blow up — but then I'm distracted by her tears. *Why she crying?* I'm thinking.

"But I saw what he did to you, Jan. I saw

it and I've carried it with me all this time," she say. And that she seen me like that make me shame before her. I want her to leave, but she crying and her tears seem like something sacred.

"I always thought something was wrong with all of us. My father, your brother, and who knows who else. What does that say about us, you know? That we come from such mess? I felt so filthy. So ashamed. The whole time I was growing up. Even after I was grown." She shrug it off, like she don't care, but she don't mean it. I can tell. "I never told him about where my father died or why he was there. Not the kind of things you want to tell you somebody you're dating, you know?" She look at me like I do. And then she shrug again and say, "And he wasn't my father. That's why I didn't look like him."

And that last little bit jab me and I can't even want her to leave no more. All I say is "Oh" and feel stupid for trying to make her feel bad about not looking like him. Even though I ain't got no daddy, I don't want to see nobody else without one.

"We were seeing a movie that day. Mother and me. We were all supposed to go, but my father's blood pressure was up. Headache. Had worked out of town for a few days. I remember that much," she say, nodding like she won a prize or something. "I was so happy to see him when he walked in that day. He never left us overnight like that. Mother said he'd gone to Dallas and I couldn't understand why we didn't go with him. When he walked in that day, I was jumping all over him. Asking him questions. Telling him about all the commotion at Grandmoan's. I guess . . ."

She go quiet for a minute and she looking at her hands. Then she say, "I imagine we were there when the police knocked on our door," she shrug. "*The Color Purple.* I imagine we were right at the part where my mother was crying. Right at that part where Mister told Sophia and Harpo that it was nice to see them together again." She kind of twist up her face and say, "I couldn't for the life of me understand why Mother took me to see that. I was young for something like that."

She stand up with her eyes fixed on my window curtains. Her suit make me uncomfortable. It look hot and inappropriate. She walk over to the window, and I don't say nothing. She reach her arms up and draw the curtains open. The room bright now. I don't know how I feel about that.

"When we drove up to our duplex, I said,

'Somebody burning trash on our porch, Momma.' And I really thought they were. I was so young."

She stand facing the window, so I can't see her face, but her voice shake and I know she still crying.

"I saw the smoke rising from that crumpled pile of dark matter and knew for sure it was a trash bag." She reach down and pull one of her shoes off by the heel. "This thing has been killing me all day."

She hold it in both hands and stare down at it like it's the first time she ever seen it.

"It's because my right foot is bigger than my left," she say. "Maybe I'm really a size nine in that foot." She laugh.

"What do you do about something like that? An eight and a half in one foot and a nine in the other." She got a sad smile on her face, and my heart go out to her.

I done heard the stories about her daddy. What they say he did to Laverne. Him going to prison. His death. And how all of it broke my aunt in more pieces than one person ought to be. I know for a fact half of the tales I done heard ain't true. The only story I know to be true is the one about the hog cause I know that's Grandmoan way. Something she done before any of us knew her. I want to hear what Lil believe, but it feel strange to just sit here and listen and not say nothing.

"We ain't get to go see it when it was at the movies," I say.

She look up from the shoe and her eyes fall on me. "*The Color Purple,*" I add.

She ignore what I just said and say, "Mother knew and I didn't. I didn't put it together right away. Looking back, I saw it in her eyes that night. They screamed it before she even jumped out of that car and ran toward the smoke. Maybe it was the musky, sweet perfume smell, mixed with the scent of leather being tanned over a flame."

She pause, bend her knees a little bit, and drop the shoe back down to the floor. It land upright instead of on its side.

"It wasn't really a smell. I think it was a more of a taste," she say after a while.

The tears gone from her voice now. A old Chevy Blazer pass the window, and the loud bass seem to rattle everything in my apartment.

"Rotting steak or greening-at-the-edges swine," she say, and I try to follow what she talking about.

She nod. "Maybe it was just that she knew Grandmoan. But whatever it was, she knew he wasn't coming back to that duplex."

And that make me think about what I

know. What I always knew. Alex raped that girl, not Soweo. Grandmoan knew it, too. I knew it when I saw his face that night. I knew by the way she talked to him. I sat behind that deep freezer and heard everything. Every secret thing.

It wasn't never Soweo. Seem like everybody but Lil know that.

I surprise myself with my own voice. "What happened to him — to your daddy — I mean, Soweo?"

She slip her foot back into her shoe and walk back toward the sofa. "He had a stroke in his cell," she say. Then she pass the sofa, heading to the front door. I follow her with my eyes.

I bring my hand to my own heart. Want her to know I'm sorry about that, but I don't say nothing.

She shrug. "He must've laid there all night before the guards realized something was wrong," she say, still moving to the front door, like she about to leave, like she about to just cut off on our conversation. And then she just pause. Stand there for minute and look back at me with a sad half smile on her lips. "He probably could've lived if he wasn't in there." She shake her head and sniff. "And I don't know how I feel about how much I still miss him and wish he had been free so he could've. So he could've survived." She shrug. "I know. I know what he did. I mean, he had to be — he was there for *that* crime," she say, and then she start back moving toward the front door.

And that make me feel guilty about everything. Make me feel like her little ten-minute lie ain't nothing compared to what I been holding. It's just wrong and I want to make it right, like she made herself right with me, but I got to do it before she leave out my house. "It wasn't him, Lil!" I yell out to her. I can hear my words crashing on top of each other, like I'm speaking in tongues. "It wasn't him. It was Alex. Soweo ain't touch that girl," I say. The words spill out my mouth fast, like low-fat milk or something clear.

She stop moving and look at me. Tears running down her face like I done cursed her. It seem like she looking at me forever, and then she smile real weak, look down at the floor, and start moving again.

I wonder where she going — if she saw something through the window I didn't or if she just want to get away from me. I think about going to the window, but I hear the door click just before she put her hand on it to pull it open.

Javon and Jazera stumble through the

door; they eyes look real scared and panicked. I move quick to where they at.

"What is it, babies? What happened?" I
ask, and I can hear my words rushing out
like vomit. I can feel tingling in my face.
Lord, not them, I say to myself. Please not
my babies, too. I can feel my lips shaking as
tears start to blur my eyes. My momma appear in the doorway. She out of breath, like
she been running a marathon or something.

"What's wrong with you?" She frown,
breathing hard. "They called you already?"
she ask, and push her way past the kids.

She done always acted so clueless. I want
her to stop acting dumb and tell me what
she let her son do to my babies.

"I didn't think you'd be one to get all
shook up," she say, still trying to catch her
breath. "But let's gone and get up there
before they do it, and we don't get to pay
our respects."

"Huh?" I'm confused. I don't know what
she talking about. They all look like something done happened. Like trauma on
repeat in my life.

"Momma," my momma say, and frown at
me again and then look over at Lil. "What's
wrong with this girl? Y'all in here fussing,"
she ask Lil before she sigh and turn back to
Javon and Jazera. I look at them, too. And I

realize they look more out of breath than afraid.

"Next time y'all beat me, you ain't getting no ice cream," she say, and they all start laughing.

"Granny, you just too old and slow," Javon say.

"All grannies is," Jazera add, giggling.

I smile and wipe the tears from my eyes. My momma put her hand on my shoulder. She gone always be clueless. She can't understand my fear, and I don't understand why she ain't got none.

"Let's go. They gone wait till we get there to say bye to her, but they say it's time. She brain-dead," she tell me. Ain't no sadness in her voice.

I'm still smiling. "I thought you took them back over there," I tell her.

I feel my smile stretch wider, and I look at Lil. My stomach start to jiggle, and I feel laughter creeping up. I don't recognize it as my own when it first come out, but it feel good and bad at the same time.

"I thought she took them back," I say to Lil, pointing at my momma.

I can't control the way my body moving on the count of my laughing, but I still try by bending it forward and grabbing hold of my stomach. I feel the tears I just wiped away come back, and I try to stand up straight again. I really don't want them to see me like this, but I can't stop the loud scream that want to pop through my throat. I see Lil arms go up and Momma grab my babies and pull them to the kitchen. I feel Lil arms come down around my shoulders, and I wrap mine tight around her back.

"Why is it like this?" I scream into her shoulder. I can hear my voice. It's muffled and sad, but it feel good. "Why life got to be so hard like this?"

I feel her rubbing my back in a way that nobody else ever have. Her voice make me want to bury myself inside her shoulder and she keep repeating, "It's okay, Jan. I'm here. I'm here."

I ain't never really cried out loud like this before. Not even when I was a little girl.

I'm glad when I hear Momma say, "Javon, take your sister to your room. I'll come get you fore we leave." I hear they feet shuffle away on the tile and wonder how they gone look at me when they get back. Lil start rocking me in her arms, and I feel the storm of my tears going away.

"He was my brother," I say into her shoulder. "Why he have to go and do that to me?"

It's quiet for a moment, except for my

375

sniffing and the deep sighs and heaving that come with real tears.

"You my daughter," Momma say, finally. "And he my son."

I raise my head from Lil shoulder, and her hold on me loosen up, but she don't let go. Momma standing in the kitchen, arms behind her back. I don't want to hate my momma, so I don't never look at her straight on. From the side of my eyes, she done always looked old and tired. I always catch glimpses of her in bright colored wind-suits that swallow her small body. She always look like some jacked-up character from the '80s movie *Breakin'*. I almost laugh when I think about her jumping down to the floor and spinning on her head like they do in the movie, but instead I let my eyes focus on her — really look at her.

She look kind of healthy and full today. Almost happy at first sight. She wearing modern clothes — yoga pants and a T-shirt — and her hair slicked back in a bun. The gray of it don't look so dingy. The hard lines on her face been there ever since I known her, but the teeth and the tears in her eyes is new. Everything about her seem new.

"What I'm posed to do? Who would you pick out of your two?" She shift her weight to her left hip, and slide her right foot out slightly. "I love all my children. Y'all all I ever had that was mine," she say. She bring her right hand around, balled into a fist, and pull it up to her hip. She look at Lil hard before she look down at the floor of my kitchen.

She bring her hand to her chest and say, "When Momma put him in that shed and he run off, it was me who made her go get him and put him away. I put him away from Wayne and I put him away from you," my momma say, still looking at the floor.

"Momma, why can't you look at me?" I ask. And I think about her looking like somebody new and me trying to get out of here. I think about Grandmoan "put-up" money and something in me know. "Why you look different?" I ask.

"Wayne was my brother just like y'all my kids. Y'all don't know what we went through in that house. What *he* went through in that house," she say. "Momma built that shed and locked him away. She hated him with all her heart." Her lips quivering, and she almost look pretty to me. Her shoulders drop down and then begin to shake in a rising and falling kind of motion. And something feel wrong about all of it.

"Momma, look at me," I say.

Her eyes stay on the floor. I let go of Lil,

377

and she let go of me, too. We standing there looking at my momma cause neither of us seen her like this before.

I finally say, "I been trying to deal with this on my own my whole life. Here you is knowing. Done always knowed, and you won't even look at me?"

When she finally speak again her voice is deep and throaty. "When Alex come home with shit in his pants that day, my first mind say it was Wayne. I knowed about Wayne. I knowed everything about Wayne. When you quiet and scared, folk don't spect you in the shadows watching," she say.

"But I erased that thought out my head. Wayne hadn't never give me no reason to think he want my little boy. Anybody little boy. And I tried not to notice. But at some point, I knowed. I knowed it in my heart. And I couldn't let my momma lock him in that shed like she did Wayne, so I ain't tell her nothing."

She breathe in deep and exhale slow, and then she put her eyes on Lil, like she want to burn a hole through her, and she say, "It's just so much I don't know how to undo it. What was I posed to do? Whole damn family have to come undone."

I look at Lil. Her eyes on my momma like she can see right through her. Her face blank. She waiting for my momma next word, like me.

Momma take her left hand and rub the back of it across both her eyes in one swipe and finally lift her head up. Even though the tears gone, her face twisted up and she almost look like she got a clue. Then it go straight. She clear the twisted look up, and her face clear of everything. Her eyes get all empty and she stare into mine.

She shake her head. "Nuh-uh. Thought I could do this, but I can't," she say, and turn her back and start messing with the empty paper towel holder on my cabinet, the one she found for me at a garage sale a few months ago. She hold it up over her shoulder without turning back around to face us. "I don't see how you can get nothing done in here without one paper towel on this holder." She put it back down and rest her palms flat on the counter, like she centering herself for yoga. She don't turn around and look at me and Lil. She don't want us to see what she feel. To know her in that way.

"Doing all this don't help nothing," she say, and blow out a deep breath, like everything getting on her nerves. "Let's go and move the hell on from all of this," she say, and grunt, pushing herself away from the counter. She start out of the kitchen toward the kids' room.

"All the talking in the world won't help this shit, January. Just move the hell on from it," she say, throwing the words over her shoulder like trash on the street. And then she disappear into Javon bedroom.

Lil and me, we just stand there, closer to each other than we ever been. Lil put her hand on my shoulder. "I'm here, you know?" she whisper.

I look down at her fancy pumps and shake my head.

She place her finger under my chin and lift my head until our eyes meet.

She shake her head slow and say, "I won't leave you again. I'm here now, Jan. I won't . . ."

"I know," I say after she cut herself off. She shift her eyes toward the ceiling and exhale. I can smell her breath. It smell good, like she chewing spearmint gum, but I ain't seen her jaws moving at all.

She drop her head back down to where her eyes with mine again, but then she close hers.

"I'm so sorry for leaving you, Jan. I won't ever leave you like that again," she say, and for the first time in a long time, I trust that she won't.

18
ALEX

I watched them drive away from the window of Grandmoan's living room. I saw the kids jump out of Jan's car and run to Julie B. I saw Lydia go to Jan's car, tap on the window, and get in. Julie B. stood there kind of smiling at them. Kind of tilting her head like she was proud, ignoring the kids as they tugged at her arms and showed her how excited they was to be with her. How much she means to them. And I just stood in the window watching cause nothing good can come from me trying to be part of what they have.

Laverne was an accident. Jan, too, but Laverne really was. One the biggest regrets I'll always have is her swinging from that jump rope. It was a Friday when I saw her skipping down Colgate. I was at the corner, coming from the snow cone house. Grandmoan had put me away, told me to stop aggravating the girls earlier that day, and I had spent the afternoon hitting prairie dogs with rocks with a makeshift slingshot. I don't know what possessed me to grab that girl. To be thrilled and aroused by her fear of me.

"Hey, boy," Granddaddy says, calling me from the den. "Thought you was coming over here to check on your old granddaddy."

I pull myself away from the window and head toward the den. The house doesn't belong on the east side anymore. Not since the updates. Although Grandmoan banned me from it after she was sure about what I'd done, I've driven by for years, making sure it was still standing, making sure they were alive. Sometimes, I'd ride by real slow and gaze at her sitting on the porch. Her shoulders slumped a little more than I remembered. She wouldn't look away no matter what. She didn't turn her eyes away from me. But there was nothing I could see in them from the car. Nothing that told me I was forgiven.

"I did come by to check on you, Grand-daddy," I say, chuckling a little bit.

He's sitting in her La-Z-Boy, snuggled underneath a thin blanket. There are holes in the arms of the chair. I can see the yellow sponge stuffing inside. His chair leans to the side from age more than it should, but he looks comfortable. And it's hard for me to believe I'm inside the house again, after all these years. I still don't know if I should be grateful to Grandmoan for keeping me out of prison or angry with her for putting me out at fourteen. I sit on the arm of the brown leather couch across from Granddaddy's chair.

"You know your grandmomma don't want you in here," he says.

His good eye is peering through me. The other, the glass one, protrudes slightly from the socket.

"I know," I reply. It embarrasses me a little that he's speaking about my banishment out loud. It's always been a silent thing. Something we all just understood.

"But Granddaddy love all his grandchildren. Don't matter y'all ain't my blood. Granddaddy don't care bout none of that," he says. "And I don't care what you done."

He reaches down beside the chair and scoops up a faded-to-green brass plant pot, and brings it up to his mouth and spits a brown thick slime into it.

"Ain't a-one of us perfect, Alex. Not one of us. Can choose sides all day, but everybody answer to God. Even her."

"Yes, sir," I say just as the telephone rings.

"Hand me that," he says. I reach over to

383

the end table that holds the old rotary phone.

After Granddaddy gets the phone, I stand to give him the privacy. Photos are all over the room. I don't remember all of these pictures being here when I was a kid. I see the framed faces of people I don't know on the coffee table, end tables, and on hanging shelves. Black-and-white framed photos mixed in with family portraits decorate walls that were once wood-paneled. When I look closer, I see that most of the photos are the stock ones that came with the frames, but there are some real ones — some that I recognize. There's a picture of her and who I assume is one of her brothers from back when she was young. She's wearing a Supremes wig and she's not smiling, but her brother is. They look alike with their humped noses and creased foreheads.

I shift my eyes to the photo beside that one. I see my own young face smiling back at me. Julie B. is sitting with Jan on her lap, and I'm standing behind her smiling, displaying two front spaces where teeth should be. I'll never forget that Sunday. It was after Uncle Wayne had started with me, but life was still good. I hadn't touched my sister yet. All the pain was contained within me. It was still all just in me.

It was the first and last family portrait I was ever a part of. Julie B. had been so proud of how nice we all looked as we sat on the bus stop that Sunday morning and waited for the Citibus to come and take us to Kmart to have our picture made.

I don't have to ask nobody for a dime today. I remember her words as she smiled wide and licked her thumb, then dabbed her wet finger at the side of my mouth. *It's gone be like this every day, one day,* she said.

I look away from the picture and see Granddaddy hanging up the phone. He doesn't say anything. He just looks out the French doors that have been installed in the den. The backyard is on the other side of the doors. The grass back there looks artificial, but it's nice. There was no grass back there when we were kids, just red dirt that made my allergies bother me.

When I first got here, I stood there, looked out at the shed, and remembered. It didn't look as torturous as it had when she banished me to it. In fact, it looked quite normal sitting in the corner of the yard. I closed my eyes to the memory of spiders, field mice, and the leaky tin roof that I slept under in my last days at Grandmoan's. About a week after she put me out there, Julie B. started coming in and sitting on the edge of the tiny cot when she brought my food at night. The first time she did that, she scanned the shed with her eyes and said, *At least she ain't locking you in. At least she ain't doing that.*

From where I'm standing now, I can't see the shed, but I can see that a huge meat smoker sits in the center of the clean, cemented patio. A little black-and-white ball of fur stands up and starts barking when he notices Granddaddy's gaze. I chuckle.

"That's Panda," Granddaddy says. "Grandmoan don't like *her* in the house, either. She couldn't handle that."

The dog must be a miniature something, yet it's attached to the smoker by a thick chain. It can hardly move itself toward Granddaddy's gaze because of the weight of its heavy chain, so it just stands there and barks.

"Panda been in that yard for years," Granddaddy says, shaking his head. "I don't care how little she look; she a outside dog." He chuckles. "Eat you up if you go out there."

I turn my eyes away from the dog and let them roam the rest of the room. There are so many new things in this place. Open entryways where doors used to be. High ceilings where they were once leveled. This

386

looks like a home. Like Grandmoan has tried to make herself a home. I tell myself this is a second chance, but I know better than that.

If I really had another chance, I would go all the way back to that day with Laverne. I wouldn't offer her that handful of Chick-O-Sticks, and then pull her into the old house on Bates Street that had been boarded up since the '70s. She only came with me because she was afraid of me, and I knew that. I liked that. She was almost shaking like a cold dog when I told her I'd punch her in the back of her head if she didn't climb through that window where I knew the board was loose. I wouldn't push her through to hurry her up, like I did. She fell through, hit the ground so hard her lip split and her front tooth broke. I didn't even flinch then, but now, if something possessed me to do a fucked-up thing like that, I would. I would flinch. I wouldn't turn her over and see her busted lip, broken tooth, and scared eyes, and still ball my fist up and slam it into the middle of her face. Or flip her limp body back over and push her yellow sundress up to where it covered up the patches of her auburn hair. I wouldn't pull at her flower panties so hard that they rip a little but not completely. I would be sad about her whimpering the way she was as I kept pulling at them till they ripped all the way off. And there is no way in hell I'd climb on top of her and shove myself in her ass, the same way Uncle Wayne had done mine so many times before.

For a long time, I thought I was better because I can't even think about what I did to her and not want to throw up. But after Samra, someone I looked at like a little sister, after my response to her body pressed against mine, I don't know if Veola should trust me around her little girls. I don't want to be who I am, but what do I do? What am I supposed to do with myself?

"Can you drive me to the hospital?" Granddaddy finally asks.

"Is everything okay?" I ask.

He lets out a loud grunt as he struggles to get up from the chair. "Nawh, son. Nothing round here never been okay. But we still got to keep on going, don't we?"

We ride in silence, except for Granddaddy's humming. I doubt he's ever been in the front seat of a police cruiser, but he's not in awe. He's humming what sounds like a blues song, and I don't know what to say to break the absence of words. I've never been close to him. It was always her. Always me and her.

And I wonder why. Wonder what it is I love about her. Wonder what she loved about me. She was my focal point before I ever realized we all needed one. My hope in her forgiveness is what has carried me across these years. All I've ever wanted to do is make things right with her. Feel like making things right with her might heal me.

Granddaddy stops humming and says, "We had to sell the hog pen on the count of y'all." He grunts and shakes his head.

"Didn't nobody want to help — stick around and see what the end was gone be. Wayne gone. You was gone. Wasn't nobody willing," he says, without taking his eyes away from the window.

"Sometimes . . ." he begins, but only returns to humming.

When I was little, they'd take me to the hog pen with them. I'd sit between them in the single cab of that old hog pen truck. Grandmoan was always the silent one. Granddaddy would sit in that driver's seat and talk about all kinds of things. His day at the chip factory, people who were sick or dying, or even the weather. He'd fill the silence with words that meant almost nothing. Most often, Grandmoan kept her eyes in the direction of the road ahead of us, and even when he laughed at his own jokes, she didn't crack a smile.

Some of his stories were interesting, like the time he told us about his friend Smitty losing his hand in one of the machines at work. He talked about blood splattering everywhere, even on the chips. About how things were shut down but he was sure some of the bloody chips made it into bags and out to the public. But I watched her ignore him and learned to ignore him myself. Even though I thought about that story — about a lot of his stories — for days after he told them, I never once said anything to him about them.

If he made a mistake on the road, swerved or stopped too abruptly, she'd tell him to shut up right in the middle of his talking. Just say *Nigger, shut up and pay attention. You kill us and I'm gone blow your brains out.* On those days we'd ride in silence, except for Granddaddy's humming.

"Nothing scare your grandmomma more than death," he says. "Ever since I knowed her, she been looking over her shoulder for him."

I don't say anything. Just keep my eyes on the road.

"I don't think she scared no more. Haven't been for a long time," he says, and then he chuckles. "Granddaddy and Grandmoan ain't never think we was gone see such a thing as black man be president. Come from a time where that kind of thing wasn't even a thought in our heads."

My mind shifts to a picture Julie B. showed me on her phone a few years back. Granddaddy and Grandmoan were seated on their living room couch. In the picture they wore matching T-shirts with Barack Obama's oversized face printed on the center. Granddaddy smiled wide for the camera and Grandmoan offered a slight close-mouthed smirk. I wished I was there with them. I told Julie B. that.

"Get to seeing change like that, death ain't nothing to fear no more. Things change that much, you know you been here too long. People fix things different from how we did it in our time. Like to talk things out. We from a different time — a silent time," he says, and sighs. "Talking it out scare her more than death. And maybe that's when death be a mercy. When you can't live in the world cause it change too much to hold your kind. Maybe it be a better place and even that's too much for you." He shakes his head. "No matter how you look at it, everything come to one promise," he says. "Every living thing . . ." He uses his whole body to sigh. "These bodies. They got to

391

perish, and it's a whole lot of mercy in that."

I park my car in a space reserved for handicapped parking and Granddaddy looks over at me. His face is blank and I can't tell what's going on with him. Him and Grandmoan have always been him and Grandmoan. I wonder if he knows how to feel or if Grandmoan is the one who usually tells him that. I want to tell him not to worry. She'll be okay and he'll be whole again. We all will.

Instead, I say, "You all right, Granddaddy? You ready to go in here?"

He shakes his head and rubs his hand over it. "She loved you, boy. Ever since you was a boy — a baby — she loved you." He shakes his head and looks out the window.

"So much hell come out of her over the years. None of y'all — none of us can't never understand how she live with herself. How she live being her," he says.

I watch him wrap his fingers around the door handle, pull it, and push the door open. I figure he'll just sit there with the door open for a while. I figure he'll at least finish our conversation. But when he begins his slow rise from the seat and heads toward the hospital entrance, I shut off the engine and open my own door. I almost have to run to catch up with him. I grab his arm and hold it firm. Hold *him* firm in place. My grandfather has always been a tall man, but his body seems to be shrinking and his back has the curve in it that most old folks have. I hover over him, and he looks up at me. We stand there for a moment. Man to man. Eye to eye.

When I speak, I can hear the desperation in my own voice. "Did she know, Grand-daddy? Did she know what was happening to me when I was a boy?"

He smacks his lips and looks back toward the hospital, and then he jerks his arm away from me and slaps me across the face with as much force as he possibly can. My jaw is ringing and I'm wondering if anyone saw — if there will be trouble because he, a civilian, has assaulted an officer in uniform. He is still standing in front of me, peering up at me, waiting. His eyes carry a fire that I have never seen in him. A fire that tells me he can strike again. Angry eyes. Almost Grand-moan's eyes. And I am shocked because I have never known him to raise a hand to anything. To see this side of him tells me a lot about time and change.

"Granddaddy?" I finally say, cradling my face.

"That's what she should've done to Wayne. That's what she should've done to you. That's what she should've done to . . ." He shakes his head as if he means to shake away a memory.

The fire in his eyes unnerves me. Neither of us is who we once were. Nothing about this is in its rightful place.

"Bible say, owe no man but to love him. This family seem to only pass down owing. Owing lives. Owing violence. Owing explanations. It's time for her — for all y'all to pay your debts," he says before turning to walk away from me.

And I dare not grab him again. I watch him walk away and speak loud to his back, "How do I pay, Granddaddy? How do I pay?"

I sit down on the curb leading up to the hospital and wonder if she thought about me before she slipped away from herself. About the night she put me out, the night I'll never forget. I don't know what I was expecting when I walked through that door. There had been so many times that I had done the wrong thing and she still received me with grace.

When I was ten, I stole from Ms. Loodney's candy house. I didn't try to hide it either. I walked right up to the makeshift display case she had positioned in place of a car inside her garage. It looked like a meat case at a butcher shop or something like that. She had any kind of candy or junk food snack a kid could ever want in that thing. From penny candy to the big bars. Mary Janes, Bit-O-Honey, Tootsie Rolls, chocolate and flavored, Now and Laters, packed and singles, Kit Kats, Mr. Goodbars, anything you wanted. On top of that case a big jar of the juiciest Best Maid Sour Pickles sat at all times.

The day I stole from her, I walked right up to that case and when she looked her bold eyes down at me, I laughed. Her hair was wild and free on her head. It was completely white with age, and for most of the neighborhood kids, the white wildness equaled madness. Her haggard face had so many hard lines it looked like they had been carved into her skin. Her long, pointy nose didn't match her dark skin at all. She looked like a witch — a real television, Halloween-time witch. So I laughed and she smacked her lips and said, "Boy, what the fuck you want?"

She hated me. Thought I was the worst thing in the neighborhood. Whenever I passed her way, we'd go back and forth with insults, but that day I had nothing for her. I'll never forget that day because it was the last day Julie B. took us to the prison to see

Dale. I'll never forget that day because it was also the day I was done being the son of a man who couldn't father me. I'd made that decision when the guards made Julie B. take off her bra and all of those men cat-called her. When it was my turn to talk, I told Dale about it and he chuckled and said, "Man, these cats in here ain't seen nothing fine as your momma. Probably not never." And I was through with him. If he couldn't protect her, even with his mouth, I knew there was nothing he could do about what was happening to me.

I didn't have fight in me for Ms. Loodney by the time I made it to her house. I was there for that jar of pickles. I needed to do something that felt good to me, so I reached up, snatched it, and ran away as fast as I could. I don't remember where I took them or if I even ate them, but by the time I got home, Ms. Loodney had visited and told Grandmoan the whole story.

Grandmoan called me into the kitchen, where she sat at the table and instructed Marie on how to shell peas. She didn't even look up from the bowl in front of her when she asked me, "What you got to tell me, Alex?"

I didn't even fix my mouth to tell a lie. I let my eyes fall to my feet and kept them there until I heard her chair scrape against the tile. She lifted my chin with her fingers when she was in front of me.

"Told that old silly gal not to take y'all to that jail. Here you come bringing that mess home with you." She sighed and said, "Don't never do nothing like that, son. We ain't thieves. Don't never take nothing and run away. You want something, you figure out how to get right. Kay?" she said. And when I nodded, she pulled me into her and all I felt was warmth and love and safe.

She made me work the money she gave Ms. Loodney for that jar of pickles off at the hog pen, but she handled the situation with so much grace that I never wanted to do anything like that again. I never wanted to disappoint her in that way.

I hear the automatic doors slide open behind me and then I hear Granddaddy's voice. "Come on, Alex. We ain't got long."

I push myself up from the ground with the palms of my hands and turn to see him waiting for me. He smiles like the slap never happened and when I'm close enough to him, he puts his hand on my back and says, "We gone all be all right in our own good time. God got a way of making sure things end up how they posed to be. Even if it don't feel good, it's all right."

And we make our way to the woman who banished me.

Granddaddy walks in the room like more of an authority figure than me. "Helen, dear," he calls out. "I done made it back. Brought our boy with me."

She is silent.

I hesitate at the door. I'm not sure about crossing the wide threshold. I can see the form of her feet covered by the thin hospital blanket from where I stand in the door. Granddaddy has disappeared into the room and is telling her about all the parts of the day that she's missed. I'm reminded of sitting between them in that old hog pen truck. I imagine her listening without looking at him. Listening without listening.

"Come on in here, Alex," Granddaddy calls me. "Come on in here and say bye to your grandmomma."

And I enter because I want to see her eyes. I want to see something in them. More than what was in them when Julie B. was sneaking her around me. I want to see her love me again. She doesn't have to speak to me. I just want to see her eyes. If I can see them, I can see everything. Her love, her regret, her forgiveness. I'm holding my hand like I'm holding a bouquet of roses, and my body is trembling. When I'm far enough in the room to see Granddaddy sitting in a chair next to the bed, I let my eyes roam to the space next to him. I don't know why I'm expecting her to be looking at me — to be giving me what I need, but I am.

My knees almost buckle when I see her eyes closed. She looks gone and something in me knows that I won't see her eyes ever again. Nobody told me she wasn't conscious. Not Julie B. Not Granddaddy. They didn't prepare me for this.

I approach the bed and stand over her, hoping I'm wrong. Hoping she'll open her eyes and give me what I need.

"She ain't gone never wake up no more, son. She breathing, but she ain't here," Granddaddy says. "I still talk to her, though. She can still hear me."

And I can feel tears coming down from somewhere deep in my mind. I shake my head and lean over her body. I look back at Granddaddy and he nods his head at me.

I swallow. "Uncle Wayne touched me, Grandmoan. He grabbed me and put himself where I didn't want him," I whisper. I lean in further. So close that my lips almost touch her forehead. "He broke me and I broke them and that broke you," I say.

There are tears in my voice and I'm seeing Uncle Wayne that day and Jan and

Laverne and Samra and Veola's little girls. "I don't know what to do," I say. "How to make myself right. I just don't know."

I stand up, adjusting my focus to her face as I come away from it. There are tears at the corners of her eyes and some are sliding down her cheeks. I can't determine whether she's heard me. Whether the tears are hers. Whether they are mine spilled onto her. There is no way to know anything with her eyes closed.

I look over at Granddaddy with a mind to tell him that it's too late, that she hasn't heard me, that she won't ever hear me, but his smile is so wide and so proud that I just don't have the heart.

HELEN JEAN

2012

Helen Jean could never quite recall when it became the truth, but she held on to the day she decided to pretend as long as she could. It was the day Julie B. took her to Alex. Thought she wasn't coming back to herself and decided to take advantage of the moment. It was that day that he held her and wept because he thought it was too late for her to know he was doing it. That was the day she decided to never let them know when she came back to herself. It was that day she decided to make them think she was gone for good.

In the beginning, she'd forget things here and there and the worried look in Homer's eyes made her sad. She wished it would all just hurry up and happen, so he could stop fussing over her and fearing what it would all mean, or so she could at least stop knowing that he was fretting over her.

The day they found out for certain what

she had known since she saw it in her father — the day they found out what she would become — Homer sat in the back seat with her, like they were royalty and Julie B. was their driver. He handed the keys over to Julie B. and said, *You drive. I'm gone sit with her. Make sure she all right.*

Julie B. had smacked her lips and replied, *She all right. Momma always all right.*

Helen Jean watched him look out his back-seat window into the redness. A dust storm was near. Red grit swirled around them, like hundreds of weak twisters. It would get worse, but they would be settled in on Colgate by then.

She allowed him to take her hand into his own when they settled into the back seat. She rarely did that, allowed him to touch her so intimately. He squeezed and she squeezed back. He turned his one-eyed gaze to her and, for a moment, she felt bad. The dead eye was her doing and she couldn't help but also feel responsible for his white hair and ashen skin.

She'd been taking on the responsibility of some heavy things lately. What Bacon had done to Wayne. That she couldn't see either of them through who they were because she was the same. Came from the same tired and broken place. She could've done more to help Wayne. To make him better. To give him a shot at being human, but sentimentality and unwillingness to see that the brother who suffered along with her as a child had hurt her son. She could've been human enough to end it all — to save them all. But she didn't. She helped spread it, so they were all the same.

And she could barely live with what Alex did to Laverne. What Laverne and Marie turned around and did to themselves. How all that mess broke Ruby Nell. And then there was Wayne's death, which had come too late and that it had needed to come at all. She'd broken the promise she made in the outhouse that night long before she handed Wayne the way to his demise. She broke it when she put him in the shed — isolation — and thought that could erase everything. She took all of their lives then, and now she would leave everyone to hold the mess she'd leave behind. Especially her Homer. He would be alone in the mess she'd made, and that was most certainly on her.

What you want me to do, Momma? he asked, patting her hand gently.

She took a deep breath and exhaled. *Well, I reckon,* she began. *What's gone happen, gone happen,* she sighed, then shook her head and smiled. "And you come along and tame me."

She felt her smile drop slowly and she looked at her hands like they were something new. *If I had done right by the first one . . .* She pounded a gentle fist into her chest. *I think it was me who was to turn all this. My children dead now, and I got to live with I done killed them.*

But, Helen Jean, he said, and she could hear the whine in his voice. *God can fix it. Don't matter about all that mess they said. Ain't no heart problems. And the devil can't have your mind.*

She touched his cheek and her hand looked so slender against his face. Her nails had always grown long and winding and her palms were never sweaty. They were dry in a way that wasn't rough and soft in a way that wasn't moist. Her eyes searched his, which danced wildly, and as she stared into them, she could see them slowing, calming under her gaze.

I'm still here, honey. For now, I'm still here.

But Dr. Kharkuli say all that —

Ain't a-one of us get to live forever, Homer. Not a one. Our bodies get tired, baby. Minds, too. Can you just be like you always been? Be what I need? And she peered at him soft as she could, soft as she knew how.

404

After a while, he nodded. *Okay, Helen Jean,* he said. *Okay.*

But the worry from that day never left his eyes.

They started a game of waiting after that doctor's visit. Most days, Homer looked at her like she would disappear before his very eyes. Sometimes, she wondered if that's how it would happen. Other times, she closed her eyes and hoped that the relief of knowing nothing, remembering nothing, would come quickly. The real forgetfulness, not the kind she thought was it in her fifties, began about a year after that initial visit with Dr. Kharkuli. The instances were so small they almost missed them. Insignificant things, like forgetting to tell Homer that the grocery store called and said there wouldn't be scraps for the hogs one day or forgetting to take her meds or the best place to hide the money that still came in the mail each month from Alex.

She didn't begin to realize that Dr. Kharkuli's words were upon her until she started struggling to remember who the name on the envelopes belonged to and why they were sending money in the first place. She didn't say anything to Homer or Julie B. She let them figure it out on their own, and nobody confirmed when they did.

It felt like losing time at first, but the pity that she felt from her husband and daughter when she came back was almost unbearable. It didn't take long before she found herself pretending that she was lost in her head for hours at a time. She'd learned that during the times she pretended to be lost, the people around her were so preoccupied with how they felt about losing her that they forgot to pity her. They only had room enough to pity themselves.

It wasn't until that day that Julie B. coaxed her into the car like she was some type of child that she got the idea to be lost altogether. Julie B. had watched her all morning that day. Kept bringing her face close to her mother's and speaking loud, like Helen Jean was losing her hearing, instead of her mind.

"Momma, you good?" she yelled in her face while they sat at the table, where she watched her eat oatmeal.

Before Julie B. knew it, her mother had cursed her. Had said, *Julie B., your simple ass holler in my face one more time and I'm gone blow your goddamn brains out.*

Julie B. gasped, moved her face back, away from her mother's, and pushed her chair away from the table. It was only then, when she stood up defeated and deflated, that

Helen Jean caught on to what she was looking for, what she was waiting for. And it was partly that she loved playing the game, loved making them pity themselves and partly that she pitied Julie B.'s very existence that she called out to her dead daughter, like she thought she was still alive.

"Marie," she heard herself say. "Marie, get in here and wash these dishes." And for a moment, she thought it was real herself. For a moment, she expected to see the girl round the kitchen corner with her eyes on the floor.

But it was only a second before she realized that she was calling down her own pain in service of Julie B. That made her feel like a mother. If she had it to do all over again, Marie was something she'd have done different. She'd have tried loving the girl and being all the things that a child like that expects of its mother. When Homer found Marie in the bathtub with her wrists split open so soon after they'd found her friend from across the street, hanging from her bed, Helen Jean knew it was all on her. She'd failed to acknowledge her in the way that she should have. She'd failed that child completely. The part that pained her was that even in the child's death, Alex won her grief. They had to be let go in the same way they come into the world. There was but six months between them.

She made her eyes as empty and as confused as she knew how and watched Julie B.'s light up when she realized that her mother was in that lost place. She let her sit back down, let her hurry her through breakfast, and then she let her daughter fold her up into her Buick and talk to herself throughout the drive.

You was yourself, you'd kill me for bringing you to him, she said, never taking her eyes off the road.

Helen Jean watched her readjust her hands around the wheel and waited for her next words. There was silence for a while and in that silence, she wondered what she would become in Julie B.'s care. She'd hardly let her finish her breakfast, hadn't washed her up afterward, hadn't even helped her get dressed before rushing her into the car.

He just want to see you so bad. Been wanting to see you and it'll help for you to be there when I tell him Jan say he can't meet them babies, Julie B. said, looking over at her.

Why he always chose you, I'll never understand. She grunted. *But he did and I got to deal with that. I got to live with that,* she said, before turning on the radio and letting music Helen Jean couldn't understand drown out everything.

When Helen Jean came to, she was sitting in a folding chair in a dimly lit room. There was a sliding door with hanging blinds that let in a few random slits of light to her right. The room was empty except for a big bean bag in the corner. The vacuum tracks on the carpet were perfect, which made her notice how clean the walls were. As her confusion lifted, she realized that she'd really lost time because she couldn't remember arriving at the place. She let her eyes roam her full surroundings and realized she was in the living area of an apartment. She heard soft voices coming from somewhere nearby, most likely the kitchen to her left, from which a bright light was shining. She carefully pushed herself up from the seat and stepped slowly in the direction of those voices, that light.

She gone die? she heard the male voice ask. *She gone die without ever speaking to me again.*

The next voice she heard was Julie B.'s. *She can hear you. You can talk to her. She come and go. This ain't forever, Alex.*

Helen Jean's feet stopped moving. She stood there in the middle of the empty room and remembered the day she dropped him off, the last time she'd seen him. Remembered what he'd done. What he'd made her do. She had been sure it was Soweo when she went to her daughter's place to confront him. Didn't believe him when he promised he'd never do such a thing. He came to that door wearing the same red eyes that the child had described to her. Wearing that dark skin that she hadn't trusted since her daughter first brought him to Jerusalem. Later, much later, it dawned on her that he'd only reminded her of her father because Ruby Nell reminded her of her mother, and men like that could only be drawn to women with weak minds. Helen Jean had been sure that Laverne's description was of him, but she realized, long after his death, long after Ruby Nell's mind was gone, long after everything had turned to ruin, that she convinced herself of that because what she'd known in her heart was that it was all on her.

And she made the decision to burn that hog, made sure Ruby Nell knew she was meant to move on from Soweo. Something in her knew it would break her daughter, but she made herself okay with that.

And then later that night, she learned the truth. That night Alex came in wearing his guilt was the first time she ever hit that child. Putting her hands on someone had never hurt her so much. She hadn't been a weak woman in a long time. Certainly hadn't been the kind of woman moved by deserved discipline or justice, but that was different. And once she did that — put her hands on him — he had opened up and cried and apologized, admitting to everything.

She could've gone to the police station and made things right. She could've freed her daughter's man and made Ruby Nell right. There was still a chance to turn that part around, but freeing Soweo would've been condemning Alex and despite everything, she couldn't bring herself to do that. She didn't realize that choosing between Soweo and Alex was also choosing between Alex and Ruby Nell until much later. Until she had testified against him, until Ruby Nell's mind was so far gone that there was no coming back, until Soweo was dead, until she dropped Alex off at that ranch. And even after that, she thought about the choice she'd made, thought about what it did to her daughter, thought about the alternative, Alex in prison, thought about more men taking from him, and she lived with what came with carrying the guilt she drove into Soweo.

She stood just outside of their voices and listened to him scold his mother. *You always too late, Julie B. Tell me to wait and Jan might let me be in her life. Tell me to wait on Grand-moan,* he said.

She couldn't see his face, but she could hear his anger. It was the same firmness that she had seen in him when he was a child. She felt a glimmer of hope spark inside her. Maybe he was still himself and they could sit down and talk, and he could show her that he was stronger than his past and be absolved of everything.

I — I'm doing the best I —

Yeah, I know, he said, in a voice that sounded more like mockery than under-standing.

Maybe he thought his mother owed him. Maybe he blamed her for everything. Helen Jean scoffed at that. Over the years, she'd had her criticisms about her daughter, but she could see Julie B. — could always see how Julie B. tried hard for her kids. It took her a long time to understand that one person's mediocre was another person's best. Julie B. had always been operating at her very best, and that she was that medio-cre was sad to her mother, but it wasn't for Alex to judge. It was weakness on his part — the owe and blame. It was weakness just like what she suspected he'd done to his sister, what she was certain he'd done to that girl across the street, and just like that she knew all of it was still there — still in him. It was only hiding. He would never again be her Alex. He *was* ruined. Would always be ruined.

Where I'm at, she called out.

The voices went quiet and Julie B. rounded the corner almost instantly.

I'm right here, Momma. I'm right here with you, she said, approaching her, paying close attention to her eyes. *You all right, Momma?* she asked.

And she knew her daughter needed her to be lost, and as much as she wanted to be angry, wanted to go upside Julie B.'s head, she needed to be lost to Alex, too. No matter how ruined he was, though, she needed to see the only child who had ever chose her.

Tell Wayne to quiet that goddamn dog, she said to Julie B. And she wanted to slap her face when a smile spread across it.

She waved her hand behind her and he emerged slowly from the kitchen. Helen Jean stared at him, trying to look confused, trying not to be in awe, trying to stay lost. It was him, the oversized toddler waiting for her in the den in an infant seat. It was him, who recognized her grief, even before he should have and loved her there. She wanted to tell him how horrible the thing he did was. How she knew it was still in him. It would always be, but she never burned a hog for him. He was the one she wanted to remember.

And she pretended to be lost before him. He stepped into the room and Julie B. flipped the light switch and the two of them — Helen Jean and Alex — illuminated like they were on a stage.

His eyes were teary when he approached her. He was a little boy and he was hurting, Wayne was hurting him. Pretending to be a good uncle. An uncle who wanted to help. And something in her had to know that — had to know it and looked away. Looked away because looking at Wayne was looking at the most shameful part of herself. She closed her eyes and she could feel the tears on her own face. She could see Wayne on top of Alex, Bacon on top of Wayne, and her father on top of it all. She opened her eyes and raised her hand to stroke his cheek.

He closed his eyes and let his cheek rest against her palm, and she wanted to stand on her toes and put her lips to his beautiful skin. Right before she fixed her mouth to tell him everything. That she knew everything. Right before she let words that had never been born walk, she remembered she was lost. That she had always been lost.

I shouldn't have let him kill your dog, Wayne. I shouldn't have let him do that, she said.

Alex opened his eyes and they were filled with horror, and Helen Jean went on apologizing to her son. He lifted his head from her palm and looked back at Julie B., who smiled as if she was handing him something beautiful. He looked back at Helen Jean, stared deep into her eyes, and it was in that moment that she thought he saw the truth.

He nodded and said, *It's okay. It's okay,* and then he tilted his head to the side and put his lips together as if he would smack them, but instead they quivered when he said, *I love you anyhow.*

She could hear the tears in his voice, and it took everything in her to hold herself and keep from throwing her arms around him when he said, *I'll always love you, old woman. Always. You been my lifeline. Even after all this time, you been it.* And he pulled her body into his and held her like a comfort she hadn't felt since the day she had to see him. That day she had to look away for good. She could hear his soft sniffling and she patted his back and said, *It's okay. She*

415

*just a dog. Just a animal. You be all right after
while.*

That was the last real day she held on to.
The last day she showed herself to anyone
for any amount of time. After that, she
couldn't be sure if she was herself or if she
was lost, but she was certain to make sure
that everyone thought the latter, until she
finally lost everything.

That was her last real thing. Alex. She
didn't know she was there when, years later,
he finally met Jan's children by accident in
the parking lot of the grocery store, where
Javon held her hand tight so she wouldn't
wander off. When Julie B. stuttered over her
words, afraid to introduce her son to her
grandchildren because of the horrible things
he'd done. When she began to sneak them
to his apartment every Wednesday that year
while Jan was working, Helen Jean was there
but she didn't notice how he would smile.
How it reminded him of the times he'd
spent with her as a boy. How he would look
into her eyes those days and only find
emptiness. She couldn't see how he tried to
be a good uncle to the kids, to be strong,
not the kind of uncle Wayne was to him.

She was there that Wednesday at that
Mexican flea market with him, Julie B., and
the kids, but she didn't see how taken he

was with how taken Javon was by all the statues at the little statue park. She simply stared at the giant roosters and frogs, Virgin Marys, fountains, all kinds of lawn fixtures, thinking nothing of them or anything else at all. She didn't notice that Buddha was the biggest thing out there. That he stood out with his white shine and his deep-thinking look. She didn't listen as Javon stood in front of the Buddha statue and asked his uncle a million questions about it. She was there when Alex presented the statue as a fixture in the middle of his living room that very next week and knew all things Buddha, but she didn't know what was going on. Helen Jean's days of knowing were behind her, and she was just there, not as a witness or a judge, but as an old woman with no shame, no secrets, and no covenant left to keep.

19

LYDIA

I'm thinking about Walter's reply to my last text: Come home, Lydia. I'll be here, as Aunt Julie B. walks ahead of us. We exit the elevator on my grandmother's floor.

I try to keep my mind on Walter because Jan's words — her truth — is just too difficult. Alex. All this time I thought he was Jan's monster. All this time he was mine. And Grandmoan. She knew. She let my mother go mad with grief and despair and she let me grow up alone and ashamed of the father I loved. She could've freed us all.

I'm inclined to turn on my heels and go home, as Walter has pressed. I don't know what my being here means anymore, not after what Jan has revealed to me.

The police questioned my mother that night, but she just sat there shaking her head, answering no to every question, and I tried to figure out what was going on. I had no idea what any of it meant. The hog burn-

418

ing in the trash bag on the porch, Mother's frantic screams, but my mother knew. She knew from the start.

"We've got everything we need, ma'am," one of the officers said as they prepared to leave. And that was that. Soweo went to jail and never came back to us. And then he was dead. Mother never recovered from that.

My mother drove us back to the east side after our duplex cleared of cops that night. We didn't park in front of Grandmoan's, though. We parked in front of the Scott house.

"Come on," my mother said as she opened the door to the Riviera. "Go up here and behave," she commanded like it was an ordinary night.

It was late. In fact, it wasn't really night; it was early. Three a.m. All of the houses on Colgate were dark and quiet. We walked up to the Scott house and my mother pushed the doorbell. Nothing happened. The porch remained dark, so she opened the glass screen door and began to bang on the wooden door, like a madwoman.

"Momma." I pulled at her shirt. She pushed me to the side and stopped banging to point her finger at me. "I told you to behave." Finally, the porch light clicked on and the door swung open.

"What the hell is —"

"I need to talk to your girl," my mother said, plainly. Mr. Scott tilted his balding head to the side, and it seemed to glow like a halo under the porch light. He peered past us to the street.

"Laverne? Are you crazy? It's the middle of the night. She's sleep—"

My mother's voice became desperate. She nodded her head back toward Grandmoan's house. "They done took him. He ain't do this. Not my man. Not Soweo," she said, slamming her balled fist into her chest. "And Momma done burned a hog on my porch cause she want me to forget him. She think he touched your daughter. Trying to make him gone. I just need your daughter to say the truth."

Mr. Scott's eyes widened with understanding, and he inhaled deeply. "I'm sorry. I'm so sorry, Ruby Nell."

"I don't need your fucking sorry, Cholly. He was *your* Saturday night domino partner. I'm sorry for you. Y'all never lost. Now, I need to talk to Laverne."

"I can't let you wake —"

"Who? Who's gone?" a small voice asked. And I stood there hoping they'd tell her, so that I could know, too.

Mr. Scott turned to Laverne's voice behind him. We couldn't see the details of her struggle through the darkness, the bruises or marks that she carried from the attack, but my mother still tried to look around Mr. Scott to make eye contact with the girl. And when Laverne saw my mother's eyes, I think she understood what I was too young to see.

"Go back to bed, sweetie," Mr. Scott said softly.

Laverne didn't say a word, but she locked eyes with Mother and something passed between them that I couldn't understand then, and I'm too old to clearly remember now.

All I know is Mother's shoulders slumped and then her whole body dropped down to the ground. "No, no, no, no, no. Not for nothing," she said. And that's when she began to peel away from herself. She babbled other things — things I couldn't understand — and Laverne began to cry out loud from behind her father. I stood beside my mother, who rocked herself on the ground in a fetal position, and Mr. Scott left us in the doorway to comfort his daughter.

The next morning must have been as hard for Mr. Scott as that night was on my mother because he found Laverne's body swinging from two of her jump ropes. I'm sure he hadn't expected to lose her in such a way, but the tight knots that she had used to tie the jump ropes together and to secure them on one of the three sturdy wooden beams that he had installed himself to make her room look like a summer camp cabin displayed her determination to die that night. To find her twin bed pushed away from the center of the room and her desk chair lying on its side must have been so hard for him. Mr. Scott and his wife probably would have lost their minds, too. But they didn't because they had each other.

And weeks after that, Marie followed her best friend. The saddest part about that is it was as if nothing happened, as if someone had inconvenienced the present suffering by saying the wrong thing, as if she grabbed the heels of grief reserved for others and all that remained were leftovers in a room full of greedy people.

And now, I know Soweo — my father — didn't do it. He didn't rape Laverne, and he didn't deserve jail or my shame. That makes me feel more cheated than losing him in the first place.

Aunt Julie B. and the children approach the door before us. They walk in without knocking. My heart starts beating fast. I wonder if this is really the day she dies. I wonder if she knows it. If there are such things as heaven and hell, I wonder which one awaits her calloused soul. I walk into the room before Jan and I know instantly that there will be trouble. Alex is standing there talking to the children and Aunt Julie B.

And just like that all of this is real to me. I remember the bathroom and passing him and being afraid that he would know that I knew what he had just done and what that meant for me. He would be handsome if I could get rid of the image. His head is shaved bald and I can tell it's because of balding by how perfect the light bounces off the top of his head. His skin is blemish free and shiny and his beard is full of gray speckles. He looks like a good person in his police uniform. He stands up straight like he wants to salute us, and his shaved head makes him look clean and official. I forget for a moment what he's done to Jan — what he's done to me — and I think about what his mother said was done to him.

". . . so I punched him right in his nose," Javon says, finishing up his sentence. Alex's smile is wide, but it disappears when he see me and Jan.

"Get away from him," Jan hisses.

"Jan, what's your problem —" Aunt Julie B. begins before she is cut off by Jan.

"You is, Momma. You my problem. Always been my problem," she says, pointing at Aunt Julie B. "Get away from him," Jan commands Javon again. Javon's face is confused but he obeys, and Jazera follows as they file over toward where we're standing.

When the children are safe beside me, Jan begins to walk over to where her mother and Alex are staring at her in amazement, close to Grandmoan's bed. She cuts into the space between her mother and Alex and turns her body toward her brother.

"I ain't scared of you no more," she says to him through gritted teeth. "I ain't gone never be scared of you no more."

I see a flicker of something I can't read pass through his eyes. He tilts his head slowly and I hear the bones in his neck crack.

"I'm . . ." he begins, and then he drops his face to the floor. The room is quiet. He nods his head until his eyes land on Jan again, and I watch the two stand face-to-face. They are so close it seems they'll embrace. I'm sure they will when Jan's lips begin to quiver. That's when I notice her whole body is shaking.

Aunt Julie B. is just standing there, like she is trying to decide whether healing or hell is taking place. I can tell by the plea in her eyes that she's hoping for the former, but I can also tell by the way her hands extend as if she's about to catch something that's falling that she's preparing for the latter.

"Okay," he says. "I understand. I know. I can fix it. I know how to fix it now."

And Jan's shaking body begins to vibrate and a rumbling sound, something like a moving garbage truck begins to flow from her throat. She places her hands on her stomach and lets her upper body sway back, like she's taking a big breath. When her body comes back forward, she lets the first wave of hysteria go right in her brother's face.

"Fix it? You sick. You — you like a animal. That's what you is," she hisses, and the laughter stops. "You ain't no better than a nigger — than a stray dog off the street." Alex looks down at the floor. And we all go quiet again.

Finally, he softly says, "Excuse me," and moves away from her. "I need to use the bathroom." His face is different from what it was when we first walked in. In fact, he looks a little pale and deflated. I almost feel like reaching out and embracing him. Forgiving him for her. For myself.

Then I realize he's coming toward me. I'm still standing in the doorway. I remember that day in Grandmoan's bathroom. I can feel my body tremble. I exhale when he turns to the bathroom door, just before reaching me. The trembling stops.

Alex opens the door and disappears inside the bathroom.

"You ain't got no right," Aunt Julie B. says to Jan before swallowing and shifting her eyes in way that tells me she doesn't even believe her own words.

"She wouldn't even want him here," Jan spits back.

"Get out of here," a voice commands from further inside the room — the side I can't see. And the bickering stops instantly.

"Granddaddy?" I call out, stepping completely into the room. I pass the bathroom door and stick my head around the corner. Jan and Aunt Julie B. head over to the entrance of the room, away from my grandfather's voice, where I'm standing with the children, and I walk in the direction of his deep, tired voice. I hear the door close after my cousin, my aunt, and the children. I can't see them exit from around the corner, but I know they're gone because I no longer hear the shuffling of their feet. Granddaddy is seated in the chair right next to my grandmother. I approach him and he spreads his arms open. I lean over into him and he folds me inside of them.

"I knew if ain't nobody else come, you would," he says. "You never was one to hold on to things."

I start to cry.

He begins to rub my back and whispers, "Don't come back to this place. Don't ever come back, you hear? Ain't nothing for you here."

I push myself away from him. "But Granddaddy —"

"Go back to your people. I know they ain't perfect, but your momma chose you, gal," he says, tilting his head to the side.

I'm not certain he can see the question in my eyes, so I let out a confused "Huh?"

He points his finger at me. "You was a choice. For Soweo and your momma. She was troubled. Broken. But they still chose you as best they could," he says, and sighs.

His words crash into me and I realize that my mouth is open like a hole or a tunnel to nowhere.

He shakes his head. "Ruby Nell wasn't never able to get one before or after you.

Begged her sister and God allowed you to be."

His words come together in my head, like scattered puzzle pieces. *Choice. Never able to get one. Begged her sister.* I can feel my own eyes widen and my heart begins to race. "She didn't give birth to me," I say out loud.

"I always thought you should've knowed it," he says.

He shakes his head again. "It don't matter too much, but it matter a whole lot when you trying to know. You was meant for who took you. Who loved you, child."

I feel my lips quiver. "Aunt Julie B.?" I say, looking at him. When he nods, I look back at the door.

"Ruby Nell carried you, though," he says, looking at me and pointing a finger at his heart. "Soweo and Ruby Nell. They was the ones," he says. He nods at my grandmother. "Don't think she even know the truth about that. Nobody was supposed to, but Grand-daddy pay attention."

I don't say anything. I think about Aunt Julie B. and her kids, all in Grandmoan's house and I think about Jan's little legs dangling off the bed and how they could've been mine. Granddaddy can't know what I've gone through. How I thought I would become my mother. That she had passed her illness down to me. How each time one of my babies died I thought maybe it was for the best because of that. He can't know how angry I feel I should be, but how for the first time ever, I understand that it could've been so much worse. I can feel myself becoming more than a fragment, and I decide that this is a piece of the puzzle that I'll keep for myself. My parents had their issues and those issues became my issues — those issues shaped me, and they will always be mine. If my aunt can keep that part of herself, I'll keep that part of mine, too.

"Your grandmomma," he says, interrupting my moment of understanding. "This old gal give me love and family like I ain't never had it," he says, nodding in my grandmother's direction.

He nods toward her still body again. "This kind of death be like a cleansing rain. I want you to leave here and don't you never come back," he says with finality.

I nod and we both stare at her. She looks like a peaceful woman — a human being. Her skin is pale, almost green, and her lips look like they have already been embalmed. Her hands are pinned beside her, and I place one of mine on top of one of hers.

"She ain't all bad, you know?" Grand-daddy says. My eyes stay on her face. "Her daddy mess up her mind real good. Took me a long time to figure that out, but folks lose all they secrets when they forget they trying to keep them." He squints his eyes and tilts his head a bit. "Ain't hard as she want to be," he says. "Built herself up to forget everything. To forget that Wayne was her daddy's child." He closes his eyes and sighs. "Wanted to build a world where men wasn't ruling her. Breaking her all the time," he says.

I shake my head. "Her father raped her," I say, looking down at her still body, and suddenly she doesn't look frightening to me. She looks like someone who got everything wrong because she had been wronged.

"You were just a broken thing yourself, huh," I say. I want to tell her that I think we all are and that we can only pass that on.

And I see myself back in the hospital bed after the death of my last child. I'm smiling and Walter's face — his eyes are draining of patience, understanding, and comfort as I try to cover my smile. My joy. And it dawns on me that it *was* a type of joy and that's why I won't let him touch me anymore. I love my husband. I want to be a good wife and give him what he needs. I want to give

430

him the legacy that he and his family find so important. But I want to keep something for myself. I don't want to be a mother. I don't want to be mine and I don't want to be hers. I don't want to be anyone's. Not ever. And I don't know what that means for me and Walter but I know what it means for me.

I lean down and kiss my grandmother's warm cheek. It's the first time I have ever kissed her. As far as I know, she has never kissed me.

And then, something in the bathroom explodes. Granddaddy and I both jump, and I think about the time Grandmoan got drunk and shot a hole through the bathroom wall while chasing Granddaddy. I remember how he ran outside and all of us children looked on as if it were some sort of game and how we knew it wasn't by the way his good eye and bad eye scanned over us with fear when he realized that running out to our driveway placed us in the line of fire, and he retreated back into the house when her curses were close to emerging from inside the den. That's when we heard the explosion, the gunfire from inside the house.

I look down at Grandmoan. She's not in the bathroom this time. Granddaddy is not there either. He's not balled up in the corner, right next to the toilet, hiding from her bullets, loving and fearing her too much to do anything outside of that. They are not in the bathroom at all. Alex is. I hear the toilet flush. I don't want to move. I know what it is. I imagine brain matter splattered on the wall. Half his skull gone. He's over. I imagine his body falling over on top of the toilet handle. I imagine him finally dead.

Jan, Aunt Julie B., and the children burst back through the door, sliding around the corner, eyeing Grandmoan's body still in her bed.

"What was that?" Aunt Julie B. asks.

I shrug and point back to where they came from. "It came from in there — in the bathroom."

Her eyes widen and I know she knows, too. "Alex," she says, and rushes back around the corner. Jan is right behind her, and the children follow Jan. "Alex, baby. What you done done?" I hear Aunt Julie B. say before I hear the bathroom door click open.

Granddaddy and I scramble after them, toward the bathroom. I hear the heavy door bang against the wall before I approach the bathroom, and then I hear Aunt Julie B. scream. Jan is standing frozen in the doorway when I make it to the door, and the children are trying their hardest to get a better view around their mother's body. I feel Granddaddy's tall frame coming up behind me, and he must see something inside the bathroom that Jan's body is blocking me from seeing.

"Good Lord. What that boy done done?" he says out loud.

Aunt Julie B. sounds like my mother long ago, chanting no.

Jan finally unfreezes and turns to look for her children. "Come on, y'all. Let's go home. Ain't nothing in there to see," she says calmly, and I can tell she's had enough.

I watch as she shuffles past and rushes them out the door, just as a nurse comes running in. When I turn my head back to see what's going on, my hand instinctively flies up to cover my mouth.

Alex is sitting on the toilet with his pants dropped to his ankles. He looks like he's in a daze. His mouth is open. Slack. His eyes are focused straight ahead. It looks like he's staring straight at me, but I know he's somewhere else. His shoulders are slumped forward and one of his arms hangs straight down to the side of his body. The other is bloody and resting in his bloody lap.

I hear the nurse's voice behind me. "Excuse me, ma'am." And I shuffle my feet over a little bit. "My word," she says, and backs away. "I'll be right back." And she's gone.

I see Granddaddy walk away too, but I can't. I stand there gazing at Alex as he gazes at something invisible to me.

Aunt Julie B. is kneeling in front of Alex. She is babbling incoherently when the nurse returns with the other nurses and a doctor. I'm leaning against the doorpost and Alex is still gazing straight ahead. He sees me but he doesn't, and I realize that this is the first time we've locked eyes since I saw him on top of Jan — on top of his sister — on top of my sister. My brother on top of my sister. I think about how much I've hated Soweo because of what I thought he did to Laverne.

And then I think about what Alex must be fighting to do this to himself. To harm himself in this way. And for the first time ever, my heart goes out to him. "I'm sorry," I mouth to him, and I hope he catches it and understands. I really hope he receives it and understands.

"What happened, exactly?" one of the nurses asks me, and I just shake my head.

"Let's just get him to an OR, right now," somebody orders.

"We're going to have to move you, sir!" somebody shouts in his face as they kneel down beside the toilet. Alex doesn't break his stare, and drool is starting to drip from his mouth.

I move from the doorway and stand there for a moment. My hand is still covering my mouth. I decide to go search for Granddaddy at Grandmoan's bedside and round the corner of the room. He has drawn the curtain that hangs around the bed closed. I know he'll be there and he is. He is sitting on the edge of her bed with his back to me. I can't see Grandmoan's face, but it looks as if he's gazing down into it. As I approach him from behind, I see that a huge white pillow is completely covering her face, and his big hands are resting — no, pressing on top of it.

"Granddaddy," I say. "What are you doing?"

"Thought I told you to leave here," he says, without turning to face me. I step back, almost in shock myself, and turn toward the door. I'm ready to run, but hospital workers are filing out the door behind Alex and the people carrying him. As I pass the open bathroom door, I see Aunt Julie B. on her knees splashing her hands through the bloody toilet water.

"He flushed it. Oh my God, he flushed it. My baby flushed his manhood away." She is hysterical. I know I can't help her, and I know I don't want to.

I stand there for a moment and a nurse comes back through the room door.

"Is this where they just brought the young man from?"

I nod, and she turns into the bathroom. She walks in on my aunt's chanting "He flushed it." I continue toward the door. When I place my hand on the handle, I hear laughter erupt in the bathroom.

"My son flushed his dick down the toilet!" Aunt Julie B. screams, and then her own laughter follows again.

I open the door and walk out. When I cross over the threshold, I exhale. I close the door behind me and hurry down the corridor to the elevator. I dig my phone out of my purse as soon as I get on, and search for Walter's last text. I find the text he sent asking me to come home. I hit reply and type:

I'm coming. There is so much to say. So much.

Then I hit send.

20
JAN

I hurry my kids out the elevator. My body feel like it's about to come undone. Javon firing off questions about what done happened, but I can't open my mouth cause I'm gone lose it.

The automatic hospital doors open to let us out. I push my babies through the door. I don't stop moving. I can't stop moving cause I might fall apart.

I'm praying to God that I can keep it together till I get home, but I can't stop seeing Alex on that toilet with all that blood. All his blood. All mine cause we the same. I can't stop thinking about how mad I still am with him, but how much I wanted to wrap my arms around him and forgive him when I was right there in front of him. How much I felt like a traitor to myself for still seeing him as a brother. For wanting to understand him. For wanting to forgive him and feel sorry for him.

437

When we make it to the car, I open the passenger door and help Jazera in without saying a word. Javon get in the back and he done gone quiet. He don't even complain about taking the back seat. I make my way round to my door and take a deep breath fore I open it and get in. When I'm finally in that seat, I turn around and take a look at my babies.

They so safe and innocent and that make me proud. Proud of myself for being the type of mother I been. I done did so many things different from my momma. Left the place where I growed up to make a safe place for me and mine. And I'm dreaming, and dreaming lead to doing, so that's something. I wonder if Grandmoan ever had a dream. If my momma ever had one. I don't want to just survive no more. I'm dreaming about a future where we good in all the ways we can be, and I know that's something I can be proud of.

My babies ain't got no idea of all we done walked out on. They got no idea of what I'm running from. But I know. I know how the past can follow you. I don't want that for them, but something in me know that if I keep them here that's what they'll get. And just like that I know. I can make it in Dallas on my own. I can leave all this behind me and give my kids a new start. A life.

I don't need Grandmoan money to do that. Never did. I done lived my whole life like this. Poor and broke and scared. I'm not gone die now just cause I don't have her money. I'm gone struggle, but that's all I know anyway. I can make it without it. I know I can. Just like that, I make my decision. We going. We got to.

I stick my key in the ignition and turn it, but the car don't say nothing. I look around at the kids and then I turn it again. It still don't say nothing, so I just let my body fall back against the seat. Then I think about being here, outside the place where everything I want to leave behind is, and I sit up and let my hand fall hard on the steering wheel. Then I let it fall on it again. And again. Until my slaps turn into punches and my closed mouth turn into shits. I can feel myself crying again. Just letting all of it come out, and I can hear my kids saying "Momma" cause they worried about me through all this. I'm worried about me, too. Seem like I can't stop crying today. Laughter and tears is all I got today. But it feel so good to let go in this way. Even fore my kids, just letting go and being something real seem like the right thing to do.

After a while, I stop and they stop calling

my name, too. I tell them to roll they windows down and I roll mine down and we just sit there in the hot quiet of the car, sweating a little and thinking a lot.

I don't know why Grandmoan who she is, but I ain't got to understand her. Sometimes we don't get to understand things. People. We just got to try to be better than the things that spit us out. I don't know why my momma like she is, but I love her and got to keep on with it. I can't make the people I love no different. I can't change the past. All I can do is love myself and my kids enough to move forward. Love my people where they is and fight like hell not to let nobody else mistakes — nobody else pain — break me ever again.

And I don't recognize my own voice at first when I look in the rearview mirror, peer at my son, and say, "Javon, Alex did something ugly to me a long, long time ago. Kay, baby?" I watch him nod. "I'm coming to realize that he might not be no bad man, but he did a bad thing. And I can't trust him with y'all." I twist my upper body in the seat so that I'm looking at them both. I see questions forming in they eyes, so I say, "Right now you just too young to understand it. But I promise to tell y'all when you get older. I promise I won't keep nothing from you. And don't y'all never keep nothing from me, you hear?"

They nod and say, "Yes, ma'am," and I say, "We ain't gone keep stuff from each other in this family. We gone talk about stuff. Can't protect each other if we don't open our mouths."

I look out the open window, and I know this town is over for me. "We moving, y'all. We moving to Dallas. Momma gone go to school. Give y'all a better life," I say, and I wait to see how they gone respond.

And they quiet, and I get scared. Wonder if I done said too much. Wonder if they think I'm lying like the other times, so I turn away from the window and look at them. Both of my babies wearing smiles so big, I can't help but smile, too. And just like that, we gone be all right.

21
JULIE B.

When they pronounced Momma dead, wasn't nobody there but Homer. I had made my way down to the nurse station to find out where they took Alex. To find out how they could fix the mess he made of hisself. Now, we sitting in this room with her body, waiting for something Homer say ain't gone happen. My elbows resting on my knees and my head in my hands, Homer sitting next to Momma with his legs cross, holding her hand like they on a date, smiling like she here.

"I know you want to wait on them some more, Julie B. Want them to see her. Say good-bye, But they gone, darling. They ain't to return to this place. They trying find they own —"

"Stop talking, Homer, just stop," I say to him without even lifting my head. "I'm trying to think."

"Nawh, Julie B., I think this one time your

442

momma want me to keep talking and you to keep listening."

He ain't raising his voice. He calm as untouched bathwater, so I just sit there. Got no real intention of hearing nothing he got to say no way. I'm worried about my kids. Alex shot his dick off. Flushed his whole manhood down the toilet. Had the nerve to tell them folks he don't want to do nothing to fix it. Punkin took them kids and it feel like something final. And Lil, I ain't never really had her, but she run after Punkin like they belong together, and I guess what's getting to me is that ain't none of them see enough in me to run here. To run to they Momma.

"Everybody want to say bye, show the dying that they here and they somehow living on in spite of everything," Homer interrupt my thoughts. He sigh so loud I lift my eyes up and see him shaking his head.

"Alex come here to get what he needed — to get an answer on what he needed to do. Lil come here to get answers about who she is so she can let it go," he say, and let his eyes peer into mine, and I know he telling me more than just that. It feel like he judging me.

"And that sweet little January, she come here to be released from it all. To give them

443

kids what we ain't give her."

"I don't know what to do, Homer." I look back down at my hands. I can feel the tears clouding my eyes and I try to make them stop. If all them coming to the hospital for something — coming to Momma for something — something wrong with what I gave. And I always knowed that. No matter how much I doubted it when Wayne first touched my baby, I knowed. And when I realized how nervous Punkin was around her brother — my son — I knowed that too. I thought by keeping that — making sure my momma didn't know — I was saving them from what Momma had done to Wayne. Thought by not telling her that my brother was spreading through my children — that he had already got to Alex — I was doing something good. I thought I was saving them by not doing nothing. By picking Alex up from school myself when I could get Momma car. By putting Punkin in the bed with me after I knew about Alex ruin. After Laverne, I thought I was saving Alex and Punkin by letting her send him away. And Lil, leaving her be seemed best with all the mess we had going on in that house.

But all that mess — all that doing nothing — it's still with them. It's still hurting them and it done gone so far I don't know how to fix it. "I just want it all to be right. I thought we could come here and see her and burn a hog and make all that old stuff right," I say, and I hate that I'm crying. I sound so weak to myself.

"Why Julie B., that's your plan? That's the most foolish thing I done ever heard. You can't change nothing what happened, but you can go to them kids and do a honorable thing." His voice go down to a whisper. "Tell them what you know and unburden yourself." He slam his fist on the arm of the chair and raise his voice. "Tell them!"

And I jump a little bit and look over at him, shaking my head, and then I close my eyes. "I can't tell them that, Homer. I can't tell them I knew all that stuff. I can't tell them I thought I was doing stuff to protect them — I can't tell them those things cause they still got hurt, Homer. Nothing I did saved my babies. And I left Lil out there alone."

"That's part of growing good, Julie B. We all make mistakes. Ain't that right, honey?" he say, shaking my momma's hand and looking at her lovingly.

I want to tell him she dead. She gone cause it seem like he ain't getting it. Not by the way he holding on to her.

He nod in her direction. "She died feeling

bad about all them men claiming you as they child. Couldn't find the words to tell you no matter what they say, Jessie B. was your daddy."

I begin to weep into my hands. I can't stop.

"She said so many wrong things to you before she come to that. Before she understand that it was what you needed to stop carrying your uncertainty. Julie B., we all got mistakes we ashamed of. Ways we done wronged. Only way to live clear through that is to make them right. Go to them."

He stand up and walk over to where I'm sitting. I feel his hand on my shoulder. And when he say, "Homer here for you, Julie B. As long as God allow me to be here, Homer be here for you." And I wrap both my arms around his arm, like a child clinging to a father they don't want to leave, and I put my face in his arm and let out a scream into it.

He use his free hand to rub my back and he tell me in a soft voice, "Get it out, girl. Get it out cause we gone be all right."

When my screaming die down and I stand up, I let my eyes roam up to his face. He look tired, but he wearing a crooked smile and his eyes look like a comfort. And I'm standing there, gazing at him, not knowing where the words coming from but I know I have to say them cause they the truth. "It's always been you, Homer. Since you come along, it's you who been my father." And I mean it cause even though it ain't never meant nothing, it mean something now that he all I got left.

He nod and smile — blush really. "I know it might seem all bad to you right now, but being in y'all life, witnessing it — that's been a honor. All y'all belong to her." He nod in Momma's direction. "All y'all belong to me."

And all I can do is nod. I don't know if I can do what he thinks I should, but I know I still got him if I ain't got nobody else. And I still got Tricia. And I still got to mourn my momma. I got breath in my body, so there's still time. We'll figure everything else out tomorrow.

ACKNOWLEDGMENTS

My deepest gratitude is due to my brilliant agent, Samantha Shea. Thank you for challenging me to be better and write stronger. I feel so blessed to have you on this journey with me.

Gratitude to my outstanding and insightful editor, Amber Oliver, who, from the very beginning, understood this book at its core; and to Phoebe Robinson for creating this beautiful space that allows the safe production of so many beautiful words. I'm grateful to the Tiny Reparations art team for a lovely cover and to the rest of the team for believing in and appreciating this work enough to see it to production with patience and grace. Special thanks to my copy editor, Amy Schneider.

For the time and space to write, I am beyond grateful to the following institutions and their staff, who welcomed me so warmly: Kimbilio Fiction Center, Hedgebrook, Yaddo, and Art Omi. I am especially grateful to MacDowell, where I completed several drafts of this novel. Thanks to Bread Loaf Writers' Conference.

Thank you, Clay Reynolds, for allowing me into that very first workshop at University of Texas at Dallas and for seeing something in that first very rough draft. *Perish* was birthed in that class. And you have stood in my corner ever since. You are a wonderful friend.

Many thanks to the colleagues and friends who workshopped this novel, particularly Sobia Khan, Susan Norman, Scott Branks, Cameron Maynard, Sanderia Faye, Lily Ounekeo, and Andrew McConnell.

Gratitude to Kima Jones for being a powerhouse, a generator of fresh, genius ideas, and my Friday night movie buddy.

Finally, I am indebted to my family for the ways in which they have cared for this book by caring for me. My husband, Arnold, I will always be in awe of your love and support; my children, Jeremiah, Jordan, and Dymond, for sharing your mama with this book; my parents, Clyde and Lydia, for all of the ways you both nourish me; my sisters, Nene and Shay, and my nieces, Bria, Carrington, Morgan, and Faith, for all the laughs and all the light; my father-in-law,

Lloyd, and his beautiful wife, Joy, for your calls and encouraging words; and Levi, for making me something I've never been when I needed change the most.

ABOUT THE AUTHOR

LaToya Watkins's writing has appeared in *A Public Space, The Sun, McSweeney's, Kenyon Review, The Pushcart Prize Anthology,* and elsewhere. She has received grants, scholarships, and fellowships from the Bread Loaf Writers' Conference, MacDowell, Yaddo, Hedgebrook, and *A Public Space* (she was one of their 2018 Emerging Writers Fellows). She holds a PhD from the University of Texas at Dallas. *Perish* is her debut novel.

The employees of Thorndike Press hope you have enjoyed this Large Print book. All our Thorndike, Wheeler, and Kennebec Large Print titles are designed for easy reading, and all our books are made to last. Other Thorndike Press Large Print books are available at your library, through selected bookstores, or directly from us.

For information about titles, please call:
(800) 223-1244

or visit our website at:
gale.com/thorndike

To share your comments, please write:
Publisher
Thorndike Press
10 Water St., Suite 310
Waterville, ME 04901